The novels of
MICHAEL KANALY

thoughts of god

A metaphysical novel of murder that pits two modern-day hunters—men of the streets—against each other, while at the same time takes you into the notebook of God, where questions—answerable and unanswerable—build to a dizzying climax of earthly justice and cosmic vengeance.

virus clans

A story of evolution, where the viruses themselves reach an extraordinary level of intelligence, multiplying only as they see fit—and deciding that to be the perfect hosts, humans will have to be changed . . .

Ace Books by Michael Kanaly

THOUGHTS OF GOD
VIRUS CLANS

virus clans
A Story of Evolution

MICHAEL KANALY

ACE BOOKS, NEW YORK

For Jude and Sean: "Twice blessed is the man
who can call his sons friends."

This book is an Ace original edition,
and has never been previously published.

VIRUS CLANS

An Ace Book / published by arrangement with
the author

PRINTING HISTORY
Ace trade paperback edition / March 1998

The Putnam Berkley World Wide Web site address is
http://www.berkley.com

Make sure to check out *PB Plug*,
the science fiction/fantasy newsletter, at
http://www.pbplug.com

ISBN: 0-441-00500-4

ACE®
Ace Books are published by The Berkley Publishing Group,
a member of Penguin Putnam Inc.,
200 Madison Avenue, New York, NY 10016.
ACE and the "A" design are trademarks
belonging to Charter Communications, Inc.

PRINTED IN THE UNITED STATES OF AMERICA

10 9 8 7 6 5 4 3 2 1

Come with me,
Into a land where Virus Clans
whisper light-wave thoughts,
Planning complicated cancers
in which to house their young.

prologue

Moonlight leaked through the window. White bright, like clean sheets snapping on the line in some television ad for laundry soap. Even as the moon grabbed his hand and pulled him toward the window—demanding to be looked at, moving him as easily as it pulled the ocean tides—the image of laundry soap stuck in Bracken's mind. Reminding him that he absolutely *had* to wash some clothes soon. If not, then he would surely sink ever more deeply toward the reality of becoming an actual, full-blown bum. That thought made him look around the house with a critical eye, and he grimaced at the clutter and outright filth in which he currently lived. It was not, as the voice of his mother whispered across the decades, the way he had been raised.

No, he admitted, his present circumstances had nothing to do with the way he had been raised. You're living in fucking squalor, the part of his brain where the image of his mother still dwelled admonished him. While the fact of the matter was undeniable, given the clothes, books, papers, and assortment of overused dishes and coffee cups heaped about on every conceivable surface, his current wretched state was not entirely his own fault. At least that was the rationale, the lie Bracken kept telling himself. The house, strictly suburban middle class, had always been kept neat and clean by his wife. With, he freely admitted, only occasional help on his part. Now that Rebecca had left him, things had certainly gone to hell. That was not entirely true either, he admitted to himself. Things had been going to hell long before Becky packed up and, presumedly, moved to her mother's condo out on the Island. Fleeing from him. From the madness which had become his life. And the truth of the matter was, he hardly blamed her.

The moon, full and sharp against the midnight sky, cast gloomy, ghostlike shadows across the lawn. It penetrated the bony, bare branches of the trees, reminding him of leaves unraked. Of the yard, which he had once tended with care, now in the same state of disrepair as his house. And the yard work wouldn't be done, Bracken knew. Not by him, anyway. There was simply no time. No time for anything anymore. Except, of course, for one thing. The Madness, as Becky began calling it, before she, too, had become another ghostly shadow, an inhabitant of his former life.

The ceaseless clatter of the computer on the living room desk fought the moon for his attention, and won. These days, it always won. Sighing, he returned to the machine, to the thing which had consumed his life these last months. Consumed it literally, he knew. It had eaten away at his very existence. Taken his wife, his job, everything. Until he was left with only this dust-mired clutter of a life. At times, he felt almost crushed by it all. Lifted momentarily by glimmering hints of success, of a break-through which, he honestly believed, would turn every-thing around. The puzzle, once solved, would restore all he had lost. Becky, his career. His life. Then the moment would pass, as quickly as a lightning flash burning through the summer air, and he would be left only with the ashes of his failure.

The computer stopped its run and he leafed through the pages of the printout. Hopeful this time would prove to be the charm. That the translation program would fi-nally work, unlocking timeless secrets, opening doors to undreamed-of knowledge. Saving him from the dismal, encroaching swamp of personal disaster.

"Goddamn," he whispered, staring again at the con-fused chaos of numbers and symbols, as familiar to him by now as his own name. And he knew, once again, the bitter, crushing weight of his own failure.

He was close—so fucking close. He could feel it, taste it. But somehow the answer seemed to barely elude his grasp. Like clutching at a mountain of sand. Like catch-ing fog in his hands and trying to mold something tangi-ble out of the vapor. The solution to the puzzle, he knew, was right in front of him, floating at the very edge of his consciousness, but he simply could not grasp onto it. But it was there. He was certain of it. Certain . . .

Yet, he admitted to himself, he had been just as sure weeks, months ago. Before his life had been taken over and systematically destroyed by this *Thing*. He sat down in the chair, staring at the computer screen, at the twisted jumble of meaningless crap—the last page the computer had printed. Stared, once more, into the face of failure. His failure. At the inability of the translation program to make sense of the protein molecules he was feeding it. Encoded molecules, filled with unprecedented knowledge. And it was right there. Right at his fingertips. Only neither he nor the machine was able to make the slightest sense of it.

"Bastard!" he swore, slamming his hand down on the corner of the desk. Instantly sorry, knowing his uncontrolled action could well cause the computer's internal drive to crash. Not that it mattered all that much, Bracken admitted. The whole fucking thing was useless. Failure, like a heavy stone around his neck.

And it was undoubtedly going to get worse before it got better. *If* it got better, he felt obliged to remind himself. Thinking that, he actually laughed, shaking his head. Yes, it was damn well sure to get worse. Maybe Becky was right, he considered. Maybe the whole thing was Madness. His money was almost gone. The savings he and Rebecca had built up over the years, vanished. The mortgage payment overdue, and he was desperately afraid even to begin balancing his checkbook. And this afternoon, the power company had left an ominous message on the answering machine, demanding payment or they would be forced to terminate his electricity. Which would, he was aware, make it extremely difficult to run another translation on the computer. He imagined himself, sitting in the dark, in his filthy clothes, waiting for the finance company to repossess the house and toss him out into the street, lock, stock, and computer. Actually, he realized, they'd probably repo the computer, too.

Yes, in the morning he definitely had to go to the bank and get some cash. He backed out of the program and shut down the machine. He poured himself a drink from the dwindling reserves in the liquor cabinet and went into the bedroom. The bank, in the morning. Get some cash. In the dresser drawer, under a pile of papers where Rebecca used to place his clean underwear and folded socks, he fished around and found the gun. Not a big gun. A little .32 caliber, bought over Becky's objections, to protect the house against some imagined intruders. That had been . . . when? He couldn't recall. His brain, once so sharp, now seemed clouded by the events of the past weeks. He inspected the release mechanism of the weapon, making sure he still remembered how it worked. Five or six years ago, he thought. When his life had been normal, and at the time it seemed a reasonable thing to procure a gun to protect his wife and home. How was that normal? he wondered.

Perhaps, the suggestion crept into his mind, he had realized even back then the magnitude of the storm that was eventually to overtake him. Perhaps, in some deep, hidden part of his brain, he had known that one day in the not-too-distant future, he would be sitting on his empty, lonely bed, his life piled around him like the wreckage of a car crash, broke and despondent, considering robbery as his only viable alternative. Surely not the way he had been raised, he thought bitterly. And up until a few weeks ago, he would never have considered the rash, perhaps insane action he was now contemplating. But there really wasn't any other way out. Things had disintegrated to a point way past rational.

In the morning, he would have to go to the bank. There was simply no other alternative. Well, there was one. He took a long pull off the bourbon and toyed with the gun. He could slip the barrel into his mouth and pull the trigger. Would he hear the sound before he died? The loud explosion, the roaring in his ears, even as his brain poured out of the other side of his skull? Would he smell the gunpowder? Mostly, he wondered, would it hurt? For how long? And did it really matter?

Fear caught him, and he stopped the train of thought,

shutting it down before he actually convinced himself. His hands, he noticed, were shaking. He laughed again, a short, barking sound. This was really crazy. Was he actually going to let this *Thing* kill him? No, all he had to do was go to the bank in the morning. The truth was, he was in too deep. He couldn't stop now, even if he wanted to. Bracken put the gun on the table beside the bed, turned out the light, and curled up to get some sleep. The bank, in the morning. Get some cash. That was the only choice left. And maybe, in the end, this was the way it was always meant to be. He considered that thought for a moment as his mind hung on the murky edges of sleep. Who knew it would all turn out this way?

It hadn't always been like this, of course. At least that's what he told himself during his increasingly less frequent rational moments. In the beginning, he had loved his work, loved his wife, his job. It was a curious thing, to lose all that. Oddly enough, he was not entirely clear on how it all happened. Who knew? he thought.

I knew, he realized suddenly. Maybe not in the very beginning, but soon after it all started.

I knew, he said to himself, drifting toward the abyss of sleep. And the truth was, he had known, but somehow was powerless to stop it. Life is a long, slow train wreck, he thought sadly. And his last thought, before he fell into the dark well of sleep, was a question:

Jesus, how had it all come to this?

one

It began almost four billion years ago, when two separate, seemingly unrelated events took place thousands
of light-years apart, in the galaxy which would come to
be known to some of its inhabitants as the Milky Way:

In the outskirts of the Galaxy, in the Fourth Spiral Arm,
on a newly formed planet spawned by a small yellow star,
it began to rain. For half a billion years, since its formation from the swirling clouds of dust and gases left from
the birth of the star, the planet had undergone a series of
spectacular changes. It added to its mass through an almost continuous bombardment of asteroids and mete-
orites as it traveled through the debris left in the wake of
the sun's birthing. The surface of the planet melted under
the intense heat of its own gravitational forces, and as the
differentiated world began to cool, vast clouds of gases
were released from the interior, streaming to the surface,
shrouding the planet, forming a thick atmosphere hundreds of miles high. Over millions of years, the saturation

point was reached, condensation occurred, and it began to rain. The rain fell in great, swooping drops, splashing against the hot, rocky surface of the planet, turning instantly to steam, rising back up into the cloud cover in a hissing mist. Slowly, the rocks began to cool, and in the harsh, jagged cracks and crevices, water began to collect in shallow pools. Under the darkness of the shrouded sky, it rained without pause for ten thousand centuries.

At that same time, thousands of light years away, in the more densely populated regions of the Galactic Disk, the gravitational fields of two stars touched, then intertwined. The stars began a slow dance around one another, a waltz in the depths of space. At first, their powerful gravity fields pushed gently against one another, like opposing fog banks rising up from some dark, unimaginable ocean. The fields grappled, then locked together, as each star sought dominance over the other. Each step of the dance drawing them closer, toward an embrace which promised either cataclysmic disaster or shared brilliance.

In this crowded sector of space, theirs was not an uncommon meeting. Here, in the great disk which formed the core of the Galaxy, suns often sparred with one another to establish their solitary positions in the night sky, to carve out homes for themselves and their planets. As often as not, however, the encounter ended in disaster. Such was to be the fate of a small, blue world orbiting one of the opposing stars. A world on which life had spawned, where evolution passed through its complicated maze, producing a species of intelligent creatures:

The stars paraded across the sky in a swath of brilliant light, their glow competing with the twin moons as the Sun's Children rose in the eastern sky. Celonious, Watcher

of the Sky, Predictor of the Seasons, began his nightly
trek away from the fires of the village, walking toward a
hut on the rim of the summer valley. The hut, built of
stone and wattle, was his second home; and in truth, at
this late stage in his life, he found himself looking forward to the solitude of his nightly duties. To be removed
from the demands of his four mates and the gaggle of
children he had sired. He thought this and smiled to himself, considering the undeniable charms of his latest
mate, a gift from the Valley Lord for his part in the boun-
tiful harvest the People enjoyed at the time of the last
gathering. It was, he knew, a foolish gesture on the Lord's
part, as there was little chance that at his advanced years
he would impregnate the female. Although, he admitted,
that fact did not stop him from trying. His smile, which
he tried unsuccessfully to wipe from his mouths, was one
of lust and sensual pleasure, both of which were un-
seemly to one of his high position, and so might be dis-
pleasing to the Gods of the Sky. Celonious, who knew
well the power of the sky, was not one to take chances
when it came to angering the Gods, and so pushed those
thoughts into the hidden chambers of his brain. Still, her
touch lingered across the scales of his body like the sweet
drippings of honey birds, and the smile lingered. He
hoped that the Gods, ancient and demanding of youthful
sacrifices, would not mind his dalliance. After all, had not
his own father brought him into the world as an old gray-
scale, the last of many striplings? Perhaps the Valley
Lord, who was well versed in the History of the Lineages,
was not so foolish after all.

But there were other, more important duties to attend
to this night besides the wishful meanderings of the flesh.
Celonious cleared his mind for the task at hand. The days
of the Second Planting were not far off, and it was im-

portant that the star patterns be read correctly. The Second Planting was no trifling matter, as the numbers of the People had increased considerably under his guidance. And in no small measure due to his own fertility. He smiled again, unable to help himself. He was indeed as foolish as a stone in the fields, he thought to himself as the hill rose before him; steeper, it seemed, each night he made the trek. His years, numbering now some twenty hands, were catching up to him.

His apprentice had made the climb before him, lighting torches in front of the hut and wax candles within, so the Watcher of the Sky might study the parchment scrolls upon which the movement of the stars and their position during the seasons was recorded. Entering the hut, Celonious balanced himself on his thick tail and spread the summer scroll out on the rough-hewn table, which ran the length of the far wall. Other scrolls were rolled in their cubicles above the workbench. They were the work of his lineage, from the time of his father's father, and of others before—a trail of knowledge, carefully gathered and closely guarded, for they were the basis of his People's survival. They were also, Celonious knew well, the tails on which his own power rested. The scrolls were a continuing work, entrusted to him by the Elders at the time of his father's passing, and they held many secrets. Some barely hinted at, others revealed in great detail.

Celonious's apprentice, the third son of his second mate, glanced eagerly over his shoulder, the old Watcher noticed. Celonious also took note of the fact that the young green-scale was oozing mucus from his breathing mouth, and so was afflicted with the coughing sickness now plaguing the village. He motioned for the boy to stand farther back, least he splatter the scroll with a chance exhale. The apprentice ran a tongue across the affected orifice and nodded, taking a discreet step away from the table, clearly not wishing the task of copying the detailed scroll onto another parchment should it become stained through his carelessness.

"At the time of the Second Planting, this is the star to watch," Celonious said, pointing with a carefully filed claw. "Her name is the Pearl, and when she intersects here with the Paw of the Worm, it is time for the seedlings to be covered."

The apprentice cloaked his breathing mouth and glanced closely at the parchment, raising the scales of his forehead in understanding. Celonious nodded, studying the scroll. He pondered for a moment, trying to decide if the young male was ready to learn some of the deeper mysteries. But there was danger in much of the scrolls' knowledge, teachings which were in direct opposition to the preaching of the Holy Ones, who believed that the world on which the People dwelled was, in fact, the center of creation. Celonious's father, he recalled, had whispered to him one dark night in this very hut, that he suspected their world existed as a tiny speck in a vast sea of stars and planets. Celonious himself had come to the conclusion that this was indeed the case. He had even plotted a counting system which, he believed, proved his father's theory. But he decided the green-scale was too young yet to be exposed to what would undoubtedly be considered blasphemy, and so kept the knowledge to himself. There would be time later, when he had prepared the apprentice further. The Holy Ones, he knew from experience, were not to be trifled with, and Celonious did not care to end his days banished and starving in the Dust Lands.

"Come," he said instead. "We will find the Pearl and check her progress."

The boy helped him off his tail, which these days was often stiff and unresponsive. Fortunately this infirmity had not reached other parts of his body, Celonious thought, a picture of the Valley Lord's daughter dancing across his brain. Perhaps if he finished the sighting early, he might still get back to the village in time to share her nest.

"Come along now," he said, making it seem as though the apprentice was the one caught in the slow vise of time.

Outside, the night had deepened. The multitude of stars were caught like frozen raindrops against the black sky. Below them, the fires of the village were banked for the night, the young ones collected into their pods. The soft, moaning prayers of the Holy Ones drifted on the breeze, keeping the Night Demons at bay. As always, Celonious found his breath numbed at the brilliance of the stars. He almost told the apprentice that he suspected they lived in the heart of a star swarm which was but one of many such swarms, stretching farther into the heavens than anyone could imagine. And one day, the People might find a way to visit these undreamed-of places, flying like birds to the Sun's Children and beyond. He was about to speak of these dreams, when the green-scale's eyes narrowed and the membranes protruded from his forehead, focusing on a point of light, three heads above the horizon.

"There." The apprentice pointed, his voice quivering with the excitement of discovery. "What is that bright star? I did not see it on the scroll. . . ."

Celonious stared up in the direction the youth's claw indicated. His own membranes fluttered, allowing him to focus on the place the green-scale pointed.

"Do you see it?" the apprentice asked.

"Yes," Celonious whispered, staring at the bright point

of light, which he knew with certainty had not been there before. A wave of confusion caused the earth to move under his feet and he almost stumbled. The plotting of new stars and their inscription on the scrolls was part of the Watcher's work, but this . . . this star was much too bright to have gone unnoticed. As he stared Celonious imagined that the star grew even brighter before his eyes. Was it some sign from the Gods? he wondered. At once he made his way back inside the hut, pulling scrolls down from their niches, his new mate washed from his mind like a pebble in flooding waters.

The next night the point of light was definitely brighter, and brighter the next. Celonious now stayed in the Watcher's hut both day and night, scribbling counting figures on many pages of parchment. He sent his apprentice to the Valley Lord with an urgent message to begin the Second Planting, even though it was not yet time. For the counting figures showed, beyond a shadow of doubt, that this new star was moving directly toward them. And at a speed that was all but unimaginable.

It was, in fact, a sign from the Gods, Celonious concluded. And it was a portent of disaster. He hardly noticed when he, too, began coughing, the mucus running from his breathing mouth, splattering the parchment.

In the bodies of their hosts, the virus clans multiplied, the strategy of planned mutation now discarded in favor of rapid propagation. Encoded protein molecules were sent forth, reaching each clan in turn. As had happened in the past, a time of change was approaching, and survival depended on increasing the clan's numbers to their maximum levels. This they did with an efficiency known only to those of the hive.

• • •

In the Fourth Spiral Arm, after thousands of years of ceaseless rain, the skies above the fourth planet finally cleared. The sun cast long, sweeping rays of light through the dissipating clouds, sparkling on the waves of newly created oceans. Water, miles deep, now covered the surface of the world. The sun, aided by huge volcanic eruptions deep within the earth, began the slow process of warming the vast sheets of water.

Meanwhile, over millions of years, the tectonic plates ground against one another as they floated on the liquid mantle, miles beneath the oceans. Like tiles pushing against each other, the plates collided, their edges sliding upward, pushing the waters aside to form islands of rock protruding above the waves. Volcanic eruptions blasted through the seams of these collisions, spewing a flood of melted basalt up from the bowels of the earth, expanding the islands of rock into continents. These, too, were pushed along by the relentless action of the tectonic plates. The continents themselves crushed together, then ripped apart, forming mountain ranges, rift valleys, and shallow seas which flooded the shore lines of the ever-changing landscape. Gases from the volcanic explosions also rushed up from the underground chambers of the differentiated planet, creating an atmosphere of methane and carbon compounds. An atmosphere in which oxygen was but a trace element. The warm air and moisture rising from the oceans were cooled as they passed over the newly formed landmasses, creating colossal storms which battered the shorelines and churned the shallow seas, mixing minerals from deep within the planet with acidic oceanic waters. Along these shorelines, in the warm, coastal waters, thin sheets of mud and slime floated on the surface, forming a bridge between water

and land. The sheets of slime formed, then were broken
apart by storms, only to re-form again and again. The
process repeating itself over and over, for millions of
years. In the slime beds, which extended for miles around
the rocky shoals of the continents, molecules of nucleic
acid combined with specks of trace minerals washed
down from the basalt landmasses. As the molecules and
minerals floated on the surface of the shallow seas,
warmed by the penetrating rays of the sun, these chance
encounters also repeated themselves, again and again,
over millions of years. The building blocks of life, touching one another, fusing briefly, only to be torn apart as gigantic storms ripped through the slime beds. Then, in a
moment of unrecorded time, in an instant which was to
forever alter the history of the planet Earth, molecules of
nucleic acid and trace minerals came together to form a
microscopic string of genetic material, which through reasons of chance or fate, survived to become the molecular
platform on which all life on Earth is based. An instant of
time, a fusing of chemicals, a chance encounter—one of
uncounted trillions . . .

And five hundred million years later, the seas teemed
with bacteria. Tiny, single-celled creatures, possessed
with the unique ability to replicate themselves. This they
did, creating generations beyond counting, filling the
oceans, exploding into the empty environmental niche to
which they were born. Three and a half billion years ago
the oceans of the earth were ruled by swarms of one-
celled animals, whose dominance was assured by their
own simple method of reproduction.

Celonious was dying. The mucus filled his lungs and had
now turned into a bloody froth on the edges of his breathing mouth. After weeks spent brooding over the scrolls,

he had finally been carried from the Watcher's hut and wrapped in the pod of his rebirth. Each day now, the Holy Ones came to pray and chant over his failing body, as they did for all the many hands of People now afflicted with the dread sickness. A plague, the Holy Ones decreed, which was caused by the Dark Star now encroaching upon their lives.

Each day the apprentice also came to stand watch over his master, his father, whom the young green-scale would be forced to replace. Even though he himself knew he was far from ready to assume the task. Fortunately, however, the Second Planting was now complete and the harvest was really a question of ripening, rather than an accurate reading of the stars. But in the spring . . . in the spring, the apprentice knew he would be forced to wear the mantle of the Watcher. It was a thing he feared, even more than the coughing sickness. So he wiped his breathing mouth clean of the dark-stained mucus and came each dawn to the pod into which Celonious had been sewn, in the hope the Old One might wake and answer some of his many questions. Although, he admitted, that hope faded with each passing day.

He stood in the doorway of the dwelling of Celonious's first mate, listening as the Holy Ones sought to repulse the evil of the Dark Star. That, in itself, was a curious thing, he thought, glancing up at the pale blue of the morning sky. For the invading star was anything but dark. It could now be seen clearly even in the light of day. A bright halo hanging above the horizon. The People, he noticed, barely left their huts these days, hiding in terror from the apparition which brought this plague upon them.

It would be centuries, at best, before the technology of the People advanced to a level where the illness could be identified for what it actually was—a vast, almost unprecedented expansion of the virus community which lived in parasitic harmony within the bodies of the People. The One becoming the Many, again and again. Until by the sheer weight of their numbers, they decimated the immune systems of their hosts. This was an unfortunate occurrence for both the People and the virus clans themselves, as it interrupted an evolutionary process which had been taking place for aeons. A process of uncounted generational mutation and natural selection. A process which had finally achieved a much-sought-after goal— that of a two-part, segregated brain. The Many had been close to becoming ONE. But the damage to the hosts was unavoidable, as the clans' survival mechanism had been activated.

Although they were unaware of the fact, the People would not have centuries to improve their technology. And the green-scale apprentice did not need to worry about the Spring Planting.

The Dark Star, as she was so named, carried no planets within the long, looping sphere of her gravitational field. She did, however, bring with her a vast collection of cosmic debris—clouds of dust and huge chunks of dead rock, the size of small moons, circled in the outer reaches of the Dark Star's field. As the two suns pulled toward one another, caught now in their mutual webs of magnetic and gravity forces, one of these asteroids—a monstrous clump of solid iron, hundreds of miles across—intersected the orbit of the planet.

It came in the night, even as the colliding stars struggled to attain equilibrium between themselves. An iron fist of rock, its mass accelerated by the converging stars. The apprentice, sitting on his tail outside the Watcher's hut, saw it briefly, for an instant, as it entered the planet's atmosphere. A flash of light, blinding in its intensity. A sharp pang of fear danced across the apprentice's brain, rattling his scales. His membrane filters closed over his eyes, even as the gigantic chunk of metal slammed into his home world. Even as the explosion vaporized him, and all the People. The asteroid continued its thundering path through the sky, striking the planet, delivering a terrible, killing blow, as both planet and asteroid were pulverized into bits of rock and dust. So great was the impact that a large volume of rock and planetary dust was thrown clear of the impact area. Thrown clear, even, of the gravitational forces of the colliding stars. This cosmic debris, once the home of evolved, intelligent life, was propelled by the force of the explosion off into the depths of interstellar space.

Had any thinking, rational creature observed this cataclysm, they would, undoubtedly, have come to the conclusion that life on the planet had been completely obliterated. And for all practical purposes, this was indeed the case. However, drifting on the fist-sized rocks and grains of dust, tiny submicroscopic organisms clung, attached by gluelike molecules of protein to the floating debris. In a static state approaching suspended animation, these microbes drifted through the endless, timeless night of space. Behind them, a few centuries later, despite their best efforts to achieve equilibrium and form a binary star system, the two suns collided in an even more shattering explosion, sending radiation and huge, flaring comets out into the silent, all-enveloping darkness. Several of the comets passed through the dust clouds left from the destruction of the planet, picking up bits of rock and granules of dust in their own gravitational fields. Carrying the debris with them on their long journey through the vastness of space.

t w o

I began with a phone call, which took place in the middle of a war:

The war was being waged on a scale incomprehensible to the human mind. A single battle, which would mean complete annihilation to the vanquished and total victory for the conquerors. The losers in this epic struggle would be slaughtered mercilessly. Their home ravaged as a prize of war, their offspring put to death, as well as their rulers, soldiers, and workers. Those few who managed to surrender might live for a time as slaves, but in the end even the memory of their hive's existence would be wiped from the face of the earth.

It was a war fought on a single front. A brutal, headlong assault on the defenses of those under attack. It was a war which began only hours ago, but whose outcome was already decided. . . .

The invaders came upon the target colony early in the day, even as the sun's rays dried the morning dew. Their scouts crossed a trail of scent molecules left by foragers, who themselves had happened upon a potential food source that very morning. The trail was left so that other workers in the colony might find their way to the food source with a minimum of wasted time and effort. Efficiency was a prime directive, built into the creatures over millions of years. Their existence, their success as a species, revolved around this model of efficiency. The chemical trail left by the foragers was but one link in this long chain of survival strategy. It was, however, a strategy with which the invading scouts were well versed. Even those among them who had never encountered such a trail knew its meaning instantly, the knowledge imprinted into their genetic code since the moment of their inception. They had been fed and trained for this specific function—to seek out and destroy any nests which were not their own. They were warriors unlike any others. Their allegiance unquestioned. Their ability to forfeit their lives, if necessary, in the line of duty was also unquestioned. They were, in essence, killing machines. And like tiny, living robots, they went about their task with an inexorable will.

As the first scouts crossed the trail of the target colony, as their antennae touched the scent molecules left in the wake of the foragers, their pincerlike jaws opened and closed in anticipation of the coming battle. The lead scouts advanced along the trail, backtracking to its source, while others of their kind returned to the home hive, to relay the information of the newly discovered scent trail, and to bring back with them the invading horde.

As the lead scouts advanced they encountered stray foragers along the way. These they killed quickly, effortlessly, leaving behind twitching, headless bodies, which staggered about in mindless confusion, even as the severed heads looked up at the rising sun with dead, lifeless eyes. At the mouth of the target colony, the scouts continued their slaughter, snapping the bodies of their victims as easily as a human being might tear paper. Meanwhile, belowground, panic spread through the tunnels and chambers of those being attacked. Defenses were marshaled, soldiers poured out from the underground colony, swarming over the invading scouts; who, unmindful of the overwhelming numbers against them, continued to cut and slash with their murderous, viselike jaws, until they, too, were lifeless husks, broken and twitching in the dirt of the tunnel mouth. But even as they died the horde from their home hive was advancing along the scent trail. An army marching off to war, terrible and indomitable. Each entity of the invading horde existing for a single purpose—the destruction of their enemy, whose very existence had been unknown until that morning.

In the face of this approaching menace, the target colony rushed about hoping to shore up their limited defenses. Soldiers patrolled the outer edges of their territory even as scouts went off in search of information about the invaders. Workers frantically sealed off chambers beneath the ground to protect the queen and their young larvae. The sun had not yet dried the granules of sand at the main entrance, when the invaders fell upon them. A swarming battle line formed as the defenders rose up to meet the charge. It was a silent battle, despite its incredible ferocity. And it was fought without mercy. Bodies from each faction littered the ground by the hundreds. As the defensive line was pushed back workers from belowground were ordered into the fray, and they went forward fearlessly, even though their deaths were all but assured, as war was not the function for which they had been designed. They were food gatherers, tunnelers, gardeners, nursery workers, and royal attendants. But they, too, went off to be slaughtered, in the vain hope that their numbers alone might be sufficient to stem the tide of the invasion.

The warriors of the invading horde, however, knew their work well. Before the sun was halfway up the sky, the final defenses of the target colony had been breached and the horde poured into the tunnel mouth, where the killing continued, unabated, until the royal chamber itself was broached. There, beneath a swarm of tearing, snapping jaws, the queen and her attendant king died. At this point, the plundering of the target hive began in earnest. Food stores were ravaged. The egg cases of the vanquished, the final victims of the war, were carried off to the home hive, where they would be hatched and used as slaves for the duration of their short lives. In the end, the target colony would be left for worms and beetles to inhabit, until the tunnels themselves finally crumbled, and all traces of this once-thriving community vanished.

Gary Bracken was raking the leaves out of the flower beds around the side of the house, trying not to think of an advertising jingle he'd heard on the radio that morning. A stupid bit of music and words which had somehow gotten stuck in his head and refused to leave: "Burger Barn, Burger Barn. Get yourself down to Burger Barn. . . ."

Christ, he was even humming the damn thing, he realized. Amazingly, he found his stomach grumbling. Well, it was almost lunchtime, but he'd be damned if he was going to Burger Barn, ever again. They ought to outlaw that kind of subliminal shit, he thought, pulling the dead leaves away from the foundation of the house, being careful not to rip up any bulbs that might be growing unseen in the tangle of winter leaves. Not that there was much chance of actually disturbing any potential flowers, he knew. Becky had vigorously planted tulips over the last few years, each time with pitiful results. He would, on occasion, kid her about it, asking if she thought there were rows upon rows of flowers surrounding the house, all growing inverted with their petals opening up deep in the ground. She did not take the joke well, even though her so-called black thumb was legendary even in her own family. She gardened about as well as he did yard work, he knew. But she did cook a mean hamburger, he thought, grinning to himself.

"Burger Barn, Burger Barn. Get yourself down to Burger Barn. . . ."

It had to be the almost mindless task of yard work that turned his brain to mush, he rationalized. Sometimes he actually found himself counting the rake strokes, multiplying and dividing them to see if there was some kind of optimal pattern. Can you say Rainman? he asked himself, laughing quietly, thinking about what the neighbors probably thought: Gary Bracken, now there's one happy man when he has a rake in his hands.

As he worked his way toward the corner of the house, his eyes detected movement in the budding grass near the oak planter. Naturally curious—and, he admitted to himself, ready for any momentary diversion—he moved over for a closer look. Ants, swarms of them, locked in a life-and-death struggle that was already in its latter stages. Red fire ants, he saw, had invaded a colony of black harvesters, and were even now in the process of emptying the colony of its young, carrying off the larvae to their own nest. An entomologist by profession, a bug man in the common vernacular, Bracken was always fascinated by these tiny creatures. A fascination he carried with him from his earliest childhood memories, and one he had gladly turned into a lifelong study. Yes, the predatory *Solenopis invicta*, vicious and warlike in their behavior, had clearly stumbled upon a nest of Common Black ants, *Tetramorium caespitum*, by their proper scientific name, and were now in the process of decimating the weaker species. The bodies of the victims, broken by the terrible jaws of the attackers, lay strewn along the damp ground. And the victors of this ant war were looting the defeated colony, carrying away the black ants' young as the ultimate prize of war.

God, but they were amazing, he thought, leaning closer, unmindful of the red ants crawling across his sneakers. Tiny, supposedly mindless creatures, organized on a scale that defied human logic, carrying out a plan of action that required the participation of hundreds, perhaps thousands of individuals. All acting in concert with one another, each somehow knowing its specific task. Each individual an integrated part of the whole. Each ant a tiny gear in the vast machinery that was the hive. How did they know what to do? he found himself wondering. Was it instinct or some unknown form of intelligence which controlled their movements? And how do you tell the difference? Questions which he had spent a large share of his professional life studying. Questions, he knew, to which there seemed to be no answers. It was, he suspected, a thing beyond human understanding. The mentality of the hive. Completely fascinating, utterly incomprehensible.

It was 11:45 on a spring morning in suburbia. A Saturday, and Gary Bracken was watching an ant war, as he had dozens of times during the course of his life. Watching as the world was about to change for him. Even as it had for the vanquished colony.

Eleven forty-five. He remembered looking at his watch as Rebecca called to him from the back porch.

"Gary! Phone for you. It's Kurt from the lab."

"Coming," he called back, standing up, suddenly realizing he was making a conscious effort to straighten his back. God Almighty, he thought with a grimace. Thirty-five years old and he had to actually think to straighten up. He remembered his father slapping him on the shoulder several birthdays ago. The old man, laughing.

"Well, kiddo, it's all downhill from here," Bill Bracken had said, grinning, nodding his head in that sanctimonious manner all good salesmen cultivate.

Bracken heard his back snap into alignment. Damn, but he hated it when the old man was right. Then he remembered the old man was gone, buried in that tiny cemetery outside Plattsburg. Beside his mother, both of them dying young—at least it seemed that way to him. Why did he keep forgetting they were dead? he wondered. That saddened him as much as the remembering.

Becky was holding the screen door open for him. It was strange, he thought, how she didn't look a day older than when he'd married her, almost seven years ago now. Her long, reddish-brown hair tossed casually over her shoulders. Those blue eyes—they seemed to be winking at him in an unspoken invitation, raising his spirits. As always, he was struck by the fact that she had somehow consented to marry him, when it was perfectly obvious she could have had anyone she wanted.

"What?" she asked, smiling at him, secretly enjoying the way he looked at her—like a schoolboy passing the local strip joint, she thought.

"Nothing," he said, oddly embarrassed that he had been caught staring at her. She was, after all, his wife, for God's sake. "Kurt say what he wanted?"

Rebecca shook her head. A call from the lab on a Saturday was certainly odd. He hoped one of the refrigerator units hadn't quit again. It'd be hell to get a repairman to come down on a weekend. Not to mention the cost. Or the potential loss of cultures, he thought, hurrying now to the living-room phone. Kurt Eez's image was frozen on hold on the screen. A young kid, barely in his twenties, fresh out of grad school. Bracken pushed the hold button and the screen reset, showing a room in the research lab. Kurt was staring at the readouts from the electric-scan microscope. He turned back to the phone screen as it beeped.

"Hey, Dr. Bracken." Kurt greeted him with the nonchalant grin of a person who had yet to encounter the grim realities of protocol in the scientific research world.

Bracken nodded back. He never liked these new phone systems, with their face-to-face cameras. Phones, he thought, were for talking and listening, not watching the other person as they spoke. It was, he realized, something his father would say.

"What's up?" Bracken asked, brushing the dirt from his hands onto his pants. He always felt like he should comb his hair and brush his teeth before talking on the damn phone. "The cold units holding temperature?"

"Oh . . . sure," Kurt said, looking over his shoulder at the bank of gauges, as if suddenly remembering he was supposed to check them every hour. Damn phone screens, Bracken thought, now worried about Eez and the weekend crew doing their jobs. "Yeah, they're fine," Kurt said, turning back to the screen. "Something really strange came in on the data readouts. I thought you'd want to know, so I double-checked the numbers and gave you a call."

"What about the readouts?" Bracken asked, suddenly

realizing that Kurt Eez was barely able to contain his excitement.

"Well . . ." The kid was hesitant, Bracken saw. Almost afraid to give his interpretation of the readouts on the chance they might later prove to be false. A common failing, Bracken knew, among those working on their first research project. He immediately cut Eez some slack, realizing that the failing existed even among those who had been in the research for a decade or more, like himself.

"Spit it out, Kurt," Bracken said, trying to sound kindly, fatherly. Maybe he should consider hiring a babysitter for the weekend staff. A most unkind thought, he knew. "What have you got?"

"Well, it seems the computer identified a reoccurring protein code," Eez said, his face and eyes frozen on the screen. "It appears as though we have definable communication."

"Between who?" Bracken asked, his mind suddenly caught in a whirl of possibilities.

"Not who," Kurt said carefully. "It's more a question of what, I think. . . ."

a molecule of time
Day One

The comet moved through the depths of galactic space, as it had for almost half a billion years. During the course of its journey, the comet covered thousands of light-years; a free-flying, frozen rock of water, minerals, and gases. The Gods of Luck or Fate had kept it from more than a fleeting encounter with the gravitational fields of the many stars it passed. As it entered the realm of the Fourth Galactic Arm, however, the comet's luck was about to run out. Flashing across the cold, dark night, the head of the comet was tugged briefly, then pulled inexorably into the far-flung fields of gravity and magnetism emanating from a small, inconspicuous yellow sun. As if pulled by the hand of God, the comet began to fall toward the tiny point of light, like a raindrop falling from the dark clouds of space.

Trailing behind, attached to a speck of dust in the comet's long, sweeping tail, the One followed in the comet's wake, as it had for half a billion years. The One, which was really one of a handful of survivors now drifting through the cosmos, escapees from the planetary destruction millennia past, existed in a timeless, suspended state—incapable of thought, unaware of its destination or location or the vast amount of time which had passed since the beginning of its journey. Impervious to the cold, requiring neither air nor food, the One traveled with the flotsam of a world long vanished from the memory of the Universe. Attached to the speck of dust by molecules of its own thin outer shell, the One was also drawn into the gravitational arms of the small, insignificant sun.

It might seem to the casual observer that all life in the Universe is based on a seemingly impossible series of chance encounters. Indeed, given the vastness of the Universe, this may well be the case. It may also be that stars are Gods, all-knowing and omniscient within their fields of influence, and using the tools of radiance and gravity, set in motion the chemical encounters required for the existence of life. It may also be that there are other factors at work, unseen and secretive, gently guiding the forces of Nature, thereby increasing the odds of those seemingly impossible chance encounters.

Whatever the case, whatever the reason, the cosmic debris on which the One lay dormant was pulled past the orbits of the outer planets, swinging toward what would undoubtedly be a final, fatal encounter with the fiery halo of the yellow sun which had given birth to this solar system. But again, for whatever reason, be it chance or divine providence, the One and its train of debris fell through the elliptical orbit of the sun's fourth planet, the water world. By chance or providence, the comet's head passed close to the planet's own gravitational field and as it swung by on its journey into the hot belly of the star, the clouds of rock and dust in its wake brushed against the thin atmosphere of the water world. Granules of cosmic debris were pulled away from the comet, pulled down into the thin atmosphere. Glowing brightly for a few brief seconds, most of the debris was burned to ash by the friction of layered air. But by chance or divine intervention, the speck of dust on which the One traveled was shielded from the full force of the atmospheric collision. The dust particle had traveled across oceans of time and space, always in the protective shadow of a clump of iron, a meteorite which also survived the encounter with the water world, slamming in a blaze of heat and energy into the soft, yielding ocean—carrying with it the speck of dust to which the One was attached.

The dust particle hung suspended in the saline waters. Around it, swarms of bacteria moved, like microscopic schools of fish. The One, awakening from its millions of years of suspended animation, came slowly to the state of awareness which marked the individuals of its species. That is, the One's protein molecules recognized the existence of an environment conducive to life. The One recognized, also, the soft probing inquiries of the bacteria, as these organisms investigated the speck of dust to which it was attached. These, the One's instincts told it, were potential hosts. And so it loosened the protein glue which had held it to this boulder of dust for a time impossible to imagine. For a while the One floated free in this new world, this place of oceans and teeming bacterial life. Then, a single bacteria, one of uncounted trillions, happened by chance to brush against the One, and the virus found a match between the carbon-based life on this planet and the long-dead world on which the clans had formerly lived. It clung to the bacteria, as it had once clung to the tiny speck of dust, probing its defenses, searching for an opening into the cellular mass. The One found this opening easily and quickly, as the bacteria swarms had never before needed a defense against this form of invasion. The bacteria, many times the size of the invading virus, was unaware of this intrusion. Once inside the host, the One moved to the strings of DNA which defined the genetic makeup of the creature. There, in a feat of engineering which was not to be duplicated on this planet by any other living creature for three billion years, the One inserted its own genetic strings into the host's reproductive code, overriding the cellular instructions which had been the basis of the bacteria's makeup for five hundred million years. So began the process by which the One would become, once again, the Many . . . and the Many would eventually become ONE.

The bacteria reproduced, as all living things are programmed to do. The changes in its genetic code, however, caused it to produce not other bacteria, but rather more viruses. From across an ocean of time and space, from a single survivor of a destroyed planet, dead now for millennia, the virus clans lived again. The first step taken. The One becoming the Many.

three

Gary Bracken was in his car before noon. A quick kiss on the cheek for Rebecca, a promise that he would try to be home for dinner, and he was grabbing his keys, heading for the door. Dirty clothes and all, fighting the urge to push the accelerator down as far as it would go. Definable communication? Between viruses? And not merely the usual cellular exchange of DNA or RNA, Eez had said. But protein exchange between individual viruses.

"You're sure about this?" Bracken had said, knowing that he was already going to spend his Saturday at the lab, whatever Kurt Eez's response.

"Seems like it." Eez shrugged his shoulders, and Bracken was on his way.

Encoded protein molecules? he wondered, weaving the car in and out of the Saturday shoppers. Couldn't be, he rationalized, his mind racing faster than the car's four-cylinder engine. Encoded molecules, his brain kept repeating. Like the same data-string molecules the next generation of supercomputers were going to use? The computer model, which once would have been as alien to him as video phones, had occupied his thoughts ever since the lab had landed a government contract to study the new technology. The next computer revolution, he knew, would change the way the world used the machines. The storage of material through electronic bits and bytes was about to become obsolete. The new wave would be data storage on encoded protein molecules, a technology that seemed fantastic, even though it was already at hand. And his laboratory was playing a role in its development, however small, he admitted to himself. Oddly enough, his background in the field of insect communication seemed to serve him well in this new field. Bees, termites, and ants all used protein molecules to impart information to the hive.

But viruses? He shook his head, braking for a stoplight. Certainly they used protein molecules to feed information into infected cells, utilizing that form of communication to affect the DNA strings in the cells they invaded. That was the reason behind Bracken's insistence that the lab study these microscopic creatures, in the vague hope that they might gain some insight into how the exchange took place, and somehow be able to transfer the process into the computer systems being developed. But the molecule exchange was only supposed to happen between viruses and their hosts, not between the individuals themselves.

Behind him, a car beeped and Bracken realized the light had turned green. Viruses were invaders, cellular pirates, tiny parasites, he thought, pushing the car forward. Somehow, they restructured the cell to mutate, most often to reproduce more viruses. The protein molecules they used to achieve this admittedly complex function were only used within the host cell, or so the conventional thought ran. Cellular invaders, chemical communication. Bracken's mind was drawn to the ant war he had witnessed only a few minutes before. And how were viruses different from ants? he found himself asking.

He suppressed the urge to call the lab over the car phone, even though it was one of the old talk/listen devices. No, better to let Kurt and the other weekend assistant do their work without interruption, that way they'd have the information ready for him when he arrived. Good God, communication between viruses? He tried to recall what little he actually knew about these tiny, ancient scourges of humanity. These microbes who had defied all but the most basic intrusion into the mysteries of their lives. They were, supposedly, the most primitive forms of life, simple bits of protein and nucleic acid. In truth, many in the scientific community still refused to recognize them as living entities. But what they did was truly remarkable. Viruses were somehow able to invade living cells and change the genetic code of the host, reorganizing the DNA strings to their own devices. And they were communicating with one another? Like ants or bees or termites or supercomputers?

No one would believe it, he realized suddenly. Kurt Eez was right to be hesitant. The data would have to be irrefutable. And what if it was? he allowed himself the thought. God, the funding! The practical side of him took momentary control of his brain. Bracken had, after all, spent a good portion of his professional life laboring under a cloud of too little resources for too much work. There would be money for new equipment, new projects. The whole world would be knocking on their door. Communication between viruses?

Then the real question came to him, in an instant of shocking clarity so blinding that he almost drove off the road:

What were they saying to one another? he wondered.

A truck blared its air horn at him, and Bracken realized he had swerved into the transport lane. He jerked the wheel and forced himself to attend to the more immediate business of arriving at the lab alive. There would be plenty of time for speculation later, if the readouts should actually prove true. Which they wouldn't, the rational part of his brain told him. But, Good Lord, what if it was true?

As soon as he walked into the lab, Bracken realized he should have made the phone call from his car. Eez and the graduate student who worked the weekend shift were both staring at a computer screen. The electron microscope was projecting an image of what Bracken knew to be an active virus culture. A common cold virus, one of a dozen or so the lab was working with.

"So, what are they saying?" Bracken asked, in what he quickly realized to be an ill-advised attempt at humor.

Kurt Eez looked up at him in confusion.

"A joke," Bracken said, slipping a lab coat over his dirty work clothes. Kurt looked relieved, the other kid laughed. And they really were kids, Bracken reminded himself, even though Eez had his doctorate—the ink hardly dry on the sheepskin—and the young woman was a senior grad student from Columbia University. Eez he knew fairly well. But the other, Mary Ann Meade, if he remembered her name correctly, was a stranger to him. An intern getting a little on-the-job training over the course of the spring semester. Bracken saw her a couple times a month, and then only in passing. But if this communication thing was real, Ms. Meade would really have something to build into her thesis paper, he thought.

"What have you got?" Bracken asked, getting down to business, making his way past the clutter of tubes and vials to the scan readouts. In the back of his mind, he didn't actually believe Kurt's assumption of communication. But then, a hundred years ago no one knew how ants or bees or termites communicated, he reminded himself. A hundred years from now, the textbooks might just have a notation about the research being done right here, in this little government-funded, backwater laboratory. Who could tell? That was the exciting part of research. Whenever you fired up the beakers, a professor had once told him, anything could happen. Of course, in this case it wasn't beakers or test tubes, but a secondhand electron scanning microscope and some leftover computer equipment the military didn't want anymore. All of which, in Bracken's mind, made the whole scenario even more unbelievable.

"Here, on the overnight printouts," Kurt said, gathering up the stack of computer paper, spreading it out over one of the few clear surfaces on the counter. "The computer identified a reoccurring string of protein molecules being circulated within the culture."

"That's nothing new," Bracken said, taking a quick glance at the red-circled lines Eez had highlighted. That was, in fact, the standard mode of operation for viruses invading a cellular body. It had long been identified as the means through which a virus reencoded the DNA structure of a target cell, forcing the cell to mutate when it divided, or to create more viruses. A bizarre, yet highly efficient means of reproduction. Bracken often likened it to the cuckoo bird depositing its eggs in the nest of another bird, thereby forcing the other bird into parenting its young. He began to think that perhaps Kurt Eez had indeed jumped the gun. Surprisingly, he felt a strange sense of relief. The other implication was almost too mind-boggling to consider.

"No, it's not," Eez said, looking a bit rattled, but determined to continue. A moment later it was Bracken's turn to look rattled. "But here, the computer followed the protein string and determined the molecules were being passed directly to other viruses in the culture, not to the target cells. You can see the progression here on the next page. . . ."

Kurt pointed and Bracken blinked, staring at the lines of code. Jesus, he thought, was it possible? His mind began processing alternate possibilities.

"A computer malfunction?" he asked, realizing he was groping. "Maybe the protein string was passed to the cells in the culture, and then picked up by the viruses?"

"I checked that before I called you," Kurt said, his voice sounding hollow. Like a man standing on a cliff, shouting into a ravine to see if there was any echo. Bracken thought he heard the echo in his ears, which were suddenly ringing, as though some high-pitched machinery had been turned on in the lab.

"Like ants?" Bracken heard himself whisper. The thought made his skin crawl. The human body, after all, was filled with millions of these microscopic *things*. Tiny creatures which did not even meet the current, admittedly limited, definition of life. Viruses used no oxygen, did not appear to eat or secrete or reproduce on their own. They simply existed as barely recognizable bits of protein and nucleic acid. Which were, Bracken knew, the building blocks of life. And it did indeed appear as though they were *talking* to one another.

"Ants?" Kurt Eez asked. Mary Ann Meade turned her

head toward the conversation, as if she, too, was disturbed by the implications.

"Forget it." Bracken pushed the thought aside, wondering how he should proceed. Should he call in the senior members of the research team? Pull Jacoby off the golf course? Yank Terrance Stampe away from that young nurse who was helping old Terry deal with his current midlife crisis, in ways Bracken didn't even want to think about? No, there wasn't any need for that just now. He had enough bodies in the lab to set up a control experiment. To prove or disprove this truly incredible chain of events. Secretly, he knew, he was hoping for the latter, despite all the glory and research dollars such a discovery would bring. On the surface it seemed like such a benign thing. Virus communication. Even as he set the wheels in motion, Gary Bracken found himself wondering if the outside world would really want to know about this, once they realized the true implications. He thought not. Curiously, Bracken found himself hesitant to continue. Were there some things human beings are not meant to know? He thought briefly about Oppenheimer, Kistiakowsky, and the others of the Los Alamos crew. They found something they didn't want to know. But Bracken was, in the end, a scientist. It was his job and he took it seriously.

"You folks ready to do some real work?" he asked, using his best fatherly tone.

What *were* they saying? he found himself wondering.

a molecule of time
Day One + 2 x 10 ^9

Timeless. The Many separated, each becoming the One. These also went out into the world, which was ripe with hosts. For the seas swarmed with bacteria and floating sheets of plantlike slime. The hosts' DNA strings were cut and fused in an endless variety of patterns. More often than not, the mutated bacteria died and were absorbed back into the food chain. These beings, sacrificed to the continuation of the virus clans. But there was an endless number of hosts. Occasionally, through the process of experimentation and selection, new changes were inflicted on the hosts which gave the mutated bacteria a decided edge in the constant struggle for survival. Gradually, the landscape of life in the oceans was altered. Diversification and specialization, which assured exploitation of the watery environment to its fullest. The genetic material in the bacteria offered an endless canvas on which the clans could work. Over countless millennia, the bacteria swarms were altered into a vast array of multicellular creatures—annelid worms, sponges, jellyfish, bottom-dwelling tubular colonies of bilateria, single-shelled clams, armored mollusks. The oceans became filled with crawling, burrowing, free-swimming entities possessing external shell casings, feeding chambers, and the first simple nerve structures. The single-cell code changed to create multicell organisms, offering the Many even greater opportunities to propagate their clans.

The alterations to life on this new, rich world were not limited simply to bacteria and the countless adaptations they spawned. The sheets of cellular slime from which the bacteria rose also held genetic material which could be cut and fused into endless, twisting patterns. These cells, too, fell under the clan's sway. Over billions of years, floating swarms of algae were created through the endless mutations of the Many. And these, in their turn, were altered to produce kelp beds, mold spores, and multicellular photosynthesizers. Colonizing, reef-forming plants, some of which utilized the muddy seafloors, others floating free to be washed up on the rocky beaches, carrying with them the Many. The land, empty and barren, offered endless possibilities for expansion. And so the Many came ashore, wrapped in the cellular cocoons of their plant hosts. The memory of the One locked away in their own proteins and nucleic acids. The Many, timeless and infinitely patient, filled the land with grasses, flowering organisms, vines, and trees. Millions upon millions of years passing as this process took place. The clans, all but immortal, using time itself as a shaping tool. And for all that long epoch, work continued in the seas. Experimentation and natural selection, as mollusks and sea worms crept across the dark floors of the ocean depths. As free-swimming organisms evolved gills and fins, and the Age of Fishes began. Within each individual entity, the virus clans rode the tide of the explosion of life.

Even as the hosts were mutated, so, too, did the clans change and adapt to the various life-forms being created. As the differences between plant and animal became more pronounced, the genetic makeup of the Many was altered, producing members of the clan selected and designed to prey upon specific entities. Some were created to target the genetic codes of the algae and their offspring, others the multitude of animals which had recently been brought into existence. The adaptations in the clans themselves were also designed to exploit specific environmental niches. Survival being the first, most primary instinct. And when times of dying came, as it does to all worlds where life has spawned, diversification ensured the survival of the basic DNA structure being evolved. It was both a simple and complex plan, built into the clans' instinctual need to survive. The One, becoming the Many. Changing, adapting, as they molded the world around them. But even as they themselves changed, the clans retained the basic protein codes of the One. Even as they spread to all the shallow seas and deep ocean beds, even as they became separated by uncounted leagues of water, even as they invaded the land, the clans retained their molecular connection to the One. Everywhere they gathered and became entwined in the complicated matrices of their kind, encoded protein molecules were exchanged—the history, the vast accumulated knowledge of the clans, as yet unreadable to the Many, were passed to each succeeding generation.

It had begun, at first, as a cosmic accident. The One in its instinctive need to produce the Many, altering the genetic

code of a single bacteria. The mechanics of this alter-
ation, passed down to succeeding generations through the
protein molecules housed in the viruses' own genetic pattern. Softly, like whispers in the night, the clans shared
their findings. Their history, their billions of years of accumulated knowledge required the development of a
complex neural system to read these specifically encoded
molecules, and so could not be accessed. Not yet. But
other information, such as the simple genetic bonding of
DNA strings could be imprinted upon each individual
member of the clan. The knowledge of the double helix,
opening like a flower, like the pages of a book. The clans,
timeless, learned their trade over aeons, becoming master
builders, artisans in the submicroscopic arena of genetic
engineering. Alien to this world, they made it their own.
Creatures dwelling on the atomic level. Tiny gods at play
in the fields of DNA . . .

Two billion years after the One's arrival, an amphibian
crawled up onto a sandy beach. Two billion years of mutation and adaptation. The landscape and atmosphere altered.
The life-forms themselves changed beyond recognition.
The tiny amphibian breathed the oxygenated air, scurry-
ing away into a marshland populated by giant ferns, surrounded by conifer trees. There, she laid her eggs. And
now the real work began.

four

It was almost midnight. Bracken winced looking up at the clock. He called Rebecca sometime around seven, promising to be home soon. She accepted the news with a distrust born of past experience. At social gatherings, Becky often made the comment that her husband could be convicted of bigamy in any court in the land—that he was married both to her and to his work. It was a statement not always made in jest, he was aware. But fortunately she was always quick to forgive him.

"It could be worse, I guess," she often said, when he finally made his way home after a typical fifteen-hour day. "At least I know you don't have time to be fooling around with other women."

The fact that, lately, he hadn't been fooling around enough with her went unspoken, but was acknowledged by both of them. And he'd promised to cut back on the long hours at the lab. A promise made more times than he cared to think about. And now this . . . this odd anomaly which had stuck its head so unexpectedly out of the sand. Kurt Eez was right, he saw, watching the latest round of print-outs pouring out of the computer. There was clearly some form of molecular exchange taking place between the culture colonies, and therefore, probably, between the individual viruses.

Before he'd sent the weekend staff home in the early hours of the evening, they'd set up an experiment to verify the preliminary readings. Two colonies of the herpes simplex virus, HSV1, the type that causes cold sores in humans, had been placed in the same culture dish, separated by microfilters designed to keep each colony segregated on its own side of the culture. The protein molecules in each colony painstakingly typed and matched, not an easy task, even using the government-surplus machinery. But once that was accomplished, low-level radiation markers had been injected into one colony's molecule scheme. And now, according to the computer, those marked molecules were showing up in both colonies, even though the viruses themselves had been kept apart by the filters, and even though they had been separated by what would amount to thousands of miles on a human scale. What this meant, exactly, Bracken wasn't sure. The only thing that could be said with certainty was that individual virus colonies seemed to be capable of exchanging protein molecules. A capability which was, supposedly, beyond their limitations. But was it actually communication? He kept going back to the ants, which was hardly surprising, given his scientific specialty. Still, the similarities were amazing, and chilling. It all invoked questions too vast to consider, at least without further proof.

Even so, Bracken was unable to stop his mind from wandering. Was there some sort of primitive organiza-

tion on the subcellular level? Indeed, was it primitive at
all? Could the social organization of ants be considered
primitive? They were hunters and gatherers, engineers
and builders, gardeners and domesticaters of other insects. If that was primitive, then what made human civilization any different, any better? Art and the ability to
communicate on an intellectual level were the common
responses, he knew. Language was said to be the key to
civilization. The primary thing separating man from the
beasts. Well, that assumption might very well be out the
window, Bracken thought, looking over the readouts.
What was language? The strange, intricate dance of the
honeybee to show its hive mates the location of a food
source? And wasn't the lab itself developing language,
so complicated it could barely be recognized by human
beings, to allow the supercomputers to read encoded
protein molecules? A thing done with relative ease by
ants, bees, termites . . . and now, perhaps, viruses. And
who knew what passed for art in the world of the ant?
Or in the microscopic world, for that matter, he thought,
staring at the image of the two virus colonies on the
electron scan screen. Could genetic engineering be considered an art form? What if disease itself was the
viruses' means of calling human attention to themselves?

The thought sent a particularly cold chill through
him. There were radio telescopes, he knew, scanning the
heavens looking for signs of communication from alien
life-forms. What if we're looking in the wrong direction? He heard the question sliding across his brain,
bright and diffused, like an oil stain on a calm lake.
What if . . .

He looked around the lab, suddenly realizing that he
was very much alone. Through the blinds, streetlights

fought the encroaching darkness but won only small, circular-shaped victories. Shadows played across the corners and angles of the lab, like one-dimensional animals chasing themselves in a slow-motion dance. He knew that whatever was going on here could wait, and that he should be home with Rebecca. Human beings, after all, needed companionship during the dark hours of the night, if only to keep imagined demons at bay.

"See you fellows on Monday," he said, tapping the computer screen, laughing at his own dim humor. He shut the electric scanner down, stored the cultures back in their dark, temperature-controlled vaults, and set the computer into its security mode. The machinery would not only alert the authorities if the premises were violated, but would also put in emergency calls to Bracken or the other senior lab people if there was a problem with any of the temperature controls. There was even a fail-safe device that set off an alert if the computer itself experienced a shutdown.

"And what if the fail-safe device breaks down?" Bracken had asked, when the system was installed. "Do we have a backup emergency plan for the backup emergency plan?"

He had been dismayed when neither Jacoby nor Stampe realized he was joking.

"Good night all," he said to the empty lab, turning out the lights, locking the door behind him.

Rebecca was watching the end of a movie he'd rented that morning before starting the yard work. Bracken sat beside her on the couch, helping himself to a handful of her popcorn, amazed it was still the same day he had visited the video store.

"Making a house call?" she asked, in what he thought

was an inappropriate attempt at sarcasm. Then he looked down and realized he was still wearing his lab coat.

"Maybe we can find you a hospital gown and play doctor," he suggested, which earned him a fading grin and Rebecca's much-practiced roll of the eyes.

"I don't think so," Becky said, shaking her head. "We can play the restaurant game, if you want. I saved you some supper. It's in the fridge."

"Thanks, I appreciate the thought, but we ordered pizza at the lab," Bracken said. "I could use a drink, though. You want one?"

"Why not?" Becky said, pushing the rewind on the VCR as the movie credits rolled by on the television screen. "It *is* Saturday night, after all. Or Sunday morning, by now, if one was keeping track. Which I'm not, of course."

Bracken winced again, splashing water into their Scotch and ice.

"I know. I'm sorry," he apologized. Rebecca, as she usually did, ignored any apology that was halfhearted, at best.

"So, this is some kind of breakthrough?" she asked, picking up her glass, sliding by him toward the kitchen. As usual, Bracken found himself captivated at the way she moved, like a breeze blowing through an elm tree. The smell of her perfume wrapped around him like soft, invisible tentacles. Was it a calculated thing, he wondered, this effect she had on him? After all, they had been married now for almost seven years. Even as the scent of her faded and he heard her rinsing out the popcorn bowl in the sink, he realized that human beings also communicate using scent molecules. The thought caused him to take a large gulp of his drink.

"Could be," he said, knowing he had just sounded as noncommittal as Kurt Eez on the phone that morning. So he explained further that the research seemed to have uncovered an unusual protein exchange between virus colonies. He left out the possible implications of this discovery, as he himself was still considering them.

Did communication denote, on some level at least, intelligence? Was there in the virus community, as in ant colonies, some sort of social order? A hive mentality? A communal mind? What *were* they saying to one another?

Indeed, Bracken wondered if these questions could ever be answered. And did the human world—so sure of its place in the hierarchy of the planet—truly want to know the answers? Viruses lived by the trillions, side by side and inside mankind. How would people react to the news that some microscopic intelligence was living inside them? Not well, Bracken thought. Not well at all.

"Sounds like a stretch from your research parameters," Becky said, ever the pragmatist.

If she gave any consideration to Bracken's unspoken questions, she kept it to herself and cut right to the business end of things. Hardly surprising either, Bracken thought, given the fact that Rebecca was the lab's principal grant writer, and so knew more, by far, about the business end of things than he did. He borrowed freely on her expertise in obtaining the necessary government funding for the lab's projects. Shamelessly, he admitted. Worming her way through the twisted lanes of bureaucracy seemed to be second nature to his wife. It was very close to an artistic gift, Bracken thought. A gift appreciated and handsomely rewarded by the universities and museums who contracted for her services. The fact that Becky made considerably more money than he did had, at one time in the early days of their relationship, been a sizable thorn in his side. But it was a thing he had long since come to terms with, especially since her income allowed for a much more comfortable lifestyle than he would have been able to provide as an ill-paid beaker pusher, eking out an existence doing hand-me-down genetic research. Work the big laboratories and university hotshots were simply too busy to handle. Besides, Rebecca never seemed concerned about the income disparity, and certainly wasn't about to give up her career simply because her husband's male ego overshadowed his common sense.

"Maybe a little stretch," Bracken admitted. "But the industrial agency is flexible, particularly when the research yields results."

That was true enough, both of them knew. It was only five years ago that the United States had established the Bureau of Industrial Research, following Japan's successful example of providing technological development funding to the private sector. Even if it took the politicians damn near fifty years to come to the conclusion that the way to expand the job market in the United States was to make American companies competitive in the world marketplace, Bracken often complained. So five years ago, with the infusion of funds, the research market took off. While Gary Bracken and his associates hadn't gotten in on the ground floor, at least they squeezed themselves through the door, carried across the threshold on the shoulders of Rebecca's bureaucratic artistry, Bracken freely admitted. Centrifuge Labs—a name Bracken had fought, in a losing effort against Jacoby and Stampe, on whose reputations and cash resources the laboratory had originally been founded—was now contracted to the BIR in a massive national science project, aimed at bringing the new generation of supercomputers, the protein readers, into the realm of reality. To Bracken, who had previously been involved in genetic research, specifically fruit-fly mutations, the work was exciting and offered possibilities university research couldn't touch. Namely, that he was as close to being his own boss as he was likely to get; answerable only to the senior partners, Jacoby and Stampe, and, of course, the BIR oversight committees, who were conveniently distant, and like most bureaucrats, holed up in their Washington offices lobbying Congress for more money. It was an arrangement Bracken found to be much to his liking.

"It's your authority problem," Becky often told him, usually when it was time to fill out the renewal forms for Centrifuge's grant dollars. "You never respond well to authority."

Bracken, not wanting to argue, lest he have to fill out the seemingly endless reams of paper, could only shake his head in agreement. Besides which, his run-ins with the research board at Columbia were well documented and filed away in Rebecca's mind, giving him no room to maneuver.

"It's kind of odd, don't you think, that someone who rails against authority would end up working for the supreme authorities—the government?" Becky slipped the final knife in with smooth precision as she went about the complicated procedures involved in keeping the lab running.

"I don't work for the government," Bracken always protested, in what he knew was a losing effort.

"Gary, my boy," Rebecca would say, smiling, "Centrifuge Labs has got their hands so deep in the government pocket, the two of you are practically going steady."

As much as he wanted to, even as she laughed at her own joke, Bracken knew there was no denying it. The BIR was clearly a silent partner in their enterprise, and probably a damn sight more than that, he admitted.

"Did you call any of your esteemed colleagues?" Becky asked, pulling him back to the kitchen and his half-empty glass.

"Not yet," Bracken said. "I'll tell everyone on Monday. It's all very preliminary at this point, anyway."

"Monday?" Becky said, feigning amazement. "You mean you're actually going to take a day off? Maybe spend some quality time with your neglected wife?"

She moved closer to him, a most alluring look in her eyes. Bracken sighed, putting his glass on the counter. She ran a hand across the collar of his lab coat.

"Did anyone ever tell you how impossibly sexy you are?" he asked, reaching for her.

"Not in a while," she said, the words whispered in his ear, and he wondered for a moment how one drink could make his head spin. She pulled away, walking toward the bedroom, turning out the light as she went.

"Coming?" she asked suggestively.

And he laughed, shaking his head, following her like some sort of trained dog. He was damn lucky she didn't ask him to jump through flaming hoops or sit up and beg, Bracken thought, because he probably would've done it. He barely realized he was following her scent trail into the bedroom.

Later, as they curled up together, the crumpled sheet pushed down to the bottom of the bed, she pressed against him, both of them wavering in the murky state between waking and sleep. The fog of their lovemaking touching them like a soft mist.

"So," she whispered, lying against his chest. "What do you think the little buggers are saying to each other?"

His eyes popped open and he looked down at her, caught off guard by her question, by the sleepy, matter-of-fact manner in which it was asked.

"I don't have the faintest idea," he said, and in seconds Becky was asleep. Bracken, however, lay awake for a long time, staring up at the shadows drifting across the ceiling. It was a question, he realized, which might better be left alone. It was a lot like asking if the shadowy patterns passing above him held their own deep, secret meaning. Even if they did, would you really want to know? he asked himself. Somewhere in the depths of the night, he, too, drifted off to sleep. Above him, the shadows moved, until the sun rose and melted them away.

a molecule of time
Day One + 1.253775 x 10 ^12

Working feverishly, the small mammal dug out from the collapsed entrance of its burrow. Beneath its feet, the earth still trembled, vibrating from the shock of the impact. The shrewlike animal, of course, had no idea, no inkling of the colossal events reshaping the world. It knew only the terrible fear of being buried alive in its underground nest. Even now, as it smelled the air above and frantically pushed aside the heavy dirt with its sharp claws, the fear of the unknown caused its rib cage to heave in panic. The last of the collapsed earth was finally pushed aside, and the animal filled its lungs with life-giving air.

Days had passed since the thundering explosion which shook the planet to its foundations, causing the collapse of all the entrances to the underground burrow. At first, fear kept the tiny creature frozen in its sealed chamber. But as the air grew sour, as hunger and thirst twisted its belly, the shrew had begun its frantic effort to reach the surface. Survival instinct overcoming paralyzing terror as the ground shook and slid beneath it. And now, gulping the hot, sultry air, the creature's efforts were rewarded. Life was a thing to be fought for, to the exclusion of all else.

Aboveground, the world was dark and shadowy, even though the animal sensed that it was not yet night. Not yet time to forage. Still, blinking its wide eyes in the gloom, its senses began searching for the small insects and bits of carrion on which it fed. Smoke and ash drifted down from the cloud-strewn sky, whispering confusing messages to the animal's small brain. One thing, however, penetrated the haze with frightening clarity—the roars and grunts of the great beasts in the valley below. And with those sounds, an odd smell drifted on the hot, smoke-filled breeze. It was the smell of fear, and it permeated the whole of the world.

In the valley, where the wide, slow-moving river made its way to the sea, the scene was one of panic and confusion. The great beasts were in a state of terror which approached the small mammal's own fevered pitch, when it had been trapped in its burrow. They milled about in their herds, roaring at the fact that the earth kept moving beneath their feet. Huge, smoking fissures opened in the aftermath of the asteroid's impact. Volcanic eruptions exploded into the darkened sky, on a scale unknown to the planet for millennia. These, spewing forth their own smoke and ash, added to the atmosphere's already heavy burden of dirt and dust particles. The sun now seemed absent from the sky, as were the moon and stars. For months after the impact, no creature would bask in the glory of the sun's brilliance. No creature would forage in the moon's ghostly light. Night now came with the darkness of a shroud, lit only by fires spewing forth from deep

within the earth as they reflected off the clouds of smoke
and dust. The rain came down in sheets of sooty mud.
And so it would be, for generations.

The shrewlike mammal, mercifully unaware of these
harsh facts, snatched a passing moth from the air and fed,
listening to the confused, milling sounds of the herds
below. It was as if the great beasts somehow sensed that
the end of the world was at hand. And indeed it was.

In the first days and weeks following the asteroid's
impact, surface temperatures rose dramatically, as the
cloud cover sealed in the earth's heat. But as seasons
passed, with the sun's rays unable to penetrate fully the
thick layer of dust and ash which had made its way into
the upper layers of the atmosphere, the water world
began to cool. Thick stands of tropical plants fell victim
to the combined effects of the cold and lack of direct
sunlight. The great beasts themselves, those who fed
upon the plants and the mighty predators who followed
the herds in the long, complicated food chain, began to
decline slowly in numbers. Those beasts who dwelt in
the sea also felt the effects of this cataclysm. The massive sheets of plankton were unable to sustain themselves, bringing about a further collapse in the carefully
constructed, interlocking system of plant/animal,
predator/prey.

But as terrible as these events were, the worst was yet
to come—for the cataclysm, sudden and unexpected,
caused the activation of the virus clans' survival instincts.
Survival being the first, primary goal. And so, within the
bodies of their hosts, the clans multiplied. The Great
Dying, initiated by the impact of the huge asteroid, became greater still. And once begun, it continued unabated
for centuries, until ninety percent of all the life that had
been created—from the huge thundering beasts who

dominated the earth for 165 million years, to the smallest mollusk living in darkness at the bottom of the ocean— were extinct. Vanished from the face of the planet in what amounted to an instant of Galactic time.

The tiny mammal, barely the size of a present-day mouse, finished its meal. Both stomach and lungs satisfied, it listened for a moment to the confused, panicked roars of the great beasts in the valley. It smelled the air, which was thick with smoke and the overpowering scent of fear, and retreated back into the safety of its burrow. In the coming months, it found a boundless supply of carrion on which to feed. As the smaller, warm-blooded reptiles who once hunted them began to disappear, the offspring of the tiny shrew flourished, each generation bringing forth ever greater numbers of its species.

And many cycles of time later, when the skies cleared, when the dust and ash had settled to the ground, covering the bones of the victims of the Great Dying, a descendant of this mammal poked its head above the mound of earth protecting its burrow and blinked at the light of the sun, breathing the fresh air of a new world.

Within the bodies of their hosts, those who had survived the holocaust, the virus clans began their work again. Timeless and infinitely patient. Rebuilding their resources, as they had in the past, and would again in the future. The One, searching for the cells it had been programmed to mutate. The One, becoming the Many, seeking to become ONE.

five

"It's impossible," Jacoby said, shaking his head. Carefully, Bracken noted, so the long sweep of hair that grew out of the side of his head and covered his bald spot wouldn't be shaken loose. "Viruses aren't even living organisms."

"Well, that's debatable," Terrance Stampe commented, even though he seemed to agree with Jacoby's main point.

Bracken just shook his head. He had expected this reaction from the two senior partners. Jacoby and Stampe each had a couple decades on him, both in terms of age and of years of scientific experience. And there was, undoubtedly, a seniority system, long established and firmly entrenched, within the scientific community. The fact that Bracken's wife procured Centrifuge's grant money counted little when it came to questions of expertise. Plus, Bracken was an entomologist, a lower-class scientist, particularly in Jacoby's estimation, he knew.

Never mind what the data seemed to show, they were going to stick together, chained at the neck to the "old boys" network, Bracken thought. Which was probably an unkind assumption, Bracken realized even as he watched them in their autopsy of the material. After all, hadn't he done the same thing when Kurt Eez first called him?

The three of them were alone in the conference room at their regular Monday-morning meeting, at which Bracken was somehow required to bring doughnuts. It was a pattern they had fallen into early in the partnership. Bracken, who had been pleased to have the two men, both esteemed in their fields, invite him to join the endeavor, clearly realized he had been accepted in a subordinate role. Jacoby and Stampe simply saw it as the younger associate paying his dues, as they no doubt had done in their days as fledgling researchers. But Bracken knew he was no novice, having published in at least as many scientific journals as the two of them. And now, he felt, it was time to assert himself.

"I think we have to put our prejudice aside and look at the data for what it is," he said. At this interruption, they stopped their one-sided debate and stared at him.

"The data is, to say the least, preliminary," Jacoby scowled, pointing out the obvious.

"Agreed," Bracken said, defusing the argument before it could blow up in his face. "But the implications are undeniable. There was, or seemed to be, protein transfer between two virus communities. Whether it was accidental or part of a cross-infection process, it still needs to be looked into."

Stampe took a long pull at his coffee, as if it were laced with brandy, which Bracken sometimes suspected it was in the afternoon hours. Still, Terrance Stampe nodded in what seemed to be agreement.

"That may be true." Jacoby reluctantly gave some ground. "But to call the process communication seems to be premature, at best. Viruses obviously do not have organized thought patterns. Surely you're not suggesting—"

"I'm not suggesting anything," Bracken said. "I'm only presenting what the data showed. It's true that in the conventional sense, viruses might not fulfill what are commonly recognized as traits of living organisms. They don't reproduce on their own. They don't eat or breathe or excrete, or do any of the things we attribute to life. They are, however, experts in the field of genetic engineering."

Jacoby, a baptized and confirmed Darwinist, huffed at that comment, as Bracken knew he would. But the older man did not deny its validity. Nor could he, as a scientist. Viruses were unique organisms, almost alien in the context of the natural world. At least using terms which scientists like Jacoby and Stampe recognized as the universal attributes of life. But it was, in Bracken's opinion, a limited viewpoint. The universe was vast and largely unknown, even if some chose to ignore that fact when the occasion suited them. The truth was, the very existence of viruses and their unique properties presented a myriad of problems for traditionalists in the scientific community. Simply put, given their limited facilities, viruses should not be able to do what they did. The virus, in its many shapes and sizes, was in the end only a few strands of genetic material, surrounded by protein molecules and nucleic acid. Their very existence had only been confirmed with the introduction of the electron-scan microscope in the 1930s. The discovery of the double helix, which the viruses have been using like giant Tinkertoys for billions of years, didn't occur on a human level until the fifties. The DNA code itself wasn't broken down, even on its most basic level, until the 1960s. And today, research was still in the infant stages. Facts Bracken could have used in his argument, but didn't, as Jacoby knew them as well as anyone.

While some in the scientific community were starting to consider the possibility that viruses were alien to the indigenous environment of Earth, this viewpoint, he knew, would have been scoffed at by Jacoby and Stampe. And really, it had no bearing on the facts at hand. But there was still the very real possibility that all life on Earth had been introduced in microscopic form from outside the planetary boundaries. The origins of life were, at this point anyway, an unanswerable question. Even to hint at such a thing would have meant skewing the argument in impossible directions, and Bracken was a good enough chess player to realize that was not the way to get what he wanted.

"I'm not suggesting we completely alter the parameters of our work," he said, making every attempt to sound conciliatory. "Only that we divert a small portion of our resources to investigate the phenomenon."

Jacoby and Stampe had the look of cattle being gently loaded into trucks which they suspected might be heading toward the slaughterhouse, Bracken thought, suppressing a grin. But in the end, they nodded their reluctant approval.

"I'll agree, for the moment anyway, on the condition that we keep the whole thing quiet," Jacoby said. "If word got out, we'd likely end up being laughed out of town."

"Agreed," Bracken said, having no intention of letting

this potential discovery leak out into the world before Centrifuge Labs was ready to claim full credit. It somehow slipped his mind that Copernicus, fearing ignorance and superstition, had only allowed his findings to be published when he himself was on his deathbed. Or that Galileo, along with a whole host of his fellow scientists, had been tried and imprisoned by the Inquisition.

"Well, I don't like them," Mary Ann Meade was saying as Bracken came into the lab. She and Kurt Eez, he saw, were having what appeared to be an animated discussion as they prepared the evening's culture dishes. Bracken was running a new series of experiments to see if they could isolate the protein molecules being transferred within the virus communities. It was tedious work, even tapping into the fed's big-brain computers in Atlanta. Basically, it was an extension of their previous identification process, only this time they were hoping to catch the viruses in the act, and with luck isolate one or more of the transferred proteins.

"Don't like who?" Bracken asked, smiling a greeting at the two young people. He decided they all needed to get better acquainted, since it seemed they would be spending a considerable amount of time together. Bracken himself opted to work the night shift for a few weeks, both to avoid the crush of the lab's daytime activity and to keep the project under wraps for as long as possible. Kurt and Mary Ann immediately stopped talking, and all three suddenly found themselves surrounded by a fog of uncomfortable silence. Bracken was struck by the very real possibility that they had been discussing members of the senior staff. So much for shoehorning yourself into other people's conversations, he thought, his entrance smile frozen on his face.

"Viruses," Kurt Eez said, groping his way around the edges of the fog. Bracken raised an eyebrow. "Mary Ann doesn't like viruses."

"They're creepy," she said, sounding as if she were attempting to apologize for some imagined social blunder.

"I agree," Bracken said, grinning wider. "They're definitely creepy critters."

He moved over to the bank of equipment and saw they had almost finished preparing the setup on the cultures. To his relief, they were also smiling back at him, the uncomfortable moment passing into the forgotten depths of linear time.

"So we're about ready to start the identification run?" Bracken asked.

"Almost there," Kurt said, turning his attention back to the culture dishes, sliding them into the electron scan for the initial phase of the experiment.

"Viruses are actually quite astounding creatures," Bracken said as he sat down at the computer station to log on with the Atlanta data banks. Access to the big mainframes was one of the many perks of contracted government work. "Have you had a chance to work much in the submicron field?" he asked, directing his question to Mary Ann Meade, who truly seemed uncomfortable even touching the culture dishes.

"Just the basic undergrad work. But I'm familiar with all the procedures," she quickly added.

Bracken nodded, realizing he had put the young woman into a defensive position, and looked for a way to rectify his mistake.

"This will be a good experience for you, then," he said. "And you don't have to worry, we're not working with anything particularly dangerous here."

Meade, he saw, was trying to brush away her apprehension, helping Kurt Eez set up the scan parameters.

"But you're right to be cautious." Bracken nodded. "Like you said, they're pretty creepy."

Mary Ann grinned, a little, he thought.

"The textbooks used to teach that viruses were among the first life-forms," Bracken said as he hooked into Atlanta and the big-brain machines at the CDC computer center began the complicated task of identifying and marking the various protein molecules in the two virus cultures. Bracken thought it might be a good idea to see where his assistants stood, both in knowledge and principle. "That is, until someone realized that they were parasites and needed other fully formed entities to reproduce."

"Which means that viruses developed sometime during the Age of Bacteria." Kurt Eez took the ball, having been through these sorts of tests with Bracken before. "Probably early on, but definitely after life was already fully entrenched in the primeval seas."

"Actually, prokaryotes appeared relatively soon after the earth became hospitable to life," Mary Ann interjected, catching onto the game quickly, which pleased Bracken, who disliked working with slow people. She was referring to the most basic subdivision of life, in which bacteria, the simplest of cellular organisms, were classified. The next group were the eukaryotes, organisms defined by a more complex cell structure, principally a separated, isolated nucleus. The latter group comprising all the other many forms of life, from amoebae to human beings. All of which went unsaid, much to Bracken's relief, as this was knowledge any competent undergraduate in biology would have readily at his command. "Fossil evidence puts the time frame at around three and a half billion years ago, give or take a year or two," Mary Ann said, smiling.

"Interesting, isn't it?" Bracken said. "That the oldest rocks we've been able to find show fossil evidence of organic organisms. Almost as if the earth itself came with the blueprints of life."

The scanning microscope and the computer equipment made their humming, electrical sounds. Bracken clicked on the visual monitor, and the viruses themselves became visible on the screen. Looking, he thought, like tiny, lifeless lumps. Like a picture of sterile moon rocks. Bracken knew that the failure of this viewpoint lay not with the seeming inactivity of the viruses, but rather with science's feeble attempts to peer into the submicroscopic world.

"So what are they?" he asked, both to himself and his two assistants. A long moment of silence followed as each considered the question. There was no good answer. Only theory and conjecture, all of which seemed to change on a daily basis within the scientific community. This was true whether one was considering the subject of viruses, or the majesty and depth of the cosmos.

"Degenerate genetic material formed from discarded DNA strands and loose cellular proteins?" Mary Ann Meade offered, shrugging her shoulders when the men looked over at her. "Hey, don't blame the messenger. I read it someplace."

Bracken laughed, enjoying the fact that they seemed to be developing a dialogue between them.

"Maybe," he said, studying the screen. "But that doesn't account for the fact that somehow viruses are able to do something even we're only beginning to understand—to reengineer the very structure of life. What are the odds against a few strands of RNA or DNA coming together with that sort of instinctive knowledge built into their own genetic background? And they had to be able to do that, almost from the beginning, or they wouldn't have been able to survive."

"Okay, here's what I don't understand," Kurt Eez said. "Viruses came into existence after life was already established, because parasitic organisms obviously can't exist without hosts, right?"

Bracken nodded, already guessing where Eez was heading. The same quandary had been rattling around in his own head these past few days.

"Evolution tells us, basically, that there is a hierarchy progression, from the primitive to the most highly developed," Eez said. "Natural selection, Gould's spurts of development, all of which makes sense, until you come to these guys." Kurt tapped the screen with a pencil, looking perplexed. "These little beasties—a hundred times smaller than bacteria, with no central nervous system, no brain, and only the barest resemblance to living organisms—but they're somehow able to reconfigure DNA. And do it better than we can. It's amazing when you think about it. They're able to cut and paste the DNA strands of every living thing on the planet! Like they're some kind of outer space intelligence, or something . . ."

Kurt swallowed the last of his words, as if suddenly realizing that as a scientist, he had perhaps gone too far, and if he wanted to continue his career, he'd better be more careful about what he blurted out. Bracken watched the young man raise his defensive shields, a thing he would learn to do with increasing frequency if he stayed in the research field.

"I don't know that there are any good answers," Bracken said, redirecting the group back to the work at hand, unable to tell Eez that he himself had struggled with the same thoughts. When you considered the available facts, it did seem that viruses were indeed so different from the other life-forms on Earth, they could be called alien creatures. The thought had a sobering effect on him. "Maybe that's why we're here," he suggested. "To find some of the answers."

The computer kicked on its "ready" light, indicating the first phase of the experiment had been completed. The three, now working as a team, Bracken noted, moved to initiate the second step, marking the proteins in one culture group with low-level radiation.

"There's something else I don't get," Kurt said, a look of the terminally lost etching furrows across his forehead. "When and if we isolate one of these proteins, what next?"

"Termites," Bracken said, smiling, refusing any further explanation.

Kurt Eez shook his head. Hearing that, Mary Ann Meade mumbled something, mostly to herself.

The night ticked away its hours as they worked. It was now Day One plus 1.2775 x 10 to the 12th power, or 3.5 billion years since the first Change began.

a molecule of time
Day One + 1.2765875 x 10 ^12

The female was afraid, and she had good reason for her fear. Her belly was swollen almost to the breaking point. The new life within her, kicking, reaching out to be born. She herself was young, and this would be her first birthing. Each day, as her time drew closer, the fear became greater, until now it was almost a palpable, living thing in her mind. Each dawn, as Fire crawled from its cave at the end of the world and walked across the sky, could be her last day. And truly, she did not want to die. Particularly not in the manner in which so many of her sisters had perished. Shrieking, with blood running down the fur of their legs like water. The young ones, lodged in bloated bellies, unable to make the journey into life. She had seen First Sister suffer in this way. Hours of terrible pain, with the Elder females huddled around the birthing nest, actually reaching up inside First Sister, their arms coming away bloody and empty. Until finally, she had been carried away into the forest, where her cries and blood scent would not attract predators to the sleeping nests of the troop.

It was a terrible memory, one that crept into her awareness as she crawled from her own nest, high in the lush trees at the edge of the sea of grass. The others were coming awake beside her. Stretching their long arms, urinating onto the ground below. One of the Elder females, smelling her fear, pushed through the tree branches to the young female's nest. Brushing the fur on her swollen belly, biting at the ticks and lice around her ears. Offering comforting, grunting sounds and handfuls of fruit plucked from the mango trees in which the clan nested during the green season. The young female, calmed by the attentions of her Elder, returned the pruning favors, until the dominant male signaled that it was now time to move out onto the sea of grass to forage.

Clumsy with the heavy weight of her unborn young one, she climbed slowly from the high branches. Standing on the forest floor, rising to her full three feet of height, she scanned the bush with wide, deep-set eyes. The males, she saw, were already leading the way down the slope, away from the tree line, picking up stones and fallen tree limbs as they traveled. The young female hurried after them, her body leaning forward in a loping, four-legged trot. She caught up with the others as the clan stopped at the edge of the river and drank, keeping a wary eye out for predators who stalked the drinking places near the sea of grass. Noses flaring as they tested the shifting breezes, before lowering their heads into the swirling pools of water.

After each had drunk his fill, as they always did during the green season, the troop moved on. Scouts loped ahead, watching the sky for telltale signs of carrion birds, the winged ones always being first to find the fallen bodies of the herd animals. In the distance, clouds of dust wavered against the horizon as vast herds moved through the sea of grass. The males led the way as the females followed, grouped together with their young, picking insects from the tall, brown grass. It was the time of nesting birds, with their clutches of warm, delicious eggs. The time when grubs and larvae could be found lying on the churned-up ground, after the herd animals passed. The time of sweet, multicolored flowers—some of which could be eaten, or rubbed across the fur to attract the attention of the males of the troop. The young female watched as some of her sisters engaged in this game, even as she herself had once done. Only now, with the young one kicking in her belly, she was sorry she had. Her first flowering had attracted the attention of the dominant male, an honor among the young females, who were usually paired with lesser partners. But now their coupling had opened her to the seeding fogs of the earth, and she felt certain that she, too, would soon suffer the same fate as First Sister. To be carried from the camp, more dead than alive, to give birth or perish, as the Mother of them all willed it.

There were, as yet, no words for any of this. There was no fire, no permanent dwellings, other than nests of leaves or grass. The clan lived open to the elements, communicating through simple grunts and hand signs. Migrating with the herds, with the patterns of the seasons, as did others of their kind. They ate fruit and leaves from the trees. They searched the sea of grass for fallen animals, occasionally coming upon a sick or wounded beast, which the males would attempt to kill with their sticks and heavy stones. It was a primitive existence, yet one in which each member of the troop was given a share of the available food, and each young one was cherished and protected. Once, of course, it survived the trauma of its own birth.

The young female raised her muzzle toward the sky, testing the wind, feeling the warmth of Fire on her face. Small birds called to one another in the tall grass. Clouds larger than her two hands, passed through the deep blue above her. It seemed for a moment as if she was spinning, as if the world was turning beneath her. . . .

Her ears picked up the grunting calls of the males from beyond the next rise. Instantly, the females stopped their scattered foraging and banded together in a tight group, the young ones thrust into the middle of their protective circle. The barking sounds of short-tailed wolves quickly followed the grunting calls of the males. Carefully, the Elder females led the way up the slope. Below them, the young female saw, the short-tails were in the process of finishing a kill. One of the striped hooved beasts, who had wandered from the confines of the herd. The animal was fatally wounded, blood streaming from its hamstrung hindquarters. One of the heavy wolves had its powerful jaws clamped around the prey's throat, bending the doomed animal to the ground, as others of the hunting pack snapped at its soft underbelly, pulling intestines out like long vines onto the bloody grass. The males, she saw, were rushing forward, swinging their tree limbs at the short-tails, pelting them with stones. It was a scene of blood and confusion, as hunting pack and scavenging troop fought one another for possession of the gasping, dying prey.

The dominant male ran forward with a heavy stone poised over his head, delivering a crushing blow to the rib cage of the wolf who had its jaws around the throat of the striped beast. The stone landed with a loud thump, producing a strangled, groaning bark from the short-tail, as the air rushed out of its body. Its jaws were torn loose from their killing hold. The wolf, snarling in pain and anger, rolled on the ground, its tongue flapping, eyes twisting up, white and terrible in its skull. The other males rushed in, swinging their sticks, growling and snapping at the short-tails. And as the pack's leader crawled away, panting and gasping, the rest of the short-tails reluctantly followed. The males raised their long arms and beat their sticks upon the ground in victory.

The prey animal lay on its side, gave a long heave of the rib cage and its eyes glazed over. The females ran down to the site of the kill, the troop forming a tight ring around the fallen beast. The younger males stood watch as the others fed. Then the older males alternated with them, according to the hierarchy. The females also followed the same feeding pattern. The young ones, however, were allowed to lick the blood and eat whatever scraps their small teeth could tear from the prey. It was a scene of barely controlled chaos, although no one in the troop thought it so.

The young female tore a long strip of flesh from the front shoulder of the animal. She sat on her haunches amid the group of females, savoring the thick, fresh blood as it dripped down her throat. One of her sister's young ones began pulling at the strip of meat, and the female bit off a piece, chewing it for a moment to soften the flesh, before placing it into the small, grasping hands. Fire continued its trek through the sky. Flies buzzed, ants and beetles crawled across the carcass. Overhead, carrion birds began to gather, and this was the signal for the troop to move on. The short-tailed wolves reappeared, creeping across the grass. Soon they would be joined by other, more dangerous beasts. And so, with their stomachs full, the males grunted and began leading the troop back toward the tree line at the edge of the sea of grass. The young female hastily stuck her remaining meat portion into her mouth and followed. She chewed as she walked, enjoying the juices as they rolled down the back of her tongue. It was, she thought, like catching water in one's mouth during the first rain after the dry season—sweet and wonderful. Silently, she thanked the striped hooved one for this gift.

The troop made its way back into the nesting area in the mango trees as Fire began to end its walk, sinking into the clouds. The long shadows of the trees fell across the forest floor. Looking, the female thought, like the stripes of the hooved one they had eaten. She was considering this picture in her mind as the troop milled together, pruning and licking each other's fur, when a pain, sharp and deep, cut across her midsection. She gasped as the pain made its way down into her thighs and legs. The fear, which she had forgotten, returned like a thundercloud rushing across her brain. No! she thought, panic causing her hands to shake. Not now. Not with the darkness pressing around them. This was the worst possible time. When the hunters of the night came prowling. When the males were even now making their way up the trees to their sleeping nests.

She grunted softly, urgently, and the Elder females gathered around her, smelling her fear, sensing the time of her birthing was upon her. They pulled her arms, pushing her heavy body upward, toward the relative safety of the high, vine-covered branches. Forcing her to climb while she was still able to do so. From somewhere inside her, she found the strength, knowing that to remain on the ground, in the dark, during her birthing, would be to die.

In the high branches, the Elder females hastily pulled

together a nest of leaves and twigs, and here the young female lay, her breath coming in short, quick gasps. The Elders formed a protective ring around her, squatting in the branches, turning their backs to her as she moaned and grunted. The pain sweeping through her body, the young one forcing itself out of her, until it seemed as if her very bones were being pulled apart. The female gnashed her teeth and tried to remain as quiet as possible, lest she attract the attention of predators, even as the pain shook her like a leaf blowing in a summer storm. The head of the young one was simply too big! It was pulling her apart. The memory of First Sister, shrieking in agony, dying with the sharp scent of blood leaking from her, as it had from the striped hooved beast, kept returning to her mind. Hot and burning. Like those who foolishly touched the dancing Fire when it walked across the sea of grass. And finally, when it seemed she could bear no more, when the night itself had turned into an endless river of pain, she felt the young one push free between her legs, ripping her like a heavy stone falling through her body. Unable to help herself, she gave a last, loud grunt . . . and the young one gave its own soft cry at her feet. The Elder females seemed to wake from their vigil, turning to her, making quiet, reassuring clicking noises with their teeth as the female reached down and pulled the young one to her breast. She sighed, the fear rushing away like fog melting in the morning light. The moon had risen, shedding its soft illumination through the leaves, and the female saw her young one—the head, large and heavy, like a ripe mango on the end of a thin branch. The young one raised its head a little, only to fall back onto its mother's breast. Together the young female and her child slept, until Fire woke from its cave at the end of the world and began to walk again across the sky.

• • •

In the bodies of their hosts, the virus clans worked. Cells were mutated in endless patterns. The laws of natural selection were invoked, giving final voice to the life-and-death decisions. Slowly, over millions of years, a creature emerged possessing that most unique capacity—a complex, multifunctional brain. Fueled by this success, the evolutionary forces began to expand in an explosive fashion. Generation by generation, layers of cells were added to the brain mass of these creatures. The skull widened, the body itself grew larger, heavier. The creatures themselves began to see the world in a new light.

And still the clans continued their work. Timeless and infinitely patient. The One becoming the Many, seeking to become ONE. While there remained much yet to be done, a beginning had been made.

s i x

It had been raining buckets all morning and the Beltway traffic was its usual, predictable nightmare. Once again, Harvey Mitchell found himself cursing the government cutbacks that eliminated drivers for all but the most prestigious bureaucrats. The Bureau of Industrial Research, he argued loud and often, was clearly one of the *most* important agencies in the entire federal structure. And as head of the BIR, it was close to a personal insult that he only got a chauffeur when he was meeting with some foreign counterpart. He argued this point, of course, only in the relatively safe confines of his own home, and then only to his wife, who didn't seem to consider it the sort of argument to be taken seriously.

"Then you should bring it up to the president at the next luncheon meeting," Shirley said, always knowing the best way to shut him up.

Her husband, as Shirley well knew, was not about to do anything of the kind. In this day and age, putting yourself at odds with the Washington budget cutters was the quickest route to early retirement. But dammit to hell, Mitchell realized, he was going to be late. The wipers working overtime, traffic bottlenecked at the off-ramp for the downtown offices. Mitchell punched in the number for his own office in the high-rises off New York Avenue.

"Martha, would you call Mr. Sandborn and tell him I'm running about twenty minutes behind schedule? The traffic out here is horrendous."

Martha Graney, who had been with him for the past fifteen years, during the early days at HUD and his long stint at the State Department, where he had fought for years for the formation of the BIR, chuckled on the other end of the line. Harvey Mitchell, she knew, would be hard-pressed to be in his coffin at the appointed hour of his own burial. Mitchell clicked the phone off and cursed some more. Paul Sandborn would not be a happy camper, particularly given the circumstances of their hastily called meeting. Mitchell had argued against involving every small-time research facility in the country in a project of this magnitude, even if it was the very reason behind the establishment of the BIR. And someone like Sandborn, second in command at the National Security Agency, certainly should've been aware of the security problems involved when you farmed out this kind of sensitive work. But, as usual, no one listened to Harvey Mitchell, he thought, pulling around a tourist from Maine who couldn't seem to make up his mind which way to turn as the Washington rush hour swarmed around him like a school of migrating fish.

Mitchell finally got his car parked in the underground facility of the NSA's downtown offices, and made his way through a maze of security to the eighth floor. There, Sandborn's secretary cooled his heels for a dispropor-

tionate amount of time before allowing him into her
boss's inner sanctum. Actually, Paul Sandborn's office
was sparse by Washington standards, Mitchell noted. But
it was hardly a reflection of the man's power, rather a
function of Sandborn's military background. He had,
Mitchell knew, been a colonel in the marines, an opera-
tive for the CIA, if the rumors were true. And as Sandborn looked up at him from behind a plain wooden desk,
Harvey Mitchell believed all the hype surrounding the
man. The close-chopped hair, the gaunt, almost haunted
face. But it was Sandborn's eyes that stopped most men
in their tracks, Harvey Mitchell among them. Sandborn
had the eyes of a predatory bird. Dark and hooded, set
close together in his head. It was said that Sandborn
could glance at a person and immediately determine the
most effective way for them to be assassinated. Both literally and personally. Mitchell was quite surprised, and
somewhat taken back, when Sandborn smiled and stood
to shake his hand.

"Harvey, good to see you again," Sandborn said, seeming to mean it. All of which put Mitchell more on edge.
"Glad you could make it over on such short notice. Some
coffee? There should be a pot on in the conference
room."

Sandborn led the way to an adjoining room, all but
filled by a single long table. Pictures of past presidents
lined the walls, along with an American flag, a coffeepot,
and two mugs set on a tray in the middle of the table.
Sandborn turned on a light switch and hit a button next to
the outlet, which Mitchell knew to be a high-frequency
sound masker. It was to be one of those kinds of meetings. Mitchell had been afraid of that.

"So, we seem to have a problem?" Sandborn asked ca-

sually, pouring two mugs of what looked to be strong
Colombian brew. "Cream or sugar?"

Mitchell shook his head, feeling as though the two of
them were engaged in some obscure military ritual, where
the inability to drink one's coffee straight and black was
to be interpreted as weakness. Sandborn smiled, as if con-
firming his suspicion. Come on, Mitchell said to himself,
you're being paranoid. But then, he considered, if one was
inclined toward paranoia, this room, with its white sound
masker and hidden recording devices, was as good a place
as any to do it in.

"A minor problem, I should think," Mitchell said, sitting discreetly across from Sandborn, as if the two of
them were about to play a high-stakes chess game.

"My people tell me the computer monitors in Atlanta
picked up some unusual inquiries stemming from one of
our research facilities," Sandborn said, sipping his coffee,
getting straight to the point. One of the man's classic
trademarks, Mitchell knew.

"That's correct," Harvey said. "Centrifuge Labs is the
name of the place. A small research laboratory outside
New York City."

Sandborn nodded, as if this was information he already
had in his numerous files.

"I assume we agree on the importance your agency
puts on having its facilities operate within their research
parameters?" Sandborn asked.

"Most assuredly," Mitchell said, putting on his best
stone face. Even though it appeared he could take lessons
from the former colonel. "This, however, seems to fall
into a gray area. The research they're doing up there is directly related to the computer project. We shouldn't be
surprised, really, that one of the people associated with

the project happened to discover the protein anomaly.
Actually it was almost predictable."

"Well, predictable or not, we have to be damn careful
about where this leads, wouldn't you say?" Sandborn
asked pointedly.

"There is no question about that," Mitchell said. And
indeed there was not. "We're following the work at the
laboratory in question very closely. We're sending a
memo around to all the facilities about the importance of
maintaining strict security. We double-checked the clearances on the people at Centrifuge, and they are in com-
pliance. Nothing is leaking from their end."

"Good, very good." Sandborn sounded genuinely
pleased for the first time. "Do you have any indication
just who might be involved in this security breach?"

"I wouldn't call it a security breach," Mitchell said
carefully. "But yes, the access code used on the Atlanta
data bank belonged to a researcher named Gary Bracken.
According to our records, he's been doing most of the
core work in the facility. You have to understand the nature of these people," Mitchell felt compelled to add.
"When they come upon something new or unusual, in-
vestigation of the phenomenon is second nature. That sort
of intense curiosity is what makes them proficient at their
work."

"Yes, thank you." Sandborn smiled, and Harvey
Mitchell suddenly felt exceedingly uncomfortable. "I do
understand the mentality. The fact that we produce inquiring minds is one of the things which makes our country a world leader. In this case, however, I do think there's
an overriding question of national security."

Mitchell found himself suppressing a sigh, but still
nodding in agreement.

"So the question now becomes, how deeply did

Bracken get into the protein structure?" Sandborn's eyes
had taken on the hard, flinty look for which he was famous. *Like a gunfighter in the Old West.* Mitchell heard
the whispers about Sandborn replaying in his mind.

"Not far at all," Mitchell said, trying to put more authority into his voice than he actually felt. Who can tell,
really? he wanted to say, but didn't. This was a very
touchy subject, he knew. There were, perhaps, ten people
in the country who were privy to the recent discovery that
protein molecules were being passed between viral communities. The discovery, made only last year at the Atlanta Center for Disease Control, had been quickly
classified to the highest security levels. Those working
on the project were abruptly reassigned, once the potential importance of the discovery had been brought to the
attention of the surgeon general's staff. The discovery, in
fact, was one of the main thrusts behind the project to
develop protein-reading computers. Although Harvey
Mitchell didn't understand all the concern stemming
from what one high-level adviser in the president's confidential circle called "the discovery of the century." Neither, he suspected, did Paul Sandborn. The question was,
how much did Gary Bracken understand? There was no
way to know, short of asking the man. And then, of
course, you ran the risk of inflaming Bracken's inquiring
mind to the combustion point.

Besides, Harvey knew this was not his area of expertise. It had been a real plum for his newly sanctioned
agency to grab this high-profile assignment—developing
the next great leap forward on the technology frontier, as
the public relations people put it. But he had been ill prepared for the fanatical, almost paranoid security aspects
of the program. There it was again, that word: paranoid.
A function of government bureaucracy? he wondered.

The higher one went up on the public food chain, the more paranoid one became? Really, who cared that there seemed to be some sort of protein communication between viruses? And so what if an unknown researcher, in a laboratory no one ever heard of, seemed to want to look into the phenomenon? Wasn't that what these people were supposed to do? Harvey Mitchell certainly didn't give a damn. However, Paul Sandborn and his government kin apparently did, because the man was staring at him with those predatory eyes, demanding more information.

"Dr. Bracken, it would seem, has stumbled on the fact that the protein exchange is taking place," Mitchell said, referring to his hastily constructed notes. "It's a reasonable continuance of his work to investigate the phenomenon. However, I'm assured by people at the highest levels that there's no possible way for him to delve further into the subject without waiting for the development of the required technology, namely the protein-reading computers. It's simply impossible."

Sandborn nodded and leaned back, away from the table. Mitchell was struck with the sudden possibility that Sandborn knew more about the subject than he had given him credit for. It was taking Sandborn far too long to mull over the few facts he had presented. What the hell was going on here? Mitchell wondered. BIR was doing what it was supposed to do—what the PR people fed the news media. The computer technology was being developed at a most impressive rate, and once in place, it would bring about a revolution in the industry. Things were, in fact, running ahead of schedule, an almost unheard-of event within government circles. Stanford University, along with federal labs in Michigan and Texas, had filed confidential reports indicating that the project was approach-

ing fruition. Another year or two, tops, and they'd be
ready with a full-blown model. Yet after this meeting
with Sandborn, Harvey Mitchell could not shake the uncomfortable feeling that there was something about all
this he didn't understand, and wouldn't want to know
even if he did.

"I would suggest two things at this point," Sandborn
said slowly, as if he was giving the matter his highest
level of concentration. "First, a visit to the facility in
question to make certain this hasn't gone any further than
we believe it has. A technical person from your end,
along with a security expert from my office. Secondly,
that we interview Bracken and impress upon him the
need for absolute confidentiality in this matter. Remind
all concerned that their security clearances, and therefore
their funding, could be in jeopardy if the rules regarding
this research are not followed to the letter. Also, I would
suggest that the breach—and it is a breach of security, no
less so than a civilian stumbling across a restricted military base—be handled with some delicacy. Perhaps Dr.
Bracken could be promised some additional funding in
the research area he seems to have blundered into. We
may actually want to bring him up to date on the investi-
gation of the protein phenomenon. Once, as you correctly
pointed out, the technology is in place."

Mitchell nodded, sensing the meeting was coming to a
close. He found himself barely able to suppress a sigh of
relief. The meeting hadn't been as bad as he'd feared.

"But be certain this Bracken fellow understands that
the BIR will not tolerate deviations from its research parameters," Sandborn said, his voice indicating this was a
point to which there would be no exceptions. But in the
back of his mind, Sandborn knew that sometimes the best
way to keep a close eye on people was to place a friendly

hand across their shoulders. "We don't need a loose cannon out there eager to make a name for himself," he said, satisfied that for the moment at least, the situation was under control. "The National Security Agency considers the matter to be of paramount importance. We need to keep an eye on this, Harvey. I expect you to keep me informed."

Harvey Mitchell nodded again, although driving back to his office, he realized he was not exactly sure which aspect of the research Sandborn was so eager to protect. He had assumed it to be the new computer technology, which as everyone knew was worth billions. The virus thing seemed to pale in comparison. There was something strange here, he just couldn't put his finger on it.

a molecule of time

The boy crawled out from beneath the flap of hide which still covered the entrance of the longhouse. The sun was sending its first rays between the Twin Mountains, bringing the camp slowly to life. The main fire, banked for the night, was being raked out by one of the older boys, who would soon be given a formal name and thus be allowed to hunt with the men. The young boy rubbed sleep from his eyes and watched for a moment as the hot coals were pulled from their bed, dry branches and bark placed across the glowing embers in a carefully prescribed morning ritual. The firetender had neither the time nor patience to pay attention to one so far beneath him on the social ladder, so the younger boy moved on. Besides, it was not the firetender he wished to observe, even though he would one day inherit that task. It was the hunters who interested him.

The leader of the Hunting Band, the boy's father, was even now carrying an armload of spear shafts to the circle of stones where the men's weapons were assembled. He walked in his father's footsteps, standing quietly, respectfully, outside the stone circle.

The man picked through the spear shafts, hefting each, rolling them between his thick fingers. When he found one which pleased him, he sat down in the circle of stones, opening his tool kit. The kit was contained in a leather sack, tied by a strap around his waist. He was dressed, like the boy, in roughly sewn hides, his legs and feet bare in this, the warm season. The boy watched as his father held the butt end of the shaft between his feet and began notching the head of the spear with a thin, sharp stone. The man was careful to keep the work away from his body so the boy could see what he was doing. The child, who was the youngest offspring of his second mate, had not yet been named by the Society of Hunters, so it would have been improper to invite him into the men's work area. Also, his mother would soon call for him when she went with the other women down to the low meadows along the river. There, the women and children would pick berries and dig for cattail roots, as this was the season for those plants, and she would need his hands. But the boy seemed curious and eager to learn, so the man saw no reason to send him away. His mother, who was a practical and sensible woman from the neighboring River Clan, spoke well of the boy, praising his quick mind and his willingness to work. Indeed, the man thought the boy showed much promise, despite his youth and inexperience. The lad might one day even become leader of his own Hunting Band, he thought. Providing, of course, he was lucky enough to survive into manhood.

The boy, he noted, watched his movements closely, as the notch was deepened in the head of the shaft, until the man's eye judged it to be of sufficient depth and width. Only the day before, his favorite spear had been lodged deep in the shoulder of a wounded bison, where it was snapped during the beast's death throes. When the animal had been gutted, the man retrieved the stone head of the weapon, and this he now took from his tool kit, along with a length of dried sinew. First, he chipped away at the edges of the spearhead, dulled by its encounter with the bison's hard bones. He chipped the flakes carefully, using a rounded stone which fit neatly into the palm of his hand.

"The tip must not be cracked," the man said over his shoulder, holding the sharpened head up to the sun. The boy nodded, watching the process closely.

He turned to show the boy how the long base of the stone head was inserted into the notch of the shaft. How sinew was wrapped around the spear, holding the sharp tip securely. The man then dipped the spearhead into a bladder of water and held it there.

"Why?" he asked.

"It will become wet, then dry, holding tight," the boy said haltingly, clamping his fingers together to show he understood. The boy's eyes were wide, as he was not used to being questioned in the ways of the hunt.

The man smiled, nodding. This one's mother spoke true, he thought. The man stepped from the stone circle, carrying his new weapon. The firetender had revived the camp's hearth, and the man laid the spear on the rocks near the flames. Bones from the night's feasting lay scattered on the bare ground.

"This?" the man asked, pushing one of the bones with his foot.

The boy touched his arm below the elbow and made

the forked hand sign for bison. His father nodded in approval.

"This?" The man pointed to a spear shaft stuck into the earth, on top of which a thick-browed skull was impaled.

"The Enemy!" the boy said, working a growl into his thin, high voice.

The man roared with laughter, and the boy's face burned bright with pleasure. His mother emerged from the longhouse and called to him.

The man, whose name was Ba'ral, meaning StoneArm in the language of his people, led his Hunting Band with honor and distinction well into his thirtieth year. He was, as his name indicated, a formidable hunter—a great maker of meat and a relentless warrior, defending the hunting territory of the Twin Mountain Clans against the powerful Neckless Ones, killing them and their foul offspring wherever he found them.

As the seasons passed, the boy, however, remained something of a disappointment to him. The lad was initiated into the Society of Hunters when he reached his fourteenth summer. And while it was true none could question his bravery—indeed, his deeds were often spoken of in glowing terms around the winter fires—the young man, it seemed, would never grow to match his father's physical prowess. Even after attaining manhood, he remained thin and leanly muscled, like those of the River Clan.

In truth, Ba'ral realized as age bent him and the breath seemed to leave his body too quickly on the hunt, his son would never assume the name StoneArm when he himself passed from this world and had no further need of it. This was a thing he knew, but never spoke of, for the boy had grown into manhood retaining his curiosity and quick mind, and was an important asset to the Hunting Band, although all knew he would never become its leader.

The boy himself was well aware of the fact that he would never match his father's physical abilities. The heavy spears and throwing stones were never his favorite weapons. He became expert in the use of the sling, and could inflict much damage to both prey and enemies in this fashion. But in those seasons after his father's death, when stories of StoneArm's feats were still told around the fires of the clan, the memories of the old man's greatness with the spear stayed with him. StoneArm, it was said, could throw his weapon with such strength and accuracy that he was able to pierce the heart of a running beast and turn it instantly to meat. The young man, who now had wives and children of his own, kept these memories close to him, but knew that because of his own physical limitations, he would never live up to his father's legacy.

It was on a spring day, throwing a stone from his sling at a fleeing hare, when the idea came to him. His father's arm—an extension of the spear. Just as his own arm, twirling the stone above his head, was an extension of the leather straps of his own weapon. The arm, an extension of the weapon. The thought stayed with him for a full passing of the seasons as he sat, huddled by the fires of the longhouse, listening to the winter tales, enjoying the comforts of his wives and children.

The arm, an extension of the weapon, he thought.

On those days when the snows abated, he went to the circle of stones where the hunters worked. There he hefted the thick, heavy spear shafts, which he could never seem to master. In the bundles of wood, he found the lightest, thinnest of shafts, those cast off by the other men.

The arm, an extension of the weapon.

He notched two of these thin shafts, the head of one, against the butt of another. To his amazement, he discovered that when he flexed his arm in a throwing motion, the first shaft flew over the longhouse itself. As he practiced, perfecting this notching system, the other men came out to watch him. So, too, did the women and children. They cheered as the thin shafts arched through the air, hitting hide targets with unfailing accuracy, and the men made a place of honor for him near the fire.

The weapon he invented, using the memory of his father's strong arm, changed the entire framework of the Hunting Societies. No longer was it necessary to stalk so closely to the prey animals. The power of the flying spear was such that the beasts were unable to hear the hunter's approach, or even smell the attackers. The killing range was expanded to where the hunters themselves were no longer in direct danger from the horn and hooves of the prey. Now meat could be made while standing on the relative safely of a hillside, even as the herd animals grazed below. And the Neckless Ones—the Enemy—could be killed while warriors stood well away from their clubs and heavy stones.

This idea, so simple to use that even the slightest of the clan now had the killing power of the legendary Stone-Arm, made the young man not only leader of his own Hunting Band, but Chieftain of the Twin Mountain Clans. Stacks of bones were built all across the expanded hunting territories of the tribe, in tribute to him. And when he himself died at the advanced age of forty summers, he was buried under a mound of bones taken from the Neckless Ones. It was a mound so heaped with bones that it was said the Others saw this and fled in terror, never to be seen again in the hunting grounds of the Twin Mountain Clans. Songs were sung about him around the campfires, and his name was remembered for twenty generations.

Curiously, many years after the Great Chieftain's death, a member of his lineage—a great-granddaughter of one of his many offspring—happened to notice that dried berries interred beneath the ground like the dead, produced more berry bushes. This woman, as she grew older, tried her experiment with other plants, the wild onions and melons the people fed upon when meat could not be found. Centuries later, her discovery would change the entire culture of the Twin Mountain Clans, and, indeed, affect the whole of the world. Even though her name was not remembered, and no mounds of bones were ever raised to honor her. She was known, however, for bringing forth a great number of children into the world, most of whom survived to be formally named.

In the bodies of their hosts, the virus clans went about the business of life. Unseen, unnoticed. The matrix of the nervous system, the base of which had been laid down over billions of years, was expanded and improved upon. The neuron network of the cerebral cortex became more complex, growing and entwining like thick vines. The columns of cells folded in upon one another, creating long tunnels filled with the capacity for knowledge and memory. The hosts themselves became plentiful, offering even more possibilities for the clans to perfect their work.

seven

"This is even creepier," Mary Ann said, grimacing. "I don't care what anybody says."

Kurt Eez laughed, even though he agreed. Several days had passed since the initial discovery. During this time the team successfully captured several of the virus proteins; but, of course, no one had any idea what to do with them. Bracken ordered the molecules frozen and moved on to the next step in his still-unexplained plan. He now had his assistants swabbing the slick film from what appeared to be a gigantic, grossly bloated ant. Actually, the creature was a termite—the huge, overgrown queen of a termite hive Bracken borrowed from a nearby state-university biology department.

It was a few minutes past ten o'clock on a Saturday morning, and far too nice a day to be trapped inside a laboratory room swabbing the underbelly of a seriously disgusting insect, Eez thought. But Dr. Bracken would be in shortly and Kurt knew they had better have the swabs ready for processing.

"Here, hand me the slide," he said, grinning at the fact that his partner was so eager to get out of the way. The queen was wiggling, obviously angry at this invasion. "Actually, they're pretty interesting, for insects," Kurt remarked, picking the queen up with tweezers, returning the creature to her royal cell in the glass-enclosed hive. The workers immediately began sealing up the chamber, and along with the queen's male companion, tended to their upset ruler.

"The whole hive, thousands of little beasties in the wild, they all get their instructions from this one queen," Kurt explained, carefully arranging the swabs taken from selected areas along the insect's grotesque body. The queen, he thought, actually looked like a long piece of intestine, with a head and legs glued on. In reality, she was an egg-laying machine, able to produce thirty thousand eggs a day. That, in itself, was amazing enough in Kurt's mind. But the queen of a termite hive was far more than just a baby-termite machine. She was the heart and mind of the hive. "All the workers get their job assignments by licking the queen's body," Eez said, watching as the workers swarmed over her. "She sweats out protein molecules which somehow tell each and every member of the hive where to go and what to do. Some gather food, some build tunnels to expand the colony, others function as soldiers or tend the young. The whole process is really astounding."

"Yeah, I guess it is," Mary Ann admitted grudgingly.

She, of course, knew all that already, as Bracken had given them both books to read on the subject. Eez, she guessed, felt compelled to tell her the obvious, since he was the one with the official paper proclaiming him to be an actual scientist, while she was merely an intern. Welcome to the wonderful world of condescending researchers, she thought, biting her tongue.

Eez was handing her the swabs, which she numbered according to an eight-by-ten diagram Bracken had drawn out for them, indicating from where on the queen's body he wanted the samples taken. The swabs were then rubbed on a culture dish, and from these it was hoped the various proteins could be isolated. With a little luck and some careful observation, Bracken explained, they might be able to identify the molecular codes the queen used to dispense her instructions to the hive. From there, Bracken hoped to expand the experiment to incorporate the more mysterious protein exchange taking place between the virus cultures.

"If we can teach the computer to identify protein markers from the termites," Bracken had told them, barely able to keep the excitement out of his voice, "it might be feasible for us to work out a translation program using the virus proteins."

It was entirely possible, Mary Ann and Kurt speculated, that they might be in on the ground floor of an important discovery. And that, Eez reminded her when she got too squeamish, would apply rocket jets to their prospective careers. All of which suited Mary Ann Meade just fine. It was a long way from the Pennsylvania farm of her family to a world-class laboratory at a major university. If this place provided a path to that goal, she'd eat the damn termites if they wanted her to.

"That's it," Kurt Eez said, handing her the last swab, turning his attention once again to the overgrown ant farm which housed the termite colony. The workers still swarmed over their kidnapped queen, crawling carefully across her body to be sure she was not injured. Was she telling them in some way about her mistreatment at the hands of giants? he wondered. Was their queen's capture and subsequent return about to become immortalized in the lore of the hive? Were termite priests even now coming to the forefront, to take credit for their prayers to God and the queen's release from bondage? Eez laughed, shaking his head. He was getting as weird as Dr. Bracken, he thought.

"What?" Mary Ann asked, wondering what the joke was.

"Nothing." Kurt smiled at her, gathering the culture dishes, sliding them into a temperature-controlled compartment. "The bread's in the oven. Let's get a cup of coffee before Dr. Frankenstein gets here."

"That's not very funny." Mary Ann shook her head, following Eez downstairs to the cafeteria, wondering if this sort of warped humor was the norm in all experimental labs.

Bracken had arrived when they returned. He was checking the timer on the culture compartment, looking at the printouts from the previous computer run on the virus protein molecules. Like a tourist checking his wallet every five minutes, just to be sure it was still there. And yes, the molecules were still present. No question about it. The damn viruses were saying something to each other. What, of course, was the million-dollar question.

"Morning, folks," he said, smiling congenially. "Everything went okay, I presume?"

"Fine," Eez said, offering their boss a cup of coffee, which he took gratefully.

Bracken had become better acquainted with the two young assistants over the past days, as he switched his schedule to work during the hours when the lab was not busy with its full staff. Rebecca extracted a firm promise that he would take Fridays off, as well as Sunday. It seemed to be working out well between them, even though there was always a crushing mountain of work to be done.

"Our friends seem to be doing well," Bracken commented, leaning close to the termite container, watching with interest as they went about their own incessant labors.

Once the virus protein exchange had been confirmed, and after they'd isolated molecular specimens, Bracken shifted the focus of the experiment to an area where information on chemical instructions could be more easily assessed. He went to friends in outside biology labs in search of an insect hive he could study. Dave Harmon at SUNY had come through with this fine swarm of termites. In truth, these highly social and communicative creatures had long been a favorite of Bracken's.

"Look, she's back to producing eggs," Bracken said. Kurt Eez, Mary Ann noted, went over to show curious interest and she was forced to do her best to imitate him. They're still creepy, she thought as the three of them watched the colony engaging in the business of life. Eez was right, she saw, the damned queen was an egg-laying machine. Termites moved across her body as though they were in some kind of production line. How many termites did the world need, anyway? Mary Ann found herself thinking. More than one, and you've got too many, she thought, remembering the old joke about lawyers. A joke which was never told around any of the hundreds and hundreds of prelaw students at Columbia. She thought about that and her brain seemed to twist under the implications. When she looked up, the others were over at the culture compartment.

• • •

It was frustrating work for Bracken. Basically, the entire problem could be defined as a question of translation. Human languages, even encrypted code, could be broken down into a series of binary numbers. Values were assigned to the various letters or symbols, and through a series of hit-or-miss experiments, solving the problem of translation was usually only a matter of time. Like the Allied cracking of the German High Command code in World War II. These days, with the proper key in place, unlocking any language or code became simply a matter of feeding the information into the computer. Translation of text from Spanish to English, for example. Egyptian hieroglyphics, the Dead Sea Scrolls. Even the DNA code, the basic element of all life on Earth, was slowly giving way to computer translation.

But this was a somewhat different matter. The language, encoded in the protein molecules which drove the insects—and also the viruses, he believed—was clearly before them. He was now able to isolate the information from the queen termite's body. He could look at the molecules under the electric-scan microscope, was even able to feed targeted information back into the termite colony, and they would follow the reintroduced protein messages. At Bracken's command, termite workers could be made to tend the young, gather food, expand the hive, even in the absence of the queen herself. His team could, using the hit-or-miss method, identify the specific molecule which, for example, would tell a worker to take the queen's eggs to the nursery chamber. While this was undoubtedly a significant accomplishment, he still couldn't tell *how* the molecule relayed its commands to the specific worker. Or even more important, how the queen was able to generate this information within her body.

"How does she even know *what* to tell them to do?" Kurt Eez asked in frustration, watching as the queen controlled her colony with exacting efficiency, while never leaving the sanctity of the royal chamber.

"The workers tell her," Mary Ann said, finding herself pleased to be reciting book information back to Eez. "Protein exchanges in the food. She licks their bodies, like they do hers, I think."

Bracken could only shake his head. They knew what was taking place. The why of it remained a mystery. The protein molecules, the words in this unspoken language, were right there in front of them, but it was a code only the termites seemed able to decipher. It was in a way, he thought, like trying to understand an alien language. And the truth was, that was exactly what he was trying to do. To learn the instinctive thoughts—indeed, if they could be called that—of a species which had been in existence far longer than his own, with a social and communication structure that might as well have come from another planet.

"It's funny, when you think about it," he told Rebecca, during dinner, a rare event for them these days, he knew. Still, he couldn't help but talk shop to her, relating his blundering attempts to come to intimate terms with the termite colony. That very day, in fact, he mistakenly sent all the colony's workers down to the nursery chambers to tend the young larvae. The resulting traffic jam made the Jersey Turnpike at rush hour seem deserted.

"We're developing computers which will communicate using encoded proteins, while these little buggers have been doing basically the same thing for millions of years," he said, shaking his head in bewilderment.

"Well, don't feel too bad." Becky tried the delicate

ploy of appearing to pay attention while desperately attempting to change the subject. "They've had a lot longer to perfect the system."

Bracken laughed at his wife's joke, but the brief conversation stayed with him. In a way, bringing the problem into focus. He was trying to understand a culture that was not only nonhuman but had survived virtually intact and unchanged since before the time of the dinosaurs. And, perhaps, even further beyond that, into the dim veil of the beginnings of life on Earth. The viruses, with their short strands of DNA and their simple containment fields of nucleic acids, had somehow evolved along with the bacteria in the early, monumental explosion of life some 3.5 billion years ago. How could he hope to come to any understanding of something which had existed for that incredible length of time? Oddly, it was Terrance Stampe who gave him the encouragement he needed.

"The foundations are the same," the older man had said, during those increasingly frequent times when he took it upon himself to review the work Bracken's team was doing. "It's not unlike taking a house, or a castle perhaps, and tearing it apart from the roof down. Eventually you'll get to the brick and mortar of the foundation. And that's the same in all of us—dog, cat, termite, or human being. We're all just an expanded series of DNA codes. Sort of like gigantic, complex bacteria."

It was, in Bracken's view, a most unusual statement to hear from an old-timer like Terrance Stampe, who, the joke went, had served as Darwin's cabin boy on the *Beagle*. Still the old man seemed to have taken an interest in the project. The fact that his suggestions had not yielded results only spoke to the complexity of the problem, at least in Bracken's mind. So far, no one's suggestions had yielded results.

"It's a programming problem," Rebecca said. Even though she didn't have a true scientific background, Bracken tended to lend a ready ear to her input. She did, after all, listen to his seemingly endless ramblings on the subject. "You have to sit down and work out a computer program to translate the protein data."

"But I don't even know what the data is," Bracken protested. "I'm not a termite or a virus."

"And you're not a computer," Becky correctly pointed out.

No, I'm not a computer, Bracken thought, sitting at his desk, watching as the latest data run flashed by on the screen. What was it the professionals said about these machines? They're only as good as the information they're given. Becky was right, he realized. He was asking the machine to relay data to him in human terms, when the information the computer was being given was distinctly nonhuman. Somehow he had to get the computer to analyze the data in the same manner the insects themselves received it. Unfortunately, Bracken had no idea how to go about that.

He had to learn to communicate on the level of the hive, he concluded. A seemingly impossible task.

It was late. Again. Outside, the streetlights spread thin pools of light into the human environment. Cars passed by, adding their fleeting illumination. Kurt and Mary Ann had long since departed for the comforts of home. As he himself should do, Bracken thought, feeling as though he was accomplishing exactly nothing. The data run had again turned into a meaningless jumble of numbers as the computer told him things he already knew—the size and shape of the various proteins, their place of origin on the queen termite's body, their effect on the various workers in the hive.

How did she know what to tell her workers? His mind repeated Kurt Eez's question. Was the whole process merely a function of instinct? Perhaps he was reading too much into the simple process of protein exchange between the termites and the virus colonies.

The phone rang on his desk and he picked it up, knowing it was Becky checking to see what time he'd be home.

"Yeah, I'm here," he said, responding to her unspoken question. The tiny viewer above the monitor showed his wife dressed in pajamas, yawning, obviously getting ready to go to bed.

"Just called to say good night," she said, a soft sadness in her voice. "I can't wait up, there's an early meeting at the museum."

"I shouldn't be too late," Bracken said, apologizing. "How about I pick you up for lunch tomorrow?"

"You got it. It's a date, sailor." Becky smiled, even though Bracken was certain it was forced.

"I'll see you then," he said, feeling intensely guilty at leaving her alone so often these days. And nights, he admitted to himself. "Night, babe."

Rebecca winked suggestively at him and he laughed as she disconnected, the screen blurring to snow.

Was he crazy, or stupid? Bracken wondered, blanking his own monitor. Here he was leaving his wife alone, and for what? How much of our lives do we give up for our work? It was, he supposed, a quandary all humans faced. It was also, he realized, a thought never considered by those who lived according to the rules of the hive. In the context of a hive mentality, the individual was never a factor. Life existed, and was continued, for the good of the whole. And how was that behavior different from the human view of the world? he asked himself. We raise our young to continue our own value systems. We educate and send them out into the world, hopefully to do work that will benefit and perhaps advance human knowledge. We collect what we've learned in central depositories, then teach our children to access this accumulated knowledge. For what reason? So they might be contributing members to the whole, Bracken realized.

Sitting in his tiny office, in the middle of an office complex built by the engineers of his species, surrounded by the dark, which settled over all creatures of the earth, Bracken began to see the human race as it truly was—a hive of beings, who lived and worked for the collective good. Creatures who gathered around their fires for comfort and safety, working together to raise their young and feed their various communities. A collection of farmers, builders, nursery tenders, librarians, scientists, priests, doctors, and all the other workers who kept the machinery of civilization humming. Creatures who had somehow grown to perceive themselves as individuals, but who were really connected by the dynamics of cells and DNA each carried in their bodies. Individuals who were in reality part of a collective whole. Growing, spreading across the earth, into the seas, even into space itself. The hive of humanity. No different in their basic goals than the ants, termites, or bees. All creatures, raising their young, struggling to propagate their species. And he knew, instantly, that the secret lay not in the queen termite or her workers, but in the young. How do children and larvae learn? They are taught in the early stages of their development. Call it instinct, call it education. Call it whatever you liked. Accumulated learned knowledge. Yes, the secret lay within the young. How they were educated, how they learned to do what was necessary for the continuance of the species.

Bracken got up from his desk and walked out into the lab. He uncovered the night curtain around the container in which the hive of termites lived. He looked closely at the nursery chambers, at the workers suddenly awakened by the unexpected intrusion of light. Their first reaction, he noted, was to protect their young. Within the larvae lay the secret of life. They were the ones learning how to live within the structure of the hive. Libraries of knowledge being infused into them. Instruction on the deeper mysteries of social behavior, and the work that would be required of them. As soon as they shed the larva stage, the young termites went right to work. And the hive had no room for hit-or-miss learning. Somehow, within the nesting chambers, the laws and rules by which the young would live their lives was transferred to them. It was learning on a scale which human beings, trapped in an imagined veil of individuality, could not hope to match. It was the knowledge of survival, in its purest sense. Knowledge accumulated through uncounted generations, and imparted with hivelike efficiency. Given directly to the young either through proteins in the food, or written into their genetic code. Yes, Bracken realized, the young were the key.

"That's it?" Stampe asked, peering at the projection on the screen.

"That's it," Bracken confirmed, both of them watching what appeared to be a small, raised dot in the center of the electron scan. They were looking at an isolated protein molecule harvested from Bracken's borrowed termite colony. Specifically, from the rear flank of the queen.

"And what does it do?" Stampe asked.

"That specific molecule instructs the nursery workers on how to care for the colony's larvae," Bracken said.

"Amazing." Stampe shook his head. "A termite book on child rearing, compressed into a single molecule."

Bracken smiled at the analogy, realizing that it was about as close to a joke as Terrance Stampe was likely to get. He was surprised, actually, at the older man's interest, and his ready ear. Quietly, almost imperceptibly to either of them, Stampe had been drawn into the web of Bracken's work. In truth, Stampe's long background in the field of molecular biology had been an asset during the many unexpected roadblocks Bracken encountered. He reached over and flipped the screen to a different field, in which another protein molecule sat like a magnified grain of sand on a beach blanket.

"Another instructional molecule," Bracken said. "This one taken from the right flank of the queen. When this molecule is ingested, the insect involves itself in the tunnel-building work of the colony, once it reaches maturity."

"An engineering manual?" Stampe asked, in what Bracken knew to be a rhetorical question. It was, after all, a thing no human being could answer. Not yet, anyway, Bracken thought. "And the computer analysis has been able to discern differences between the two?"

"On the surface, they appear to be duplicates," Bracken explained. "But there are several small differences in the DNA strings which the computer has been able to detect. What these mean, we're not exactly sure. But it's a reasonable assumption that the similarities represent the social structure of the hive as a whole, while the differences provide instructional information regarding the specific tasks each worker is expected to perform."

Bracken flicked the keyboard again so the two images were shown next to one another on a split screen. It was a nothing maneuver, but Bracken thought it served as an effective visual aid. The human eye, after all, couldn't hope to tell the difference between the two proteins. Any more than the naked eye could tell the difference between a single star and a galaxy shining with a billion stars, thousands of light-years away. But the real talent of human beings, Bracken now understood, was their ability to develop machinery to overcome their own physical shortcomings.

"Since the young larvae ingest the molecules, the specifics for reading the protein codes must be internal," Stampe said, as usual cutting right to the heart of the problem.

"That's right," Bracken agreed. "An enzyme of some type, we believe. We're working on isolating it now. There are a finite number of enzymes in the larva stage. A few thousand at most. We're tapped into the Atlanta computer banks, and the tests are running on a continual basis. If we're right, we should have an answer soon. Break down the enzyme, feed the specifics into the computer, and it's entirely possible that we'll have the foundation for a plausible translation program. And then we get down to some serious work with the virus proteins."

"My God," Stampe said, his voice hushed. "You really think you can do this?"

"I'll let you know in a few weeks," Bracken said, grinning, pleased with himself, now that it appeared they had taken the first, tentative steps toward success.

Much later, he would look back on this moment and see himself like a man staring into the mouth of a long, dark tunnel. Curious, even excited by the possibilities the tunnel offered. But unable, somehow, to see the monster waiting in the darkness to devour him.

a molecule of time

The young ones lay hidden in the reeds by the Great River. Above them, on the Plain of Stones, where the mouth of Home Cave opened into the valley, there was the sound of fierce fighting. Shouts of anger and fear. Shrieks of pain. The dull, heavy thump of clubs and stone. And the high-pitched humming noises of the dreadful flying spears of the Killers. All through the day, since the terror of the early morning hours when scouts came running into the summer camp at the base of Home Cave, the terrible sounds had come drifting down the ridge to the young ones' hiding place.

Only their intense fear of the blood-maddened Killers kept them huddled together, unseen in the reeds, as the battle raged above. A few of the older children had crept along the riverbank, catching frogs and digging cattail roots, which the group now ate, cold and uncooked, as fire would most certainly have drawn the Killers to them. Once, earlier in the day, one of the oldest males, a boy of ten summers, had crawled to the top of the ridge, but he had not returned. Now, with night settling around them, the band of young ones, three hands in number, clung together for warmth. The smallest among them, whimpering for their mothers. The older children, covering the babies' mouths, whispering soft grunts of comfort. The women who had led them to the hiding place when the scouts first stormed into camp with the news of the Killers' approach had also not returned. No one came for them, as had been promised, and now night was upon them. Without fire, or the protection of the adults, the children's band knew themselves to be at the mercy of whatever prowling animals or demons might catch their scent or hear the whimpering of the most frightened among them.

Te, who was the oldest female in the band in this season, moved quietly among her charges, stroking each in turn, offering what comfort she could. At twelve summers, Te was approaching the time when she would be taken into the Circle of Women. To be given a mate and a skinning knife. To be introduced into the mysteries of the Circle. Now, she feared, that day would never come. Above her, she knew, the world was changing.

Even as the moon rose and the sparks of light filled the sky, the shouts and cries continued from the Plain of Stones. Only now, the sounds were less chaotic. The shouts and cries easily identified. Drums hammered a resounding beat in the still air of the night. The glow of a great fire reflected against the trees and brush at the top of the ridge. Te and the older children knew the truth—that the Killers had been victorious. That the stench of burning flesh drifting into the river valley was, in fact, their elders. The Killers, as was their custom, would feast

on the vanquished and then scatter the bones and ashes of
their victims to the four winds, paying tribute to their horrible, vicious gods. Te knew this, and her tears flowed
like water squeezed from the clouds. Falling on the high,
bony foreheads of those she was trying to comfort. It was,
she feared, the end of the world. And there was nothing
any of them could do about it. In the morning, perhaps,
she thought it might be possible to surrender. To offer
herself and the other young ones as slaves. If the Killers'
blood lust had been satisfied, she hoped, they might be
spared.

It was a vague and horrible hope. Even as she sat
among the youngest of her charges, she heard some of the
older children slipping away through the reeds. Realizing
the magnitude of the Killers' victory and their own defeat, they were creeping down to the Great River in the
dark hours of the night. There, she knew, they would cast
themselves into the swift, muddy waters, preferring death
to a lifetime of slavery. And she wished with all her heart
that she had learned the mysteries of life. That she had
been given her skinning knife so she might run up the
slope and plunge the stone blade into the hearts of the
Killers. Her sense of duty to the Circle, however, kept her
with the young ones. Stroking them, whispering softly in
their ears. Promising food and warmth in the morning.
One of the young ones reached up and wiped at her tears,
which only caused her eyes to cloud over and burst with
water like a summer storm. A knife . . . she would give
anything for a knife.

But in the end, none of that mattered. The Change had
come, as inevitable and unstoppable as the seasons.
For some, the Change meant annihilation and extinc-
tion. For others, it was a moment of glory and fleeting

victory. No one knew this, of course. Not Te, huddled in the darkness with her small band of children. Not those of the Twin Mountain Clan as they danced in bloody triumph during this, the final victory over the sworn enemies and rivals of their people. In time, the rain and snow would wash away the blood, and even the memory of this day. The wind and the earth would cover the bones of both the vanquished and the victors, and new Changes would come.

eight

"**B**IR investigators?" Bracken shook his head in disbelief. "They actually came to the lab?"

"On what they termed a routine inspection and audit," Terrance Stampe said uneasily. "They wanted to speak with you, but I told them you wouldn't be available until today."

"They looked the whole place over and said they'd be back Monday morning." Jacoby looked as though he wanted to fire up a cigar, but thought better of it. "What the hell's going on, Dr. Bracken?"

"I don't know," Bracken replied, truly bewildered. In the laboratory's entire five-year history of doing government research, this was the first time anyone from the BIR had ever done an on-site inspection. "Maybe it's like they said, a routine inspection."

"But then why did they specifically ask for you?" Jacoby asked the question Bracken was pondering. "They barely glanced at the computer reports, or the balance sheets. Which, thank God, were up to date. Frankly I'm surprised they're not here already."

Stampe scowled, reaching across the table for a donut, which he began to break up into small, bite-size pieces, a practice that secretly drove Bracken crazy. The regular Monday-morning meeting had turned decidedly sour from Bracken's point of view, with even Terrance Stampe shooting him hard glances. Neither of the senior partners was pleased to have government agents poking their noses into the lab's work. Even if the BIR did happen to be footing most of the bill.

"Why didn't anyone call me?" Bracken asked, feeling sandbagged. Which, by Jacoby's barely concealed grin, he knew he was.

"You said you were going to New York for the weekend with your wife." Jacoby shrugged. Stampe looked guiltily down into his coffee and Bracken knew that Jacoby had been the one to withhold the warning call.

"You could have left a message on the machine," Bracken said, not bothering to remove the angry tone in his voice. Dammit all, he took one fucking weekend off. . . .

"Didn't want to worry you unnecessarily," Jacoby said, smiling in a belated attempt to defuse Bracken's animosity. If you can't take the heat, kid, you shouldn't be in the kitchen, the older man's eyes seemed to say. Bracken felt his stomach grumbling. "Besides, they seemed amiable enough. Said they'd stop in on their way back to Washington. Something about inspecting another facility upstate."

"They were inspecting another laboratory on the weekend?" Bracken asked, even more pissed off when Jacoby shrugged again and said nothing in response.

"That did sound odd to me," Stampe admitted, eating

the broken pieces of his donut. "But their credentials were in order. I checked them myself."

What he didn't tell Bracken, however, was that the two men had "requested" that he and Jacoby keep the visit strictly confidential.

"So word of the inspection tour doesn't get around the region," one of the agents had explained.

Jacoby had, of course, agreed immediately, leaving Stampe feeling as if he were betraying a colleague. Still, as Jacoby had correctly pointed out, the lab was operating up to the Bureau's guidelines, and so had nothing to hide. Providing, of course, their junior associate was conducting his own research according to regulations. It would be interesting, Jacoby thought to himself, to see what sorts of records Bracken was keeping.

"It's the protein-molecule experiments," Bracken said quietly, voicing what all three of them suspected.

"More than likely," Jacoby said. Stampe busied himself with his coffee.

But why now? Bracken wondered. Christ, he was making progress isolating the protein instructions. In another few weeks he might actually have enough information in the data base to do a basic reading. What the hell was going on?

Before he could give any further consideration to the problem, the intercom buzzed on the table. Doris Rook, the lab's receptionist, announced that two men were here, saying they had an appointment with Dr. Bracken. Sighing, Bracken pushed himself away from the conference table. Both Jacoby and Stampe, he saw, were watching him carefully.

"You didn't happen to mention anything about the project to them, did you?" Bracken asked, this time keeping his voice under control. Both men were quick with their denials, and for some reason he believed them. He left the room, shaking his head, knowing that as soon as he closed the door, Jacoby would have a few choice words about upstart researchers who didn't know how to be "team players." Jealousy, he knew, was the eminent domain of unimaginative scientists.

Three people, Bracken quickly decided, was the saturation point for human beings in his tiny office. Still, he managed to smile and shake hands with the two BIR agents, who seemed pleasant enough, even as they offered their credentials, signaling there was no mistaking this as an official visit.

"Sorry I can't offer better accommodations," Bracken apologized, sitting behind his desk to give himself some semblance of authority. "The conference room is in use this morning."

"This is fine." One of the men, who gave his name as Dr. Franklin, nodded in what Bracken took to be a friendly manner.

"We don't go in for expensive offices around here. Always trying to use the government's money wisely," Bracken said, smiling in what he immediately realized was a poor attempt at humor. To his surprise, Dr. Franklin seemed to grin.

"We did want our meeting to be private," Franklin's colleague said, using a serious tone that suggested to Bracken they were about to exchange nuclear secrets. All of which seemed extremely silly to him, until the man asked his next question. "Do you have any recording devices in this room, Dr. Bracken?"

"No," Bracken said, amazed to find his voice jerking around in his throat like a misplaced golf ball. "Of course not. Why would you ask such a thing?"

"Procedure," Franklin replied, smiling. The man's face, Bracken realized, was a well-practiced mask. Hiding what? he found himself wondering, the small hairs on the back of his neck prickling. Jesus, what the hell was going on?

"We understand you've been conducting some rather unusual experiments in the area of protein encoding," Franklin said, making the statement sound casual, as if he had this conversation a dozen times a day. "That you've been dealing with the phenomenon of molecular exchange?"

"Well, yes," Bracken said, the golf ball jumping around in his throat. "But I don't—"

"We'd like you to be aware that government researchers at the CDC are currently conducting their own investigations into this area." Franklin's partner made the assault on his senses a stereo effect. "And that it has been classified as a national-security issue, as is the case with the entire computer encoding project."

"Yes, of course." Bracken stumbled around for words. "I'm sure you know I have my own security clearance?"

The man nodded, his eyes cold, like tiny pieces of ice. Of course he knew all of that, Bracken thought, suddenly coming to the conclusion that this guy was no government scientist. And that the CDC knew a whole lot about the transfer of proteins between virus communities. There hadn't been any reports issued, Bracken was certain of that. How in God's name did all this fall under the umbrella of national security? He wanted to ask, but knew he would get no answers. Certainly not from these two goons, who had probably come up from Washington just to shut them down. National security—my ass, Bracken thought.

"Our information also suggests that you've made some

progress?" Dr. Franklin asked, the tone suggesting he wanted to keep the proceedings on as friendly a level as possible.

"I have some tentative results," Bracken said haltingly. "But again, I don't see—"

"We'd like to help you in this endeavor," Franklin interrupted his protests, smiling at Bracken's confused response. "The government is very interested in this work, and we're prepared to offer the full resources of the Bureau of Industrial Research to help push your project forward."

No shit, Bracken didn't say. Instead he pushed back in his chair to give himself some breathing room. Franklin was smiling at him in a most convincing manner. For an instant Bracken wondered if he was wrong about the man's face being some sort of mask.

"You're serious?" Bracken asked.

"Very serious." Franklin nodded.

Bracken grinned, wondering if Jacoby still had that box of good Cuban cigars stashed away in his office.

"Making his deal with the devil, the caged man smiled," Rebecca said, after Bracken related the details of his meeting with the BIR agents. The two of them were sharing a quiet dinner at home and a bottle of high-priced wine to celebrate what Bracken considered his good fortune. Franklin and his associate had promised an immediate update on their computer equipment, as well as much-needed additional funding for Bracken's research.

"You really think that?" he asked. Sometimes, even though they'd spent years together, he still couldn't always tell when Becky was putting him on.

"Maybe." She shrugged, sipping her wine. "But did

you really have any choice? They seemed to have a pretty good idea about what you were doing."

"I know," Bracken replied. In truth, that bothered him more than he cared to admit. He believed Jacoby and Stampe, that they hadn't fed the BIR any of his research data. But somehow word had gotten out. "Something in the monthly reports might have sent a flag up at the Bureau," he said, even though he had been deliberately vague about his work, waiting until they had some hard results. He was fishing around for an explanation, he knew, but it was Rebecca who gave voice to his own suspicions.

"Maybe they're tapping your computer system," she said carefully. "You were using the Atlanta data banks."

"We were accessing with our own security code, but that's a possibility," he admitted. It was not inconceivable that some high-tech government hacker was infiltrating his coded files. It was a thing both of them understood, but left unexplored. This was, after all, a celebration of sorts. Still, Bracken knew it was something he'd have to be careful about in the future.

"So what is it, exactly, that they want you to do?" Becky asked, deftly routing the subject onto a path she knew her husband would want to follow.

"Well, we're going to continue with the computer project, of course," Bracken said, rising to her bait like a trout following a medfly hatching. "The general staff will work on the protein readers. Of course, I'm not supposed to talk about any of this."

At which Rebecca nodded, rolling her eyes. The truth was, everyone told their mates everything. It was a wonder to her any secrets got kept, anywhere. Then again, maybe they didn't, she considered.

"My team, however, has a green light to go after the

protein exchange," he said, unable to stop the grin from spreading across his face. "I don't know what's there, but the government's got the whole thing classified."

"You're still going to own a piece of what comes out?" Becky asked, keeping her practical eye pointed on the distant horizon. It was her way, and Bracken didn't begrudge it a bit. If he was in charge of the money, he knew, they'd be living out of the back of the car. Well, he would. And he'd be sleeping alone in the backseat.

"If we can pull it off." He nodded, enjoying the moment. "Our contract says that Centrifuge Labs will hold a twenty-five percent residual on any of our work that goes into the final computer project. That includes the virus protein research as well, and my bet is that'll be worth a whole lot more in the long run. Computer technology changes every few years, but the virus encoding will be the discovery of a lifetime."

"So we might be talking Microsoft money here," Becky commented, and Bracken grinned some more. "Stan Jacoby must be thrilled."

"He even shared one of his Cubans with me," Bracken said, leaving out the fact that Jacoby's congratulations had been restrained, at best. But Terrance Stampe clapped him on the back and brought out a bottle of brandy to go with the cigars.

"I assume we're talking smokes, not one of Stanley's illegal housekeepers?" Becky smiled at him.

Later, after Rebecca had congratulated him one final time, in a way only she knew how to do, Bracken lay awake, his wife curled up asleep beside him. Her hair brushing his shoulder, her breath soft on his skin. The night, dark and sheltering around them. He watched as shadows moved across the room like a fog. The night— domain of nocturnal animals and research scientists

whose brains refused to shut down. He watched as the
cold light of the moon leaked through the venetian blinds,
spilling ghostly illumination across the world, across the
foot of his bed. And he gave quiet, solitary consideration
to a fact which he had kept from Jacoby and Stampe, and
did not even mention to Rebecca. It concerned the almost
offhand remarks made by Franklin and his associate as
they were discussing the lab's future in the computer research field and the strange nature of Bracken's own
work.

"We must be careful to empathize with the critical nature of the National Science Project," Franklin's colleague said, pinning Bracken to his chair like a bug.
"Centrifuge Labs must maintain its contractual obligations with the BIR. It's critical that the protein-reading
computer be developed on schedule."

"Certainly, that's understood," Bracken said, nodding.

"And, of course, to allocate additional funding, we'll
need to review all the current material on your particular
aspect of the protein work."

Bracken hesitated. Who the hell were these guys? he
wondered. And what exactly was going on? He couldn't
just let two strangers who walked through the door flashing badges have access to his entire project.

"It's procedure," Franklin said, anticipating his reluc-
tance. "If you'd care to call the Bureau, they'll be glad to
verify."

"Maybe I should," Bracken said. "Just to be sure we're
doing the right thing here. No offense."

"None taken," Franklin's associate said, actually
sounding as if he approved of Bracken's heightened paranoia.

But in the end, his feeling proved to be of little conse-
quence. A phone call to the Washington office of the BIR

confirmed the men's identity and verified their request to review Bracken's research materials. So the two agents spent the day reading and taking notes—Bracken drew the line at photocopying. All of this he told to Jacoby and Stampe as they smoked cigars and had a drink to celebrate. But before the BIR agents left, with smiles and handshakes all around, Franklin had asked for a moment with Bracken in his office.

"I just wanted to congratulate you on the depth of your work, Dr. Bracken," Franklin said. "It's most inventive how you've tied the virus phenomenon into an area where it's possible to actually chart protein communication."

Bracken took the compliment with a grain of salt, knowing that the next step, clearly the most difficult, had yet to be made. But when he mentioned this, Franklin only nodded.

"Still, you've accomplished what others thought to be impossible, until the new technology comes on-line," he said. His words, Bracken saw, were selected with great care. "But I'd like you to be aware that there are several disturbing aspects to this area of inquiry. There is some suggestion that this is not as benign as it might seem on the surface."

"What are you talking about?" Bracken asked. "And what does the CDC have to do with this? Virus protein exchange hardly falls within the parameters of disease control."

Or did it? As the man's face turned into a smiling mask, Bracken wondered if he had stepped over some invisible line.

"Let's just say, between the two of us, you know all you need to know at the present time. And perhaps a little more. Hopefully you know enough to be careful,"

Franklin said, his voice oddly cold, sending an involuntary shiver up Bracken's spine.

It was this bit of conversation, and its unspoken implications, that Bracken kept to himself. And now pondered as he watched the moon move across the span of his bedroom window.

What were They saying? Did someone else, higher up on the research food chain, hold the key to that mystery? What in God's name did the CDC have to do with this? All around him, within them all, the microscopic world went about its own unceasing work. Timeless. He thought, for an instant, he heard them whispering, realizing the sound came from everywhere. And for that instant he had the reeling, dizzying feeling that he was in this thing—way, way over his head.

a molecule of time

Day One + 1.2774893 x 10 ^12

Serpents, thin and glowing, entwined themselves through the twenty or so digits on his hands. The man blinked, shaking his head, trying to clear his blurred vision. The movement, however, only caused things to become more muddled and confused. Sparks danced before his eyes. The sun, bright white in the dry, cloudless sky, seemed to leap down, touching his forehead, until he found himself staring into the blinding depths of a fiery cloud.

He moaned, staggering across the rocky terrain. The visions, which plagued him since the first moments of his awareness, had grown progressively worse as he aged. His given name, in fact, was Shn-En, which meant Shadow Watcher in the language of the People. Now, in the fifth double hand of his life, Shn-En found that the visions were in the process of consuming him entirely.

His fifth double hand of life . . . Shn-En grinned, mad-

ness shaking him as the world shimmered before his
eyes. That would mean how many summers . . . if one
counted all the fingers he suddenly seemed to have
grown? And should he count the serpents, now twisting
their way in an endless dance across his fingertips? He
laughed out loud, his brain unable to contain the number.
Older, surely, than the most ancient among them. And in
reality—whatever that was—Shn-En knew he had already survived longer than any of those with whom he
had learned the secrets of the hunt. His hair, once combed
and oiled, was now a long, white tangle; a mane filled
with leaves and twigs, and more than a few biting insects.
His face, the hair plucked away in the manner of his people, was lined and cracked, like old leather exposed too
long to the elements. But still he walked upright with the
strength and vigor of a young man, even if it pained him
sometimes to do so. And his teeth were set firmly in his
head. Most of them, anyway.

Shn-En had lived longer than any of his contempo-
raries and had become an old man of fifty summers. He
had survived the cold and hunger of winter. Cheated
death at the horns and hooves of the great beasts. Had not
fallen prey himself to the many hunters who sought out
the weak or the unwary. He had managed to recover from
any number of terrible wounds and broken bones. Those,
he thought, could probably be counted on his too-many
fingers. Miraculously, he had avoided the sickness and
plagues which swept through the camps of the People.
All this and more, he had lived through to reach the age
of Veneration and Wisdom. The time of his life when he
would receive shares of meat simply for chipping flint
weapons for the hunters and telling stories of his many
brushes with death around the winter fires. He would
even be given the honor of training the young men in the

ways of the hunt. All this had been before him, only to be snatched away by the one thing over which he had no control—his own Madness.

Shn-En slumped against a rock outcropping, too exhausted to travel farther. Watching with a certain detachment as his feet seemed to swell in size before his eyes, until he thought they would surely burst from their hide boots. They did not burst. But to his horror, the flesh of his feet somehow melted away, until he could see white bones protruding from the broken seams of the boots, which his multitude of fingers did not allow him to mend.

The visions, the terrible haunting of shadows and spirits which he had borne all the days of his life, had increased both in frequency and severity during the last seasons. Now they came upon him like the thunder and lightning of summer storms, pounding and shaking him until he could not stand to be in the presence of his people. In truth, he feared that his old wives and his many children—and their young wives and small children—might be in danger from him when he fell into one of his spells. Shn-En knew he no longer had control over himself or his actions. Sometimes he saw the members of his own Hunting Circle as the misshapen, mythical enemies of his People. And in these moments of intense Madness, he knew himself capable of raising his weapons against them. The urge to kill the ancient scourges, which he admittedly had never actually seen, still became like a living, breathing thing inside him. And before he committed such an unforgivable act, harming one of his Circle, or even his own flesh and blood, Shn-En fled the Dry Season camp of his clan, walking these many days until he knew himself to be far outside the hunting territory of the Twin Mountain Clan. Better, he thought, to die alone and unburied than to bring terrible shame to his lineage. Bet-

ter to end his life among the shadows and spirits who
haunted him than to enter the Nether World carrying the
heavy stone of murder.

So he sat among the rocky cliffs at the edge of the Sea
of Sand, watching the sun sink behind the horizon. He
was grateful when darkness began to fall, brushing the
terrible light and the sparks from his eyes. He was grateful, even though he had lost his spear and the tool kit containing his fire stones. Lost them somewhere during the
long days of his stumbling Madness. His hunting knife,
with its sharp obsidian blade, remained strapped to the
leather belt about his waist. Shn-En found that if he did
not look at his many-fingered hands, he could reach
down and touch the bone handle of the knife. He let his
hand play along the contours of the weapon, but did not
allow himself to pull the blade free from its hide sheath.
Later, perhaps, he would take the knife and draw it across
his wrists, or plunge it into his neck, thereby ending the
Madness. At least he hoped death would end his ordeal.

This was the thing he considered as night fell around
him. The stars pushing aside the dark clouds of the heavens. The Sun's Mate rising above the empty Sea of Sand,
bringing ghosts and shadows up from the earth, as the
Sun draws plants from the spring ground. Would death
bring an end to his Madness, or would the plague follow
him across the River of the Dead, into the Nether World
itself? In truth, he did not know. And no amount of thinking, Shn-En realized, in a moment of clarity, would give
him the answer. It was a thing People knew only after
they had passed into the Land of the Dead. And then, of
course, it was too late to do anything about it. So he kept
the knife in its sheath, hoping for some wandering spirit
to pass by and grant him the gift of enlightenment. Not
surprising to Shn-En, none came.

When he was honest with himself, which was the case more often than not, Shn-En admitted he did not really expect any wandering spirits to take notice of him. As to enlightenment, he was not certain it was a gift at all. Had not the Elder Women and Wise Men of his clan proclaimed many times over the long years of his life that he himself had been given the gift of communication with the spirits? Aside from the undeniable fact that females seemed to want his children because of his so-called gift—at least in the days of his youth—and the more aggressive men were hesitant to argue with his opinions, the gift had been relatively useless. The shadows and spirits who seemed to follow his footsteps had never given the gift of calling meat to his spear. Indeed, it seemed that because of all the shadows he saw, he had to work harder, to be more careful stalking game, than the others in the Circle. He could not smell water better than the next man, and most could read the signs of rain or snow or wind as well as he. So this gift, as the Elders were so pleased to call it, had been more troublesome to his life than helpful. Particularly now, as he had exiled himself from the clan, before the Madness caused him to do something unthinkable.

The night deepened and Shn-En heard baboons crawling in the high rocks above. If they came for him, he knew, he would be quite helpless against their sharp teeth and claws. They were strong, agile creatures, who hunted in packs like the People. They seemed to be continually angry at the world, which made them furious hunters. Without fire or his spear, with only the confusing blur of his many-fingered hands to wield his knife, the baboons would make meat of him in the quickness of the Goddess's Breath. Then he would be forced to discover the truth about the Madness following him into the Nether World. It was not a thing he looked forward to.

Madness, Shn-En thought miserably, hung over his lineage like a cloud. His own grandfather, it was said, had been touched by the spirits, but few would speak about the man in the presence of Shn-En's own father, so his knowledge was limited. His mother also, if the whispers about her departure from the world of the living were to be believed. It was said, usually by those who drank too much fermented honey, that the Sun itself came and lifted Shn-En's mother from the earth, and she vanished into the clouds at the moment of her death. Shn-En had been too young to remember, but he did not believe any of that talk, having never met anyone who actually witnessed such an event. It was more than likely, he thought, that his mother had simply wandered out into the Sea of Sand and perished, in much the same manner he was about to do. Madness, it seemed, plagued all his family from the earliest times. Songs of his ancestors, shamen and healers among the People, were sung with reverence and fear around the winter fires. He wondered if, perhaps, such Madness was not an inherent trait in all the People, to one extent or another. Many of his own children, he noticed, exhibited the same signs of spirit hauntings he himself was forced to endure as a young boy. Whether this was a gift or a curse, Shn-En was not sure.

Above him, the baboon troop called out. The sound and movement making it seem as if they might have caught his scent. Shn-En wiggled deeper into the rock ledge, but to no avail. Before many heartbeats passed, a huge male baboon dropped down from the cliffs, standing like a ghost before him. The creature swayed, baring its teeth, as Shn-En lay, entwined in the arms of Madness, all but helpless in the shadows of the ledge. The baboon growled, and its long, sharp teeth seemed to shimmer like icicles in the soft light of the Sun's Mate. Shn-En tried to reach his knife, but his many-fingered hands did not allow the movement. He blinked, the stars seemed to spin in the sky, dancing like sparks around the Sun's Mate. And then the creature was upon him, even as he heard the gentle gasp of the Goddess's Breath sighing in his ears.

In the winter camps, songs were sung proclaiming Shn-En's closeness to the spirit world. His visions and many brave deeds were honored. In time, his sons and grandsons used their own gifts and magic to lead the People for many generations. His daughters and granddaughters brought uncounted numbers of children into the world. Under their guidance, many changes came to the world.

nine

Paul Sandborn arrived at his Washington office even earlier than usual. It was 7:30 in the morning, but the Centrifuge report was already on his desk, as he expected it to be. Within some government agencies, a slipshod work ethic was tolerated, even expected. But the people working close to Sandborn knew their priorities. Their jobs came first, second, and third in their lives. All the rest was extraneous, at least in Sandborn's mind, particularly when your job concerned the national security.

He thumbed through the report quickly, then went back to read specific sections more closely. By 8:30, he had calls in to both Harvey Mitchell's home and office numbers. Damn, but he smelled trouble on this, right from the get-go. It was 9:20 by the time Mitchell got back to him, and Sandborn was fuming.

"Did you read the Centrifuge report?" Sandborn asked pointedly.

"Not yet," Mitchell admitted, knowing the futility of a

lie. Jesus, the bloody thing had just come into the office, and Sandborn was practically berating him for not getting to it sooner. The man sounded like he had a bug up his ass the size of a Volkswagen.

"Doesn't matter," Sandborn said, after a long moment of silence. "We're pulling the plug on this Bracken character."

"Pulling the plug?" Mitchell asked, groping for time. He felt like he was sliding over an icy sidewalk, trying to get his footing. "I thought we agreed to bring him on board, at least part of the way. There's a funding allocation sitting here on my desk."

"Forget the allocation," Sandborn growled. "You assured me there was no way for Bracken to go further with this protein-exchange experiment."

"That's what I was told," Mitchell protested.

"Well, it seems he's a helluva lot further along than anyone thought he would be," Sandborn said. Mitchell could tell the man was making an effort to control his temper. And not a very successful effort, at that.

"Given what I know of the situation, I should think that's a positive thing," Mitchell said. He heard Sandborn sigh into the receiver. For the first time Harvey was glad his request for a new audiovisual phone system had been turned down by the budget cutters. He would have hated to be looking into the man's gunfighter eyes at this particular moment.

"It's a matter of the utmost importance that we keep this entire project under our control," Sandborn said, his voice cutting across the phone lines like a knife. "It's strictly a CDC operation, and it must remain so. Call the head of that laboratory . . . what's his name? Jacoby. Tell him the BIR has reviewed the material and you've determined that proceeding along these lines might interfere with Centrifuge's ability to meet their contractual obligations regarding the computer project. Stress the importance of the protein readers, all that sort of thing. And tell him to pack up all the material Bracken has gathered regarding the molecule exchange and ship it to Atlanta—ASAP."

"You don't think you're overreacting?" Mitchell asked, wanting to catch the words as soon as they'd left his mouth.

"Not in the least," Sandborn snapped. "You convey to Jacoby that failure to comply with this BIR directive will result in the termination of his government contract. This is a no-screw-around situation, Harvey. Make sure the man understands."

"What about Bracken?" Mitchell asked, wanting to be sure of his orders. "Should we have the facility terminate him?"

"God, no!" Sandborn sounded exasperated. Which, in fact, he was. Each day Paul Sandborn worked with the bureaucrats in the federal government, he became more and more convinced of their incompetence. It was, he thought, as if the government intentionally went out and hired idiots, and then compounded the mistake by making it a point to put them into positions of responsibility. When he considered this theory in calmer moments, he became even more certain of its validity. It made sense, in a warped sort of way. If you were a government supervisor, wouldn't it be prudent to have people who weren't quite as smart as you as underlings? Over time, this protect-your-own-ass mentality had built a system rife with fools in high places. No wonder the country was in such a fucking mess. When he retired, Sandborn promised himself, he was going to write a book. Let the taxpayers see what they were getting for their money. Providing, of course, there was anyone left who was able to read. Providing, the thought came ominously, there was anyone left at all.

"Think it through, for Christ's sake," he said, more sharply then he intended. He did, after all, have to work with Mitchell, and there was no point antagonizing the man needlessly. "If Bracken is fired, he might go babbling to the nearest newspaper or science journal he can find. Be diplomatic. Tell Jacoby that the BIR needs its most capable people working full-time on the new computer technology. Which is, essentially, the truth. You need to bring this project home, Harvey. People are counting on you."

"I know," Mitchell said, the weight of responsibility hanging over him like a heavy stone. "I'll call Jacoby this morning."

"Why don't you call him right now," Sandborn suggested, in a tone that indicated this was not at all a suggestion.

"Right away." Mitchell repeated the order as Sandborn disconnected. He punched the intercom to have Martha ring up the number for him. People were right, he thought, Paul Sandborn was one giant pain in the butt.

In his office, Sandborn fumed for another few minutes, wanting very much to smoke a cigarette, even though he had quit three years ago. He even searched the drawers of his desk for a stray butt, but knew in the back of his mind that he had played this game with himself before. Finally he picked up the phone again, this time calling the private line of the director of the Center for Disease Control in Atlanta.

"Dr. Lang?" he asked, making certain the phone connection wasn't screwed up, that he was actually speaking to the director himself. "Yes, it's Paul Sandborn. I've got some material coming to you from that New York facility. Right, the place we've been monitoring. I'm shutting down the work they were doing. Security reasons. We've got to keep this thing quiet until we've got a handle on it. Let me know as soon as you've got something. Good luck . . ."

It was ten A.M. and Gary Bracken was enjoying his second cup of coffee at the breakfast table. Becky had gone to work an hour or so ago, and he wasn't due at the lab until two. He was considering how to spend his free time. Maybe go do a little computer shopping? he thought. Spend some of the new allocation money. The phone rang, and Jacoby was on the other end of the line, for some reason muting his image. As he listened Bracken's stomach seemed to drop right down to his toes. Not bad, the cynical part of his mind whispered. After all, the euphoria had lasted all of twenty-four hours before the rug got pulled out from under him.

Fucking bastards, he thought, slamming down the receiver, knowing why Jacoby hadn't let him see his face. The rotten prick had probably been grinning, lighting up another victory cigar even as he delivered the body blow. Bracken's head was still reeling as he phoned Becky's office. Frantic, he readily admitted, for some kind words and an emotional shoulder to rail against. Her assistant, however, informed him that Rebecca was in a board meeting with the museum heads.

"Is it an emergency, Dr. Bracken?" the girl asked, obviously sensing something in his voice. Or, more likely, the ugly, savage look in his eyes. "I could have her paged."

"No, that's all right," Bracken said, making a conscious effort to bring himself under control. Becky's shoulder would be there later, when he really needed it. Once the reality of being stabbed in the back hit him. "I'll talk to her tonight. Thanks anyway . . ."

The phone screen blanked, and he sat for a moment, his

breath coming in short, shallow gasps. As if he had been gang-tackled by the entire front line of the Pittsburgh Steelers. Bracken considered his options, which he quickly realized were distressingly few. He finally came to the conclusion that he had better get his butt down to the lab, to salvage what he could of the project, before the whole thing was shipped off to the vultures at CDC. Fucking bastards, he thought, slamming his fist on the table, spilling hot coffee into his lap. What was so critical about all this, that the government wanted it kept so goddamned secret? Obviously, he was close to something important. Something the CDC wanted buried. Why? What the hell was going on? Bracken grabbed his coat and headed for the lab, determined that whatever was going down, he was damn well going to get to the bottom of it. If they thought he was just going to roll over and bow down, they had another think coming.

"You can at least let me pack up my own research materials," Bracken said, planting his feet in the door to Jacoby's office, as if daring the man to tell him differently. Surprisingly, Jacoby spread his hands and gave in to Bracken's request.

"Of course," Jacoby said, looking as if this were a victory he somehow regretted. "The truth is, I was having the other staff members do it as a courtesy. I realize how difficult this must be, but you have to look at the larger picture. The Bureau said quite specifically that they needed you on the computer project. It's a compliment to your work, you should take it as such."

"I'm taking it like it is," Bracken snapped. "It's scientific robbery, plain and simple."

"It's a question of priorities." Jacoby shook his head. "The protein reader is an extremely urgent project. Your own work is an indication of that. The director of the BIR assured me personally that you would be offered a position at the CDC, working on the molecular-exchange experiments, as soon as the new technology is on-line. My God, Dr. Bracken, that's a career move any of us would envy."

"Bullshit!" Bracken felt rage growing inside him. Rising up like some strange beast. He found himself actually wanting to leap over Jacoby's desk and rip out the fucker's throat. The thought, the actual vision of it, sobered him. He clutched his hands, which he realized were shaking. "That's years away, and we both know it," he said quietly.

"Well, there's nothing that can be done about it at the moment," Jacoby said, again shaking his head. "The directive was quite specific, as I told you over the phone. If it means anything to you, I honestly thought you were onto something. And I hope you get the chance to work on it in the future."

Bracken glared, trying to keep himself under control. It seemed as though he could taste Jacoby's blood, hot and salty in the back of his mouth. The sensation frightened him, and he kept quiet, lest he blurt out something he would later regret. Jacoby, the consummate bureaucrat, was saying all the right things. Smoothing over an unpleasant situation with feigned regrets and platitudes while dangling the carrot of future reparations. A thing bureaucrats did with unfailing predictability. It was, Bracken thought, like spreading shit over a cake and calling it frosting.

Even as Jacoby was shaking his head, Bracken felt a hand on his shoulder, and he jumped, startled. Terrance Stampe took a step backward, as if he saw something terrifying in Bracken's eyes. But then the older man blinked, like a person who thought he had seen a ghost, but quickly realized such things did not exist. Stampe then joined Bracken in the doorway, looking genuinely sorry.

"You had better see to your work," Stampe said, nodding back toward the lab, where the day staff was busily extracting Bracken's files from the computer system and boxing up his printed data.

"You know, I could work both projects," Bracken said, in what he knew to be a last, desperate plea. It was a ploy, he realized, that was doomed to fail. The final pawn push of a chess player who knew the game was lost.

"The BIR directive was quite explicit," Jacoby said stiffly, this time not bothering to work a tone of regret into his voice.

"Come on, I'll give you a hand." Stampe turned him from Jacoby's office. Stampe shut the door behind them, as if he had somehow sensed Bracken's violent hostility. "Are you all right?" he asked quietly.

"I can't let them do this." Bracken shook his head miserably.

"You don't appear to have any choice," Stampe said, bringing him back to the reality of the situation.

"I can resign," Bracken said, wondering if that was an option. It wasn't, of course, as Stampe reminded him.

"Your research is the property of the BIR," Stampe said. "It's still going to wind up at the CDC, whether you're here or not."

"And what the hell are they going to do with it?" Bracken asked in frustration.

"I don't know," Stampe admitted, shaking his head. "It's my guess you got too close to something they want to keep confidential."

"But what?" Bracken asked. There was, he realized, no answer to the question. The answer lay somewhere in the files and data sheets being pirated away from him. "What am I supposed to do, Terrance?"

"Give them what they want," Stampe said, his voice falling away into a whisper. "But before you do, funnel everything through my office. I'll see that it's shipped to Atlanta. But before it goes, I'll copy all the files and photostat what data sheets I can."

"Christ, I can't ask you to do that," Bracken whispered even as he grasped onto this glimmer of hope like a drowning man reaching for a lifeboat on a rapidly sinking ship.

"You didn't ask," Stampe said quietly.

"Terrance, I can't thank you enough," Bracken heard himself babbling.

"Don't," Stampe said, almost snapping the words. "In the end, maybe you won't want to at all."

Why, Bracken wanted to ask? But the older man was already retreating toward the sanctuary of his office. What the hell was that supposed to mean? Bracken didn't have a clue. But the day shift was cleaning out the computer files, and he knew he had to hurry if there was any hope of salvaging the data.

Rebecca came home to find her living room cluttered with boxes and computer equipment. Gary, she saw, was moving everything into the basement.

"What in the world are you doing?" she asked, inspecting what looked to be a terrarium filled with bugs. She was further taken aback to discover the thing was exactly what it appeared to be.

"They pulled my goddamned funding," Bracken said, forcing a smile. "I'm moving the experiment downstairs."

"You're joking, right?" she asked. Bracken shook his head, and she felt her heart skip a beat. "The lab got shut down?"

"No, nothing that drastic." Bracken saw the look in her eye and set down the boxes he was carrying. He put his arm around her. "Centrifuge is still up and running. And I'm still gainfully employed."

"Thank God," she whispered, hugging him back.

"The BIR knifed me," Bracken explained. "They cut the molecule-exchange experiment out of the budget. We're all supposed to work full-time on the protein reader, and my other work got shipped off to Atlanta. But I'll be damned if I'm going to let them shut me down, so I'm setting it up in the cellar. Hope you don't mind. There really wasn't any time for discussion."

"Does Jacoby know about this?" Rebecca asked. Again, Bracken shook his head, grinning, not looking the least bit contrite. "The Industrial Research people?"

"No," Bracken admitted. "But Terrance Stampe helped me get the research materials out of the lab."

"Oh, that's good," Becky said sarcastically. "I'm sure old Terrance will be standing right behind you when the BIR comes calling."

Shades of her husband's run-ins with the Columbia research board loomed again in her mind. Those scrapes with authority had cost him a professorship at the university. But that was nothing, she realized, compared with bucking the system when the federal government was involved. Not surprisingly, Bracken grinned, knowing what she was thinking.

"Aren't there security questions here?" she asked critically. "What are the feds going to say when they find out you're backdooring them like this?"

"Nothing," Bracken said, with more assurance than he actually felt. "They won't find out. At least, not until I'm ready to tell them. Believe me, when the results come in on this project, nobody's going to say boo to me. There's something big here, Becky. And I'm going to bring it home."

"Look's like you've already done that." Rebecca stared at all the boxes and equipment. "You didn't steal all this stuff?"

"Borrowed it," Bracken said, laughing. "It's old equipment we had in storage. But it'll do. Anything I can't work out here, I'll sneak into the lab's computer systems. Not to worry, babe. It's going to be all right."

"I hope so." Becky sounded doubtful. But in the end, she found herself helping to carry the boxes and equipment into the basement workshop. Wondering all the while if this implicated her in some bizarre conspiracy against the federal government. She did, however, draw the line at touching the glass container which contained the bugs. Termites, Bracken told her, critical to the scope of the experiment.

"We'd better not be fumigating, if these things escape," she said.

"Paranoia will destroy ya." Bracken laughed, singing the words from an old protest song.

Oddly, he didn't seem to be as distressed as she might have thought, with his funding cut. In truth, he seemed to be happy, working in the cellar. Basement research, he called it, reminding her that some of the most important discoveries in science had been made by people without half the equipment he had access to.

"I'm going to fight 'em, and I'm going to win," he told her, before disappearing downstairs, leaving her alone until the late hours of the night.

Rebecca, however, found herself listening carefully whenever a car passed by in the street. Expecting government agents to come pounding on the door at any moment. It was stupid, of course. This was America, and things didn't work that way, or so she kept telling herself.

a molecule of time
Day One + 1.2775 x 10 ^12

To say that he didn't understand what was happening to him was inadequate. The fact was, he didn't even understand anything out of the ordinary was happening. The change came in a progressive series that seemed, in his mind anyway, to be based on reasonable logic.

It began with the whispers. He thought at first he might be dreaming. He always had particularly vivid dreams. And the whispering, when it first started, seemed very dreamlike. It was only later, when the whispers became actual voices, and when he realized no one else could hear them, that Duncan Hill reached the logical conclusion that he was hearing other people's thoughts. But by this time, when he finally made the connection, Hill was so lost in the confusion of sounds in his head, he had become entirely dysfunctional. Although he himself didn't see it that way at all.

He lived alone in a second-story apartment building in

Houston, Texas. He worked in a plant which made parts
for the aerospace industry, or did until it became almost
impossible to force himself into the long brick building,
with its gates and guards, and teeming masses of people.
All of whom, it seemed, were whispering about him inside their own heads. They were, of course, quite oblivi-
ous to the fact that he was hearing what they were
thinking about him, but he doubted it would have made
any difference. Their disdain, bordering on hatred toward
him, was so deeply embedded, he knew they wouldn't
have been able to control their thoughts, any more than
he could control receiving them. That part he truly didn't
understand. He hadn't done anything, at least anything he
could remember, to turn them all against him. But that
was what had happened. There was no question about it.
He could hear them, whispering. And he knew they were
whispering about him, even if the words were so garbled
he couldn't make them out, exactly. But it was in their
faces, too. The way they all became quiet when he passed
by, watching him out of the corners of their eyes. For
some reason he couldn't quite fathom, they seemed
afraid. Almost terrified of him. And he'd had more than a
few run-ins with his supervisors, when he'd started demanding to know what it was people were saying about
him.

That had been a mistake, he realized. A dead giveaway
of the fact that he could hear them whispering in their
minds. Because, of course, they weren't saying what they
thought about him out loud. They were just whispering,
inside.

So in the end, he was glad he had done what he did.
Certainly he felt no remorse. They deserved what they
got. He said this, over and over, even when the cops

stormed into the plant. Even when they dragged him out and locked him away in this tiny, stinking cell.

How many? He wasn't sure. His brain didn't seem to be able to hold that sort of information anymore. Ten, for sure. Maybe twelve. He didn't believe it was any more than that. But it could be more. He hoped it was. He would've killed them all, except the gun had gotten hot and he'd dropped it. Or maybe he just ran out of bullets. He wasn't sure about that, either. But he sure as hell gave them something to whisper about. The bastards.

The cell doors clanked. Footsteps echoed in the long corridor. All the time, at all hours of the day and night. Sometimes people came and talked to him through the bars. Sometimes they came inside the cell and chained him up. Tight, so he couldn't move his hands or arms. Could only shuffle down the long corridor, surrounded by grim-faced guards. They were whispering, too, he noticed. And they were afraid of him as well. They had damn well better be, he thought. Whispering bastards.

Within the bodies of their hosts, the virus clans worked. Mutating, manipulating the DNA structures, using the knowledge gained over billions of years. Refining the neuron system of the host. It was, however, a trial-and-error method. As with any such methodology, there were many more errors than successes, particularly at this advanced stage of the work.

Within the clans, proteins were exchanged, containing the successes and failures of the manipulations. While it was true that many of the hosts would need to be sacrificed before the key sequences could be found, the hosts were plentiful. Their numbers building over the generations, until the earth was filled with their species. It was a further truth that many of the hosts succumbed to aber-

rations of the trial-and-error method, these producing an unfortunate number of diseases and illnesses. But even this served the clan's purpose. The hosts who survived were stronger, their strengthened immune systems better able to deal with the residual effects of aberrations within the mutation field. While all of this could not be said to constitute a plan, in the strictest sense of the word—the clans themselves having, as yet, no direct link to cognitive thought processes—the pattern for the development of ONE was clearly in place. No matter that it had taken billions of years to reach this point. No matter that a great number of hosts would need to be sacrificed to attain the goal. What mattered was that now, in this time and place, it was becoming possible for the Many to become ONE. In another few generations, at most, the clans would find the key, the proper sequence of molecular structures to live in complete harmony with the hosts.

The time of Change was rapidly approaching.

ten

There wasn't any such animal as a one-hundred-percent-secure communications link. Paul Sandborn knew that as well as anyone. But NSA technology provided linkups as close to that magic number as a person was likely to find. Sandborn, after years of running covert activities for his government, trusted the security arrangements of his agency. Trusted them with his career, even with his life. This, however, was one of the few times—one of a handful of scenarios he could remember—when the phone lines and computer tie-ins weren't to be trusted. Not with what might be at stake in this particular instance. So when the director of the CDC left a message saying they needed to talk, Sandborn called for a military transport to run him down to Atlanta.

Although, of course, even a face-to-face did not guarantee one hundred percent security. Security was on Sandborn's mind a lot, lately. The truth was, he admitted to himself, things might be getting out of hand. And in his experience, when things started to go south, you could always count on an information breach of one kind or another.

It was raining in Atlanta when the helicopter settled onto the landing pad at the rear of the CDC administration building. A sergeant held an umbrella for him as the chopper door flopped open and the thin metal passenger steps were unfolded. Like he was the bloody Queen of England, Sandborn thought.

"That'll be all right, soldier," Sandborn said, turning up the collar on his overcoat. "I don't think I'll melt."

The sergeant, a stone-faced marine who looked like he chewed nails for breakfast, gave in to a small twitch at the corners of his mouth. Probably as close to a smile as the man was likely to get, Sandborn considered. The umbrella was deftly stored inside the chopper door, as if it were an M-16. Sandborn stepped outside and breathed the damp, chilly air. The actual CDC laboratories were set back along the sloping landscape, which was dotted with leafless trees and curiously green grass. Winter was able to make inroads this far south, Sandborn noted, but apparently Mother Nature drew the line at fucking up the golf courses. The rain was cold, but he liked the feel of it. Liked drawing the moisture-laden air deep into his formerly cigarette-polluted lungs. The fact was, before any important meeting, it was Sandborn's custom to take a walk outside. Providing, of course, the place he found himself wasn't under the immediate threat of any hot incoming. A walk cleared his head, allowed him a moment or two to gather his thoughts. And he sure as hell needed that today, in these deceptively peaceful surroundings.

Sandborn noticed a welcoming committee, standing under the shelter of an awning, debating whether or not protocol demanded that they venture out into the rain to greet him officially. He smiled to himself and walked toward the building, making the committee's decision for them. A little weather, he thought, and the desk jockeys huddled together like rabbits. He showed his disdain for them by not shaking anyone's hand, which he deemed a prudent measure in any case, given where these people worked. He merely nodded his head, following them into the confusing maze of CDC headquarters.

The director's office was a little too fancy for Sandborn's taste, but he realized the necessity of frills to impress foreign visitors, who expected that sort of excess in America. Sandborn did shake hands with Jeffery Lang, the head honcho at CDC, a man he had worked well with in the past. Lang was an American of Japanese descent, and one of the brightest people in government service, in Sandborn's estimation. Which was a good thing, he thought, considering the man's position. Lang, however, seemed nervous as they went through the opening formalities of a face-to-face between two men who knew and respected the other's abilities. To Sandborn's relief, the opening gambit lasted only a minute or two, before the assistants were dismissed and the real business started.

"I assume you're secure here?" Sandborn asked, shedding his coat, forgoing any further pleasantries.

Lang nodded, but turned on the standard white noise masker in response to Sandborn's unspoken request. Lang was a thin, balding man, with wire-rim glasses and a propensity for wearing loud, garish ties. Lang removed his glasses and rubbed the bridge of his nose. Not a good sign, Sandborn thought. The man was obviously tired, and perhaps a bit distraught. Evil portents all around.

"How bad is it?" Sandborn asked, pulling a chair close to the front of Lang's polished oak desk, cluttered with files and pictures of the man's family.

"You've read the reports?" Jeffery Lang sat down in his leather chair and leaned back, as if this whole affair was something he wanted to distance himself from.

"And I watch the evening news," Sandborn said. "It's all over the place. Surprising, really, that the media doesn't put it together, on some level at least."

"Yes, the incidents of violence and general instability are increasing," Lang agreed. "But it's been a progressive thing, that's why the pattern goes largely unnoticed. As the rates of violence increase, only the more blatant occurrences make the news reports these days."

"But you've charted an increase?" Sandborn asked.

"I'd say yes, but the contributing factors are difficult to nail down," Lang said. "When a postal worker, for example, goes off the deep end and takes out a group of their fellow employees, who's to say what the cause is? Job stress? The crash of the economy? Or an actual brain dysfunction? It's hard to tell, really. But yes, certainly acts of domestic violence and general mayhem are definitely on the increase. One might say they have already reached plaguelike proportions."

"But you can't tag the cause?" Sandborn asked carefully. The world was, after all, an increasingly less stable place. Perhaps, as Lang suggested, people were simply reacting to the increased stresses in their lives.

"No, I can't," Lang said, drawing a deep breath.

Sandborn felt the muscles in his legs tensing, as they always did during times when the shit was about to hit the fan. His years as a soldier in some of the world's most furious hot spots taught him to trust the muscles in his legs. Invariably, they always told him when it was prudent to hit the ground or run for cover. Only here, in this overstuffed, wood-paneled office, there was no cover. That, however, did not mean incoming rounds were not imminent.

"I can tell you a couple of things," Lang began slowly. "First, there does seem to be increased viral activity taking place in the human brain. Statistically within the general populace, not within each individual."

"Cancer?" Sandborn asked. Like most people, he had come to think of viruses as the carriers of dreaded disease.

"No," Lang said, shaking his head emphatically. "This is not, on the surface anyway, a function of any specific disease. The truth is, the majority of viruses do not cause illnesses. If they did, we'd all be dead. Actually, it goes deeper than that. If viruses killed everything they came into contact with, all life on the planet would be eradicated before the week was out. In fact, life would never have arisen past the single-cell stage."

"What about the Ebola virus?" Sandborn asked, his voice critical. "The common cold? AIDS, for God's sake?"

"Don't get me wrong." Lang held up his hand to interrupt. "Certainly, viruses have the potential to cause devastating illness. Plagues of terrible magnitude. Surely, that's true. But those are the viruses we hear about. The ones we study, however ineptly. You have to understand, we're only just beginning to understand life on the submicroscopic level. There are an uncounted number of viruses which live quite benignly, alongside and within the human population. Perhaps millions of them, whose function we can't even begin to guess at. The increased viral activity we've seen lately seems to fall into this unspecified category. There are no tumors involved, no outward signs of disease that we've been able to document. I can only tell you that the increased incidents of violence and instability are correlated with this increased viral activity. Whether or not the two are related, who can say?" Lang shrugged. His eyes, Sandborn noted, took on a tired, almost haunted look. "There might not be any correlation at all. This entire phenomenon may simply be attributable to statistical aberration."

"Like comparing apples to oranges?" Sandborn suggested.

"Sort of," Lang said, in a tone that told Sandborn how far off base he was, and also that the other man was too tired to debate the point with him.

"So, I'm not sure what we do at this point," Sandborn said, his mind mulling over a mountain of possibilities. The majority of which, he realized, he didn't really understand. Actually he was waiting for Lang to step in with some suggested course of action. Jeffery Lang, however, was only sitting in his chair, staring at him. Sandborn was struck with the sudden reality that the information session was not yet over. This time, as his leg muscles twitched, he felt a brief, involuntary flash of fear.

"There's more?" he asked, surprised to find his voice suddenly hoarse.

"Yes, there's more." Lang nodded, rubbing his hand across the long, expanded slope of his forehead. "For the past several years we've been charting a mutation that seems to be occurring in a significant number of the nation's newborns."

"Mutation?" Sandborn heard himself blurt. Visions of three-armed, no-legged babies flashing into his brain. The prescription-drug debacle of the sixties. The radiation children born to the survivors of Hiroshima and Nagasaki. The smallest victims of the Chernobyl disaster. The majority of whom had, thankfully, been hidden from the press. "You're not talking . . . monsters, are you?" Sandborn asked, finding it difficult to force his mouth to say the word. "I would have heard about it. The reports didn't indicate . . ."

"No, not monsters," Lang said quietly, and Sandborn felt

himself sink back into his chair. Jesus, Lang really knew how to throw a scare into a man. He wondered, briefly, if the man smoked. Maybe there was a pack of cigarettes in his desk? No, Sandborn realized, not the head of the CDC.

"Thank God," Sandborn said, not even wanting to consider how such a thing would complicate his life. A second later, however, Lang made him reevaluate the thought.

"The mutations are nothing visible, at least not on the surface," the man continued. "The affected children are fine, physically, as far as we can determine. They seem to be growing up to be normal, healthy kids. Their parents aren't even told there's anything abnormal."

"Then . . . what is it?" Sandborn asked, feeling as though some giant hand had just picked him up and tossed him into a maelstrom.

"There's a slight aberration in their EEGs," Lang said. "A small increase in the cycle of their alpha waves. Also, we've seen some minor changes in the outer wall of the neuron cells, in the form of an enhanced receptor. That's a tiny nodule which protrudes from the surface of all cells. Like I said, we've only been charting the mutation for a few years, so there's no way of telling how long it's been going on. More than likely, there are a small percentage of adults who are similarly affected. Actually, this might be where your real problems will be."

"In the adults?" Sandborn was trying to think of contingency plans even as he processed the information. He wanted to take a walk outside, to clear his head. Actually, that was not entirely true, he admitted. What he really wanted to do was get the hell away from the Center for Disease Control and never come back. Microbe Central, the place was called in the back rooms of Washington. Sandborn felt like they were about to start experimenting on him.

"That's right," Lang said. "An increase in alpha frequency could be extremely disorientating. By the way, some people here think it might be a result of the viral activity we've been monitoring, but for the moment the cause isn't as important as the reaction. Human beings are incredibly adaptable, particularly the very young. A child born with a missing limb, for example, will quickly learn adaptive behavior which will allow it to function in a fairly normal manner. The same is true if the child is born with a brain malfunction. That is, the brain itself will in many cases shift functions away from the damaged sector, and allow necessary information to be processed by other, healthy sectors. The point being that the young are more flexible in the way they deal with their environment. Adults with missing limbs often have a difficult period of physical adjustment, and the mature brain becomes hardwired to some extent, making function shifts away from damaged sectors less likely. So the child who is born with an increase in their alpha frequency will have a much easier time adjusting to the new field than an adult who has the change thrust upon them. In actuality, the frequency increase could provide a definite advantage in such things as memory retention and information processing, once the children learn to use the capability."

"You sound like you're selling a new computer system," Sandborn said, in an attempt to check the sudden chill creeping up his spine. The tactic seemed to work well for Lang, who gave a short laugh, but it failed miserably for Sandborn.

"That's probably closer to the truth than either of us would like to admit," Lang said, nodding, as Sandborn felt the uncomfortable chill sweep through his whole body.

"But the children, they're healthy?" he asked, searching for a positive aspect he could spin to his superiors.

"Perfectly normal," Lang said. "No difference on the

learning curve. No abnormalities that we're able to detect, other than the cell change and this minor frequency shift in their brain patterns."

"What the hell are we going to do about it, then?" Sandborn heard himself ask, as though his voice was coming from the end of a long, hollow tunnel.

"We're going to instruct the hospitals to recalibrate the machinery to adjust for the change." Lang shrugged. "What else can we do?"

What else can we do? Sandborn listened as the question replayed in his mind. Nothing, he realized, his leg muscles twitching almost uncontrollably.

Bracken came up from the basement lab and found his bed cold, even though the room itself was warm. He found, also, that it was no easy task to fumble around in the dark and get covered up, without making a considerable amount of noise. He tried not to wake Rebecca, but could tell by her breathing that she was not asleep. The cold, he realized, was coming from her side of the bed. He turned quietly to look at her. Becky, like a snowbank rolled up in blankets beside him, sensed his movement.

"So what happens now?" she whispered, keeping her body turned away from him.

"I don't know," he replied, not certain what it was, exactly, that she meant. As always, this was something he never quite understood. "I'm going to try and do my work."

"They'll never let you," she said, knowing he was not referring to his job at Centrifuge Labs.

"Maybe not," he admitted. "But I've still got to try. It's important. . . ."

She sighed in the dark, and Bracken stopped his attempt to explain himself.

"We're important, too," Becky said softly, and he thought,

perhaps, she might be crying. He wanted very much to comfort her, but wasn't sure what her response would be.

"I know we're important," he said, reaching out in the dark, his hand falling just short of her shoulder. "What can I do?" he asked.

"I want us to be like we were before," she said, her voice muffled. "I need . . ." Rebecca hesitated, as though stepping out onto deeply cracked ice. Unsure of herself, and lately of her husband, whom she now found changed beyond her understanding.

"I need you to touch me," she whispered finally. "Not just when we're making love. I need you to touch me like you used to. At odd moments, when I don't expect it. I need you to hold my hand, to brush against my arm. I want to feel your weight on my shoulders. Not always. Not even every day. Just . . . just at odd moments. When neither of us wants something from the other. Just a touch now and then."

"That's not so much to ask," he said, deeply moved by the simplicity of her request. And by the fact that he could hardly ever remember doing such a thing. Such a small, trivial gesture.

"I want things to be like they used to be," she said.

At that, he had no reply. He could only move closer and hold her, knowing in his heart that she had requested the one thing beyond his control. The world would never be like it once was. Of that he was certain, and the knowledge saddened him more than he could say. The truth was, he suspected events were closing in around them, events they could neither anticipate nor avoid. These thoughts, which he could not share with her, plagued him until the last hours of the night, when sleep finally overtook him.

a molecule of time

The walls, closing around her. As if she was buried deep underground and was unable to dig her way out. The environment around her, sterile and empty. No scents, other than her own. No sounds, other than her own. She was as alone as though she was the last creature left on Earth. Alone in this cubicle of stone, having no idea how she happened to be here, waking one morning to this strange nightmare of isolation. Hers was a social species, and she needed physical contact. Needed the safety and comfort found only within the confines of the group. And the others were out there, somewhere. She was certain of it. Occasionally, through the locked, sealed opening of the stone cage, she caught fleeting wisps of their scent. Briefly, fading. And she screamed for them to come and rescue her. Screamed in the only language she knew.

Two attendants stood nervously outside the heavy metal door. They were large, burly men, dressed in hos-

pital whites, but still were hesitant to step inside the isolation room. The woman was raging again, and one of the
men held the padded straps they would have to use to tie
her to the bed. They listened for a moment to the loud
shrieks and gruntlike sounds coming from within. One of
them slid back the covering over the small window, set
high in the door. The woman, squatting on the bed, saw
faces in the shatterproof glass, and threw herself at the
door. Screaming, clawing at the door. Calling desperately
for the others in the troop to save her from this heinous
place. This treeless, empty, lonely place. She pressed her
face against the glass, growling, baring her teeth in anger
and fear.

"Jesus Christ!" the attendant whispered, taking an involuntary step backward, even though he knew there was
no way for the woman to reach him with her snapping
jaws and clawlike fingers. At least not until he had to
open the door and go inside.

"Pretty fucking scary," his partner agreed. All up and
down the corridor the same scene had been repeated,
with varying degrees of severity, for the past several
weeks. The whole fucking place, he thought, was turning
into a goddamned zoo. A zoo filled with maddened
human animals.

Insanity did indeed seem to be the order of the day.

On a street corner in downtown Los Angeles, the music
rolled from oversized boom boxes set along concrete
steps outside the apartment buildings. Thumping, blood-
rushing music, rising up like ancient drumbeats into the
soft warm air. A dry breeze coming off the Pacific,
rustling the sparse vegetation that somehow managed to
grow between strips of pavement and sidewalk, between
close-set wooden buildings with their high porch steps.

It was a gathering place of young people, dressed in
sneakers and T-shirts, wearing hats, headbands, and jackets, proclaiming the colors of their neighborhood. Cigarette smoke and laughter, brown paper bags handed around
in the early hours of the night. Cars passed by the street
corner, playing the same thundering music. Sometimes
they stopped, and young girls would get in or out, involved
in a mating game, the rules of which were barely understood, if at all.

At the far end of the street, a car drove slowly up the
avenue, as if those inside were somewhat hesitant, unsure
of their mission. But when this particular automobile
reached the street corner, the gathering place of the young
people, all signs of hesitancy vanished. The windows,
tinted dark to shield those within from the outside world,
were quickly rolled down. The barrels of guns appeared
suddenly in the windows, spitting tiny puffs of smoke
and the snapping sounds of firecrackers. Those on the
street corner screamed and ran, diving for cover, even as
the car rolled by, spewing death and mayhem. Then, as
the sidewalk and porch steps ran with dark, thick blood,
as the sharp, burning smell of sulfur hung in the air like a
fog, the invading car roared off into the night. Inside,
there were shouts and muted gasps of triumph. Adrenaline pumping, as it always does when the Enemy is given
a taste of death.

On the other side of the world, in the cold, muddy killing
fields of a small but vicious war, bodies were thrown indiscriminately into a wide mass grave. The corpses, old
men and boys for the most part, their bodies riddled with
machine-gun fire, were stacked like wood, as though a
charcoal pit were being made. Lye was spread over the
layers of bodies. Then, when the pit was filled, a bull-

dozer rumbled across the bloodstained meadow, pushing mounds of dirt over the huge grave. Soldiers who had done the killing squatted on their haunches under the gray sky, cradling weapons in their arms, smoking cigarettes, their faces flushed. Their eyes, curiously blank, as if some of the life had been squeezed out of them as well. In the background, a church smoldered, its bell tower burned and blacked by constant, indiscriminate shelling. Even though this was, on the surface, a war supposedly fought for the glory of God.

The television set gave off its warm, hypnotizing glow in a living room in suburban Boston. As it did in living rooms all across America. A middle-aged couple sat, separated by the light and sound of the machine, watching the late night newscast. The reporter—a woman on the low curve of middle age herself, neatly groomed, fashionably dressed—gently informed the couple that government investigators had determined the cause of a plane crash in the midwest earlier in the month, in which one hundred and seventy-three people had been killed, to be "pilot error." The couple accepted this explanation mutely, then went quietly off to bed.

In the crumbling basement of a condemned building on the Lower East Side in New York, a junkie slipped a needle into his arm and carefully drew back the plunger before driving the mixture of blood and heroin into his body. The man, dirty and disheveled, somewhere in the third decade of his life, had somehow reached the conclusion that his existence was devoid of meaning and hope. He lay back on a filthy, bug-ridden mattress, pulling his torn coat around him, and slipped away into a golden haze. The dope, at least, kept the whispers and shadows away.

• • •

Outside Tremont, New Jersey, a salesman flicked on the cruise control of his automobile and fumbled for a moment with the CD player. He was on his way home after a prolonged road trip, and hadn't felt right in days. His head hurt, despite all the aspirin he'd gulped, but he'd promised his wife he would be home tonight. He smiled, thinking about her, as music filled the car—a lonesome love song, with a slight country-western twang. He blinked at the oncoming headlights. Something wasn't quite right. His head . . . he put his hand up to feel his forehead . . . just as the flash came. Like a spotlight turned on inside his brain. He gasped, softly, unintelligibly. His free hand slipping across the steering wheel, as though it had been suddenly greased. His car careened into the oncoming lane, where it collided with a truck carrying produce to the Jersey markets. The explosion was deafening, even though he never heard it.

Within the bodies of their hosts, the virus clans moved, building the links, forging the delicate matrix which would bring about the Change. As they did, madness and chaos crept slowly into the lives of the hosts. Surprisingly, these events went largely unnoticed. This was due, in part, to hidden racial memories, molecules of protein the hosts carried in the deep recesses of their brains. Times of Change had come before, of course. And the hosts were known, even selected, for their ability to adapt.

eleven

Gary Bracken came home from the laboratory at five in the afternoon, as he had every day for the past several weeks. A factory worker on the scientific assembly line. A clock-watching, lunch-bucket shift worker. But all that changed at five o'clock, when Bracken entered the tiny, enclosed world of his basement workshop, filled with pirated equipment from Centrifuge Labs. There, in his mind anyway, he started his real workday, trying to unlock the secrets of viral protein communication.

Rebecca always pulled into the garage exactly an hour later. At first, during the early days of what Becky now called the graveyard shift, he made a point of going up to greet her. They might watch the news, or eat some takeout. He had really tried in the beginning, and it seemed to work between them for a while. But always, he would disappear downstairs into his cellar lab, spending long hours on the protein exchange project, and Rebecca seemed to pull farther and farther away, until touching her became quite impossible.

"I feel like I'm losing you to something bizarre," she said. When he scoffed at her remarks, it only served to increase her cracks concerning his mad-scientist routine, and her complaints about being a test-tube widow. Rather than fight with her, he found it easier simply to forgo the evening ritual.

It was a phase, he kept telling himself. Things would be better when he achieved results, even though success seemed to be just beyond his reach. He could glimpse the answers sometimes, like a distant shadow, but when he reached for them, nothing was there. It was as though the thing itself was trying to be elusive. Almost, he thought, as if some hidden entity was trying to convince him that what he saw was a mirage. Bracken knew better. The protein exchange was real, that was certain. There was something going on, and he was going to find out what. No matter what it cost.

What if the cost is Rebecca? The thought came often in the late hours of the night. That's not going to happen, he kept telling himself even as he knew she was slipping away from him. A temporary situation, she'd get over it, once he made the breakthrough. He was close, there was no question about it. Actually, Bracken had to admit, the protein storage work being done at Centrifuge was proving valuable, leading him into areas that would have been unbroachable only a few short weeks ago. The truth was, he had incorporated a lot of the government technology into his own project. Undoubtedly something that would have to be worked out later. Perhaps after the protein-reading computers came on-line and the technology was open to the public. But even if the feds protested his use of their equipment, they had no claim on the actual work itself. The molecular codes of the termite hive had revealed themselves in a series of spectacular numerical progressions, and were now capable of being processed by the early prototypes of the protein-reading system. That, in itself, was a discovery of monumental proportions. The highlight of any entomologist's career. He could write a definitive paper on his research to this point, and make a name for himself that would dominate the textbooks on the subject for years. But it was only a partial victory.

Really, he thought, in the large scheme of things, did it actually matter that by injecting certain coded proteins into a termite community, one could pretty much make the bugs behave in a predictable manner? It might revolutionize the pest-control industry—hell, it would! Bracken knew he could stop now, patent his discoveries, and make a fortune in the infestation business. Providing, of course, the FDA and the gaggle of other federal agencies granted their approval. There were bound to be ethical and environmental questions regarding the use of behavior-altering proteins. All of which could be hashed out later. Right now there were bigger fish to fry.

Well, not bigger fish, he thought, grinning to himself, as he worked the computer program under the harsh, bare bulbs in the basement sockets. Smaller fish. Much smaller. But if one took into account the sheer numbers involved, the viral protein exchange made the bug discovery pale by comparison. And he was close to cracking the molecular code of these submicroscopic creatures. Real fucking close. He had to be careful at this point, Bracken realized. To come out and publish anything now, even to reveal the code data on the termite proteins, would jeopardize the real meat of the project. It would cause a firestorm in the scientific community. Before the ink was dry on his scientific paper, every research lab in the country would be poking their noses into the field. And this was his baby. He was going to be the one who opened the door to the unimaginable knowledge of the gene masters—the virus engineers. Hell's Bells, that was worth taking a little heat from the wife. Becky would come around, he told himself, once she realized the magnitude of his work.

Still, every morning when he drove off to Centrifuge and its assembly-line science, he considered the possibility of dumping it all and going into the bug-control business. But he was aware that if he shot off his mouth too soon, the BIR would be on him like the tax man after Capone. They'd shut him down in the blink of an eye, just like they tried to do when they first found out what he was onto. And that was the real reason he was working day and night, busting his ass in the musty basement. There was something here. Something the government knew about but wanted buried. So he kept his mouth shut and fed data into the computer bank until he couldn't keep his eyes open anymore. Then a few hours' sleep, and he threw himself back at it. Close. Real fucking close. So what if his work at Centrifuge wasn't what it used to be? They wanted drones, and that was what they got. People with no vision deserve what they get. . . .

He blinked, staring at the computer screen. He was scanning protein data into the machine, cross-linking readable termite proteins with the smaller, more complicated molecules gleaned from the virus communities. The slides and vials smuggled out of Centrifuge after the BIR bastards had tried to take him out of the loop. First cutting his funding, then limiting his access to the Atlanta big-brain linkup. They were rotten fuckers . . . but the screen . . . the scanning mechanism. Usually this procedure resulted in a blur of unreadable material, with the

program unable to interface between the two sets of proteins. Actually, Bracken was working toward building up
a larger database, which he planned to use when he began
correlating the work. And the readout was always the
same, a confusing jumble of meaningless symbols the
computer spat out when it designated an error—that
being its own inability to compare the data. The incom-
patibility factor, as Bracken had come to know the terminology. Except, he saw, for a few brief lines of code that
almost escaped his notice as the scanned information
flew by on the screen.

He thought for a moment his eyes were deceiving him.
A trick of the lighting, or his own desire to see something
that wasn't there. Couldn't be there . . . then he recalled
the page.

"Sweet Jesus," he whispered, almost falling off the
chair. Tucked in among all the thousands of lines of code,
two strips of binary numbers. He stared, in disbelief.
Adrenaline pumping, waking his tired brain. My God, he
thought, was it real? He rescanned the information and the
computer faithfully spat out the same data—the seemingly endless stream of error readouts, and two tiny lines
of progressive numbers. Two lines, out of how many thousands of unreadable protein messages? He couldn't even
begin to estimate. But there they were, by God. A hit. A
fucking hit! The first definable words, a whisper from the
submicroscopic cosmos.

Bracken leaned back in his chair, feeling as though he
had just heard the soft, incomprehensible words of God.
True, he had no idea what the words were. Of course, they
weren't words at all, he reminded himself. They were
symbols, instructions in the virus genetic code, and maybe
not even that. Given the vast amounts of data he was feeding the machine, it was not inconceivable that he had

merely stumbled onto an accidental correlation. One that meant exactly nothing. A couple lines of matching molecular structure between termites and viruses which seemed to be readable, but in reality were not. Like finding two snowflakes exactly alike in the middle of a blizzard. A meaningless cosmic error.

But maybe not, he told himself. Even if it was an accident, it was one that had happened right in front of him. A set of readable numbers, the first tentative step in a translation program. Maybe . . . maybe, he kept thinking, bringing himself back into a state approaching calm. Or at least as close as he was likely to get until he actually knew what he had. But he sure as hell had something. Easy, he thought, don't jump the gun here. He knew his equipment, thrown together from remnants of Centrifuge's discards, was not adequate to actually define the code lines. The main lab at the office, however, might be able to do the job. Surely the big-brain data bank in Atlanta. This was it—the moment of discovery. No guts, no glory. Kurt Eez had run material through the extended computer system at Centrifuge for him before. Tonight might well be the capstone to all their careers. He copied the data onto a disk and went upstairs to share the incredible news with Becky.

Surprisingly, despite his elation, he found her in a most foul mood.

"You're going to the lab at this time of night?" she asked. Only then did Bracken look at the clock and realize it was past midnight.

"Becky, this might be it," he said, not understanding that she had, in fact, heard all this before. His emotion poured out of him, and he wanted very much to take her in his arms, but she was having none of it.

"You're way, way out of bounds here," she said.

Bracken took a step back, hardly believing what he

was hearing. "No, this is it. Right here!" He showed her the disk, and thought for a moment Becky might slap it right out of his hand.

"Don't you see?" she asked, her eyes glaring. Her anger a living thing between them. Bracken stood, shaking his head, dumbfounded. "You're not supposed to be doing this! You're jeopardizing your career, and you're asking Kurt Eez to follow you down the road. There are rules, procedure for this kind of thing. And you're not paying any attention to them! My God, don't you understand? Don't you know what they'll do?"

"But it's here," he said, his excitement turning suddenly to misery. Rebecca, for some reason, was acting as though he was lying to her. Or perhaps to himself.

"You said that before," Becky reminded him.

Had he? Bracken couldn't recall. But that didn't matter, because this time . . . She waved away his argument before it could even take form.

"You're right, it doesn't matter," she said, her voice filled with animosity. Toward him, he realized, and toward his work. "The BIR drew a line in the sand, and they told you not to cross it. It doesn't matter why. The CDC, the feds in Washington . . . do you think they're actually going to let you get away with crossing that line? Christ, this is all madness. Don't you see that?"

No, apparently he didn't. Bracken whispered a profanity and grabbed his coat, not staying to see the tears form in his wife's eyes. Those with no vision got what they deserved, he thought bitterly, driving as quickly as he could to the lab.

Kurt Eez, he noticed, treated his news with a skepticism equal to Rebecca's, even if it did not include her venom.

"Jeez, Dr. Bracken, we're about ready to shut down for

the night," Eez said, when Bracken showed up at one in the morning. Mary Ann Meade began to tell him how sorry she was, but they had been told by Dr. Jacoby that the two of them worked for Centrifuge Labs, not for Gary Bracken.

All of which caused the hairs on Bracken's neck to rise up in anger. A rage, which some part of him recognized as uncharacteristic and way overreactive. He felt it envelop him with a shudder, a muscle spasm, like a sharp, oppressing cough. . . . After it passed, he looked at the beakers and test tubes he'd broken, the floor littered with small glass shards, catching the fluorescent lights like sparks, hitting his eyes, causing his head to ache.

"Dr. Bracken!" Kurt was yelling at him. "What the hell are you doing?"

He blinked, seeing the confusion in Eez's eyes, and the look of fear on Mary Ann's face. What the hell was he doing? Throwing a fit, he realized.

"I'm sorry." He mumbled a halfhearted apology. "It's the strain . . . not getting much sleep these days, and I really need to have this data checked out."

The apology, he saw, did little to soften the tension in the room. He tried smiling, but that didn't seem to work too well either.

"Look, why don't you two go along home," he said. "I'll do the run myself."

His hands were still shaking, he saw. And his head pounded, as if he was in the middle of a vicious hangover. A migraine, he thought, rubbing his forehead. All this fucking stress. Rebecca, who didn't seem to understand how important all this was. Jacoby and the BIR conspiring to cheat him out of his discovery. Well, they weren't going to get away with it. He had the proof right here with him, and he was damn well going to find out what was on the disk.

"Go on, go home," he repeated. Eez and Mary Ann, he saw, exchanged confused, frightened glances.

"You go ahead," Kurt finally said to his lab partner. "I'll stay for a few minutes and help Dr. Bracken get squared away."

Mary Ann Meade, whose choice in men up to this point in her life had been, at best, unfortunate, decided she did not need any further lessons on the subject of dangerous situations. She kept her back to the wall and slid toward the door, barely remembering to grab her coat.

"Nice going," Eez commented, almost under his breath. "You sure scared the hell out of her." And me, too, he didn't add. Nor did he need to. Bracken was aware of the effect his outburst had on all of them. In truth, he himself was more than a little taken back by his actions. But what can't be changed must be ignored, he rationalized. Particularly now, as there was work to be done. He would mend his fences later.

"I said I was sorry. It won't happen again, I promise." He smiled, not bothering to see if Kurt Eez had been pacified. "But this might be important. I caught a couple lines of correlated data, and we really need to run it through the protein reader."

"What kind of data?" Kurt asked suspiciously. "And you know the reader isn't fully on-line yet. That's months, maybe years away."

"The prototype's up and running," Bracken said, making an effort to keep his voice and himself under control. Both of which he was finding extremely difficult. "Don't jerk me around, Kurt. I work here, too, you know."

Kurt Eez nodded, submitting to Bracken's authority. Yes, he thought, but how long will you be here after word

of this fiasco gets out? And he was certain it would. Mary
Ann Meade, he knew, took her women's rights seriously.
Females of her age and political standing did not take
kindly to being harassed in the workplace. Bracken's
goose was cooked, he thought. The thought, however,
vanished into obscurity in the next second.

"I may have found a correlation between the termite
and virus proteins," Bracken said, answering Eez's other
question. That revelation, he saw with some satisfaction,
wiped the smug look off Kurt Eez's face. Eez couldn't
have appeared more shocked if Bracken had taken a
swing at him.

"You've broken the virus communication code?"
Kurt's voice fell away into a whisper of disbelief.

"I'm not sure." Bracken truly smiled this time. The old
Gary Bracken, calm and confident, rose to the surface.
"Like I've been saying, that's why we have to run the
program."

Kurt made no further protest. He took the offered disk,
handling it like some priceless artifact. Powering up the
equipment. Babbling, Bracken thought, like a kid at
Christmas.

"My God, why didn't you say so?" Eez asked. "You
should've called ahead. I would've had all this set up."

"I didn't want to use the phone," Bracken said. "The
BIR doesn't want me looking into this, you know."

"Well, sure, they thought you were wasting your time."
Eez spouted the general line of disinformation currently
circulating around the lab, Bracken noted. "I mean, if
they'd known how far along you were . . ."

Then they'd pull the fucking plug on all Centrifuge's
research grants, Bracken thought, but didn't say. It was
probably a good thing Kurt Eez didn't know the true extent of the web Bracken had drawn him into. But soon,

none of that would matter. Soon they would have the keys to unlock technical knowledge, moving mankind ahead centuries in one huge leap. The gene masters, he thought, were about to give up their secrets.

"Right here," Bracken said, pointing to the two lines of numbers in the jumble of unreadable code.

"It's not much," Eez said, trying not to sound disappointed. "Did you consider it might be some kind of residual effect? Maybe something like the leftovers of a past viral infection in the termite hive?"

"Could be," Bracken admitted. "But it might be enough for the computer to use as a basis for the translation program."

"I don't know." Eez frowned, tapping the keyboard, bringing the rest of the lab's memory banks on-line to work on the problem. "The prototype's kind of lean. If the protein reader was up and running at full capacity, then maybe. Listen, we could tap into the Atlanta bank. It'll only take a couple minutes to go on-line—"

"No," Bracken said, watching the screen, rubbing his eyes as the information flashed by. "They're monitoring us in Atlanta."

"Even our secure files?" Kurt asked, sensing for a moment the kind of trouble he might be getting into. All of that, however, was lost as the computer began to cycle the information.

"Especially the secure files," Bracken said.

The machinery humming. Symbols and numbers rolling across the screen faster than they could read them. Bracken sensed the night pressing in, until the entire world, it seemed, was focused on this moment. As though he and Kurt Eez were sitting on a stage, under the glare of a single, bright spotlight. Lincoln, he thought. They killed Lincoln while he was watching a play. The thought, abstract and absurd, did not seem so to him.

"There's something here, all right," Kurt said, trying to follow the computer's translation program. "The prototype, it's not going to be able to get too far past the two lines. There! The protein reader found the same two code lines in one of the molecules we pulled from the virus cultures. We've got a positive reference in the DNA data bank, too. It's collating the sequences now. Jesus, Dr. Bracken, that's a human genetic string. My God . . . the viruses . . . they're changing . . ."

"Changing what?" Bracken demanded, after Eez fell silent, staring at the screen, a look of fear painted across his face. "Changing what?" he asked again.

"Us," Kurt Eez said, his voice a dull, hollow whisper.

a molecule of time

Day One + 1.2775 x 10 ^12

It was late in the day when the man came upon the Dog Eaters. He stumbled on them quite by accident, as no one in his right mind, other than the authorities, would actually seek out such a dangerous, unpredictable group. But the truth was, the man himself could not be said to be entirely in his right mind, if such terminology was even applicable these days, when madness and chaos seemed to be everyday events.

His name was James Denunizito, but this was a fact which only came to light when his fingerprints happened to be run through the FBI computer. An event usually occurring after James's apprehension by some state or local authorities looking to solve a series of burglaries or petty thefts. After the prints were run, Denunizito always spent a year or two as a guest in the penal system of whatever jurisdiction he happened to be passing through. This particular scenario had taken place so often during his forty years that Denunizito had actually forgotten exactly how much time he'd spent behind bars. To a normal person—whatever that happens to be these days—such an incredible lapse of memory might seem implausible. It was, nonetheless, true. It was a further truth that Denunizito simply did not care about it anymore. Incarceration was merely part of the game. He had done bids before, and would undoubtedly do so again, so Jimmy D, as he called himself, refused to worry about it. In Denunizito's mind, if he only got caught for a third of his crimes, which was about average, he was that much ahead of the game. Hell, he'd take three-to-one odds any day of the week.

Lately, however, Jimmy D had run up against a monumental stretch of bad luck, accentuated by the fact that much of the time these days he was having serious difficulty distinguishing between what was real and what was not. He had driven his car to death on a long stretch of deserted highway outside of Carson City, Nevada, fleeing from a bungled robbery attempt at a 7-Eleven store. Having no place to go, and nothing better to do, he'd thrown his few belongings into a knapsack, burned the car for kicks, and started hiking through the dry Nevada brush country. Night settled in around him with a sudden, hungry chill, and when Jimmy D saw the light of the campfire burning in the hills, he knew he had no choice except to impose on the hospitality of whoever had the presence of mind of bring matches out into the wilderness. He was hoping to find a family of campers, or at least some kids dirt biking through the hill country. But his luck, it seemed, was going from bad to worse.

He was having trouble with the sounds in his head again, even before he topped the last ridge and looked down into the ravine where the fire was burning. The voices, which were sometimes low and haunting, other

times loud and screeching, seemed to be saying something about stars and vast explosions, but they made no
sense at all to Jimmy D, who had only the vaguest idea
what stars were in the first place. The fact that they could
explode was utterly meaningless to him. As meaningless
as the shadows and ghostly images now drifting in and
out of his field of vision.

—Bright White. Flashing in his head. Clouds of gas,
filled with sharp, needlelike icicles. Shadows of impossible configurations rising up out of the sand. Figures
moaning, groaning like the wind.

The truth was, Jimmy D wanted nothing more than to
stop walking, to burrow into the sand, and pretend the
whole, stupid world didn't exist anymore. That was tough
to do, however, with cold and hunger gnawing at his in-
sides like starving rats, so he pushed on toward the light
reflecting in the hills. But even in this semidelusional
state, Jimmy D recognized the Dog Eaters when he saw
them.
  They were an infamous band of loosely connected de-
generates and criminals, widely known throughout the
midwest. Jimmy D had even spent part of a two-year va-
cation with a long-haired, tattooed Mexican who claimed
to have once run with the Dog Eaters. The memory of
that jailhouse encounter did little to reduce Jimmy's apprehension about meeting up with such an obvious bunch
of cutthroats. But the night, with its ghosts and shadows,
cold and hunger, was growling at his heels, so he forced
himself to walk down into the arroyo currently occupied
by the Dog Eaters. Three rusty pickup trucks formed a
semicircle around the campfire, and Jimmy D thought
they looked to be having themselves a pretty good time,

drinking beer, smoking cigarettes, or whatever. Besides, Jimmy was becoming desperate for any kind of companionship to take his mind off what was going on inside his head.

—Bright White. The howling of wild beasts, just over the horizon. The smell of fear and madness, riding the night wind on the soft, flapping wings of bats. Huge, rusted wings of metal lying broken and twisted in the sand. Buildings which seemed to reach up to the sky, and beyond, to the stars themselves. Wavering, then disappearing, like a fog. Bodies, piled one atop the other, until they filled the valley for as far as he could see. Stinking, rotting corpses, giving off a sickly, phosphorescent light.

Even though the Dog Eaters had a foul rep, it really couldn't be much worse than what was flashing through Jimmy D's brain. Boiling oceans, stacks of bleached bones, the screams, wails, whistles, and grunts of voices that weren't even barely human. With all that going on, Jimmy D was hardly in the mood to worry about a group of half-assed tough guys, who would be sucking dick for protection at any penitentiary in the country. Jimmy D had seen it all, and lived to tell about it. Once you've been scared almost to death, he knew, the rest of it didn't hardly matter. Besides, these boys had fire and looked to be roasting something that smelled pretty fucking good on a spit above the flames, although Jimmy had no illusions about what that thing might be.

"Hey! You in the ravine, I'm coming down!" Jimmy D yelled, the sound of his own voice startling to him, as though he had just shouted within the confines of a very small room. The noise seemed to clear his head, though, and he sure as hell caught their attention. The Dog Eaters stopped their laughing and carrying on, staring up the hill as he slid down the sandy embankment, his hands held wide and open.

"Who the fuck are you?" one of them yelled back, the words heavy and intimidating.

"The fucking fire department!" Jimmy D shouted back, in what he hoped would be taken as a joke. It wasn't, he saw, coming closer to the circle of light, looking over the dozen or so members of the group. Young boys, mostly, he thought. A handful of spic mulattoes, with wild hair and straggly mustaches. A couple Mexicans, thin and shifty looking. A few full-blood Indians, staring at him with dark, angry eyes. A white boy or two, only recently removed from the shabby trailer parks of the dust bowl. They were a rough, dirty-looking pack, and dangerous to some extent. Knives and a handgun or two tucked into their belts. But Jimmy D had seen their kind all his life. He walked right up to the campfire and warmed his backside, wearing a grin which might have been considered a sneer in other, more proper circles.

"This is a private party, asshole." One of them stepped forward to confront him. A big, dark-skinned Mex-American who spoke with obvious bad intentions. The leader of this ragged-ass band of would-be outlaws, Jimmy D thought, turning his attention to the business at hand, which was to get himself warm, cop a beer or two, and maybe a hunk of the carcass sputtering on the fire. And later, the keys to one of those banged-up pickup trucks. All, of course, without getting himself stomped in the process. Jimmy knew he had only a second or two before that happened.

"Any of you know a dude named Raymond Black?" Jimmy asked, hoping the fucker in the joint with him hadn't been simply shooting off his mouth. "Wild motherfucker, painted up big time with demons and crosses and shit?"

As if that didn't describe every other white guy in prison; Jimmy D grinned to himself.

"Maybe." The big man hesitated, and Jimmy D knew he was home free.

"Met up with him in the Colorado pen," Jimmy said, still flashing his best fuck-you sneer. "He said if I was ever in the area, I should look you all up. Well, I was just passing by, and I saw your fire. What the hell are you cooking, anyway? A fucking Saint Bernard?"

Laughter ringing out, reverberating in the circle of light. In truth, the animal on the spit, gutted and skinned, looked like a small calf, even though Jimmy was sure it wasn't.

"A big, ugly German shepherd." The leader of the Dog Eaters returned Jimmy's sneer. "You hungry?"

"Starving," Jimmy D said congenially. "And mighty fucking thirsty, too."

"Well, shit, I guess we can stand a friend of ol' Ray's a drink," someone said, and the big fucker stared another second or two, then nodded his approval.

"What's that crazy bastard doing, anyway?" someone asked, who apparently remembered Raymond Black.

"Another four years, last time I saw him," Jimmy D said.

More laughter, a warm beer pushed into his hand. And, damn, if it wasn't the sweetest thing he'd ever tasted. The same, however, couldn't be said for the shepherd, which was tough and stringy, and smelled a little like dog shit to Jimmy D. The rest of the boys ate heartily, carefully saving the bones, which they threw onto the lawns and churchyards of the towns they passed through. A calling card, of sorts, so the good citizens of the Wild West would know the Dog Eaters had been there.

". . . so we picked up this waitress in a bar outside El Paso," one of them was saying as the stars swirled in a drunken dance above the Nevada plain. "Had us some serious peyote, and damn if that girl didn't eat a handful on a dare."

The embers of the fire bathing them all in a shimmering glow. Jimmy D, half listening, as a series of whispers and shrieks swept across his brain. The Dog Eaters, he saw, had turned into a shadowy band of bony, tentacled figures. Monsters, really, with sharp beaks for noses and layers of bone where their eyes should have been. It bothered him some to look at them, but fortunately he was drunk, so it didn't matter that much. Besides, Jimmy figured he probably looked just as bad to them.

"We took her into the desert and fucked her till she was half-dead," the storyteller continued, in obvious enjoyment of his own tale. "Then Toad, here, took all her clothes and rolled her naked out the back of the pickup, and off we drove!"

The one called Toad nodded, flashing a slow, amphibian grin, making fucking sounds with his great, wide mouth. Laughter ringing in the night. Madness and chaos parading across the land, like a loud marching band proclaiming the Fourth of July.

twelve

When Terrance Stampe came to work at 8:30 the next morning, he found Gary Bracken waiting in his office. Which was in itself odd, as this was Wednesday and there were no meetings scheduled that he was aware of. Bracken, he noticed, hadn't shaved and looked positively exhausted. The exhaustion was not unusual; the man carried that look with him often these days, like a heavy stone tied around his neck. The disheveled appearance, however, was uncharacteristic. Bracken was always professional in that respect. My God, Stampe suddenly thought, had he spent the entire night at the lab?

"It's called sleep, Dr. Bracken," he said, trying to make a joke. "It's said to have a most calming effect on the human psyche. You should look into it."

Bracken laughed, as the older man hoped he would. He also sat up straighter in the chair and ran a hand over his hair. All of which did exactly nothing to smooth over the effect of having gone too many hours without rest. Still,

Bracken's eyes were bright. Almost on fire, Stampe thought.

"We've made a breakthrough, of sorts," Bracken said, carefully placing a report on Stampe's desk.

Terrance Stampe adjusted his glasses, looking at the dozen or so computer sheets Bracken offered. It was, he saw, a printout of a data run, a single-spaced series of numbers and symbols. A massive amount of material, which was, at least to Stampe's eyes, mostly indecipherable.

Bracken was watching impatiently, Stampe saw, waiting for him to reach his own conclusion. But Terrance Stampe was a careful man, not known for jumping to conclusions in the face of insufficient facts. He was not planning to change his ways at this late stage of his life, even though Gary Bracken had the look of a man who was about to jump out of his own skin. In fact, Terrance was wondering if Bracken might not be just a little unstable. A point which really needed to be considered, as it seemed Bracken's health was becoming affected by the rigors of his personal experiment. Jacoby had picked up on it also, even if the other senior partner did not know the extenuating circumstances. Still, Jacoby didn't hesitate to bring up Bracken's exhausted state at every opportunity. So far his careful prying into the younger man's activities had not yielded results, but Stampe knew it was only a matter of time before Stanley rooted out what was going on behind his back. And then, Stampe knew from past experience, the shit would really hit the fan. Maybe that scenario was about to play itself out.

Stampe became aware of the clock ticking on his desk. Of the sunlight streaming in through the window, which seemed to be as bright as the glow in Bracken's eyes. When did the man sleep last? he wondered. He spent another few seconds thumbing through the papers, then looked up at Bracken, who was hovering over his desk like some strange bird seeking a reliable perch.

"I'm sorry, I don't see . . ." Stampe began.

"It's a protein-decoding run," Bracken said, obviously frustrated at Stampe's inability to read the material. "It's just a small piece of the data. The whole thing runs on for a couple hundred pages."

"Most of which are error messages," Stampe felt compelled to point out.

"Right here," Bracken said, pulling a page out of the report, barely able to control his excitement. "These two lines, Terrance. It's a computer-generated printout of a virus protein. And we've isolated these lines, which appear on several of the pages. Don't you see? The number progression? The protein reader has been able to give us a binary translation of these two lines!"

Terrance Stampe blinked, feeling his body almost sag in the chair. His mind, he discovered, was running down a series of corridors, all of which seemed to fold in upon one another. He blinked again, staring at Bracken. He knew he wanted to say something, but his mouth couldn't seem to make the sounds. Bracken, he saw, had a look of profound triumph on his face.

"It's not much, at this point," he admitted. "But it's the beginning of a viable translation program, Terrance. And just these few lines, my God, they're fascinating. Look, it shows the DNA string couplings, and how they're manipulated. It's all numerical, of course, but the computer is able to read it!"

Bracken's words seemed to penetrate the haze that was enveloping Stampe's brain.

"You're sure about this?" Stampe was surprised to discover himself whispering, almost as though he was in church.

"Yes, it's the real thing," Bracken said. "And that's not even the most amazing part. The protein molecules are from the virus exchange we monitored a few weeks ago. The DNA sequences in those molecules are clearly related to the cell structure found in human beings. Our computer went even further and identified the code lines as referring to DNA strings found in neuron cells. The cerebral cortex . . . the human brain, Terrance! And that's not me talking, the computer found the relationship by cross-referencing thousands of DNA samples."

"But the majority of this is still unreadable," Stampe heard himself say.

"True," Bracken admitted, finally settling into the room's other chair, much to Stampe's relief. "We need to work the program through a larger data bank, but this is the first step. Think of the implications, Terrance. We're going to be the first human beings to actually be able to understand what's going on in the microcosm. Good Lord, it's going to be like looking into the mind of God!"

Stampe felt the room swaying around him. He kept his hands flat on the desk to keep it from tilting. Terrance Stampe, who prided himself on his ability to process facts, had the unpleasant sensation that this was one set of data with which he simply could not come to terms.

"You're absolutely sure?" he asked again. "There's no mistake about this?"

Bracken shook his head, and for some reason Terrance Stampe found himself believing the impossible.

"In that case, I'm afraid I need some air," Stampe said, pushing away from the desk, feeling strangely unsteady, as if he somehow found himself at sea in the smallest of boats. Bracken, he noticed, prudently took the papers from the printout off the desk before following him out the door.

Outside, the sun was shining as it had when Stampe had come to work on what seemed to be the first true spring morning that year. Cars passed by on the street, a few people walked in the park across from the office building Centrifuge Labs shared with several other medical professionals. Stampe found himself grateful for the surge of normalcy that seemed to prevail in the world, even as he suspected that nothing in his world would ever be normal again. He wondered for a moment if Bracken was aware of the true implications of what he had discovered.

My God, he found himself thinking, we are actually going to be able to look into the very heart of the world.

The scientist in him knew that even as he watched the people walking, birds flying in the budding trees, insects crawling about in the old fall leaves, a vast, unseen world was at work around them. Within them, as well. The world of the microbe extended deep into the earth, and penetrated the layers of air above. The microbe community inhabited every millimeter of the planet, every imaginable environmental niche, including his own flesh and blood. And now, incredibly, Bracken seemed to be saying the impossible.

"This code the computer is able to read . . . You're not saying that microbes are thinking, rational creatures like ourselves, are you?" he asked, wondering at the seeming absurdity of the question, even as he felt his lungs taking in air. Air containing dust particles. Particles that, he knew, if studied under a microscope, would reveal the same living things which Bracken claimed were capable of communication. The thought was staggering to him.

"No," Bracken said slowly. "Certainly that's not a claim I'm prepared to make on the basis of this data."

"That's hardly a qualifying statement," Stampe said, forcing himself to smile. "We have to be very careful here, Dr. Bracken."

"I know," Bracken said, understanding the other man's use of his title. They sat on one of the benches in the park. Pigeons marched around in the grass. Bracken pointed with the toe of his shoe at a solitary black ant prowling the dirt at the base of the bench. "We have to look at the information analytically, making only the definitive statements the data allows."

Stampe, he saw, nodded in agreement.

"Ants, for example," Bracken said. "Can we say that they are rational, thinking creatures?"

"I don't know," Stampe responded. "Perhaps we'll find out when we run their protein molecules through the computer."

"Good point," Bracken agreed. "But we can make certain assumptions based on what we know about their behavior. Ants are communal creatures, part of what might be called an extended hive organism. They work and exist solely for the good of the hive. While the extended organism operates as a highly developed social entity, the individual on its own has no cognitive thought. It only does what it's programmed to do—find food, defend the nest, raise the young."

"But the basis for this programming?" Stampe asked.

"It's purely an instinctive behavior," Bracken said, sure of his ground here. "The colony uses survival techniques passed on from generation to generation. The various species use information gleaned from the behavioral patterns of their ancestors. It's coded into their DNA. They build their nests in prescribed patterns, forage for the same types of food as preceding generations. The individual has no input or control over its activities, other than to work within the parameters of its given tasks. We can't call the individual ant a thinking, rational being on that basis."

"No more than we can call the cells of our own bodies thinking, rational entities," Stampe commented, in a low, soft voice, as though he was thinking out loud. "Even though the cells themselves are part of a communal whole to which we freely assign those qualities."

"That's true," Bracken agreed.

The world seemed to be moving around them in a strange, shifting dance. Bracken had the odd feeling that everything he thought or believed was about to be altered in ways he couldn't imagine. Questions were about to be asked, and perhaps answered. Age-old questions: What makes human beings the creatures we are? Or believe ourselves to be? He was struck suddenly by the unavoidable fact of what he actually was—a group of cells held together by cohesive forces no one truly understood. Bits of DNA and nucleic acids, combined with water and an assortment of chemicals, sitting on a park bench with the sun shining on his face. And folded up neatly in his coat pocket was a printout detailing the activities of tiny, submicroscopic creatures, graced with the innate ability to change the DNA structure of his cells as easily as he might reach out and pluck a leaf from a tree. Creatures with the power to alter, even, that mysterious, incomprehensible part of the anatomy which separates the human species from the rest of the animal kingdom—mankind's brain. He didn't know whether to laugh or cry, or revel in his discovery. All Bracken knew was that he was tired, almost beyond caring.

"Who else knows about this?" Stampe asked, bringing the subject back into what passed for the real world.

"Myself and Kurt Eez," Bracken said. "But I impressed upon him the importance of keeping it quiet, until we've got more data." And what did Mary Ann Meade know? he found himself wondering. Only that he had come into the lab in the middle of the night, acting like a jerk. There was no sense bothering Terrance Stampe with that bit of information. He would probably hear about it soon enough.

"You know what they'll say, don't you?" Stampe asked. Bracken looked at him, not understanding. "Jacoby and the others. They'll be quick to point out that viruses by themselves are nonentities."

"Like ants or termites," Bracken said.

"Except that viruses happen to be microscopic," Stampe continued. "Your ants and termites at least have a nervous system, of sorts."

"Only because of the complexity of their bodies," Bracken said. "They both need a control mechanism to stimulate nerve endings—to make legs and jaws function, to process the information necessary to do their work. The higher orders need more complex organs. Simple biology. You know that."

"Yes, I do," Stampe acknowledged. "But that's the argument they'll use."

"I'm not sure that argument's valid anymore," Bracken said, reaching into his coat, unfolding the data sheets. "My God, Terrance, this could be a blueprint of the whole secret behind genetic engineering. And the cerebral-cortex thing, that's damn frightening."

"It is," Stampe agreed. "You need to talk with someone about it, an expert in the field. Do you know Henry Woodson over at Columbia?"

"Dr. Woodson? Sure, I did my graduate work in his department," Bracken said, smiling. "He backed me in some of my scrapes with the research board at the university, for what good it did. Political bastards. But I haven't seen him in years."

"Let me call him," Stampe said. "I'm sure he'll be interested in what you've got, although I'd caution you to keep what we've discussed here as close to the vest as possible."

Bracken nodded, realizing the volatile nature of his discovery. Terrance Stampe reached over and touched his knee.

"It's good work, Dr. Bracken," the older man said. "But I'd advise you to go home, take a couple of days off, and get some sleep. Henry Woodson can be a handful, if you're not at the top of your game."

Bracken helped Terrance Stampe to his feet and they walked slowly back to the lab. Around them, Bracken knew, the world continued its dance—birds, bees, ants, humans and microbes, and all the rest. He went home and called Rebecca, to smooth things over between them, but she was out of her office. He slept, finally, but found himself lost in a dream, dark and disturbing, in which all of the world seemed to swirl and fuse together. The distinctions between what was real and what was not blurring and twisting, until he could not tell one from the other. Until, in the dream, he was looking down the barrel of a microscope, staring at an image of the double helix as it, too, twisted and blurred. Until the microscope turned into the barrel of a gun, and he woke drenched in sweat.

When Bracken checked his watch, it was past midnight. Again. The hours had slipped away like water along a streambed. Becky had come home, and he thought he re-

membered her calling down to him, but couldn't recall
his response. Indeed, if he had made one. The computer
was off and he was reading notes he had been making.
Useless notes, things he already knew. He had the first
words from the virus community, and they only made
things more confusing. Brain cells? The cerebral cortex?
What were they doing inside people's heads? He didn't
have the vaguest idea, and the computer seemed unable
to go any further with the minuscule amount of data he
was able to provide. Something to do with thought. But
what? There was, he realized, no way to tell. The viruses
were concealing a secret, perhaps The Secret, and he had
no way of coaxing it out of them. He had come again to
the place where he had started. Not just here, with this
frustrating set of numbers and symbols, this tantalizing
glimpse into the beyond. But the place where he had
begun years and years ago, when he had first started to
formulate the questions he wanted so much to answer.

Bracken sighed, walking up out of the dim light of the
basement to the half-lit confines of his house. Becky,
long since asleep. He fixed a sandwich from leftovers in
the fridge and pulled a beer out of the vegetable cooler.
He ate, pacing around the kitchen, sipping occasionally
on his beer. His mind wandering in circles, much the
same as his body.

Okay, where is it? He remembered asking that question
in his youth, and now it had returned like some forgotten,
haunting spirit. How do you find it? The secret knowledge
that someone, somewhere, must possess? The glimmering, crystal-perfect rationale which somehow makes sense
out of life. The secret that brings order out of the chaos.
Do viruses hold the key, someplace deep in the tiny recesses of their protein molecules? The revelation—the
Grand Unifying Truth—that allows a being to see the rea-

sons behind it all; the cruelties, the joys of life. What is this existence all about? He wanted desperately to know, to understand. There had to be an answer, a reason hidden from him. Hidden from everyone he knew, from everyone he had ever met or come in contact with. Every person, he realized, was stumbling through their lives, looking for the answer. The Secret, undoubtedly subtle, perhaps obvious, but something which would reveal the hidden purpose behind it all. It seemed incredible that the answer might lie hidden in the microcosm. In truth, he doubted it actually did. Doubted, even, there was such an answer. But that had never stopped him from looking.

He had done everything he could think of to find it. He thought for a time the secret might lie in religion. In the Bible, perhaps. In the Holy-Roller, I've-Been-Saved-by-Jesus movement. But that, he came to understand, was an illusion. A delusion, really, used by those who were as confused as he was. Used to comfort and insulate themselves against the absence of knowledge. As a young man, he'd studied and read and prayed. Even spent a year in a monastery, in the vain hope that someone there might whisper the secret to him in the stone-and-stained-glass caverns, which the faithful proclaimed to be the House of God. But there were no secrets in those places, he came to realize, just the same illusions and delusions which existed in the outside world. Only there, the illusion was underscored and perpetuated by silence. God did not come to him, whispering in the dark, as he knelt on the hard, cold stone of his cell. Although some claimed to hear the Voice, he admitted. Mostly, he thought, they were either lying or slightly deranged. Either way, it did not matter. God, when He whispered to those people, revealed no secrets, uttering only commands.

He had also thought, for a time, the secret might be

revealed in the fundamentals of science. So he attended
some of the nation's best universities, earning a Ph.D. in
biology during his search. But there were no answers
there, Bracken realized some years ago. At least not to the
questions he was asking. There was an understanding
only of the functional elements of life, not its deeper
meaning. It was not a question of knowledge in the academic sense, he came to understand. Certainly, one could
learn the mechanics of life, as he had done, but in all of
that, something was missing. An empty link in the chain.
A missing piece to the jigsaw puzzle of Life. And now
. . . now had he actually stumbled into an area which
might provide those long-sought-after answers? Would
he know, even if he found them?

He wandered the house in the dark, silent hours of the
night. Rebecca, asleep in their bed, untroubled by the
mysteries he so needed to understand. Yes, he loved her.
Yes, there was his work—assembly-line science during
the day, empty speculation during the midnight hours.
And he had made an exciting, potentially profitable discovery. It seemed as though he had everything a human
being could conceivably require. Love, work, the full
range of creature comforts. Why, then, was this not
enough? Why did something fundamental, something
basic seem to be missing from his life? And it had always
been that way.

Bracken recalled with almost perfect clarity the first
time he had sex. Seventeen, and the girl was his high-
school sweetheart, even though he could now barely remember her face. But the moment he could remember
perfectly. They had waited and waited—until finally
what they both mistakenly called love exploded in a night
of passion at an expensive motel amid the ski resorts of
Vermont. Flowers and wine, a fire in the hearth of the

cabin. It could not have been more perfect. And his reaction, he recalled it so clearly, even as the girl lay sleeping in his arms. His reaction had been both bizarre and foolish: Is that all there is to it? he remembered thinking. Surely there's more? And even though there was more to sex, as he would later learn, Bracken knew that single thought was to plague him for the rest of his life. Surely there's more? Something he did not understand, but which others must.

He remembered, also, believing for a time that everyone in the world was clairvoyant, except for him. That they were able to read minds and see emotions in ways he could not. It was a belief, he admitted to himself on occasion, which he had not completely shed. That other people could see and hear things somehow closed off to him. It was, he knew, a belief which was certainly irrational, and perhaps bordered on instability. It was a thing he kept hidden deep within himself. A secret he did not share, even in jest, with the woman who had been his mate these past years. And what secret thoughts did Becky have? he sometimes wondered. This he did ask her at odd moments, usually after a second bottle of wine over dinner. She always laughed, as if she believed he was simply trying to entertain her. She denied having any such secrets, although he suspected that was not entirely true. Everyone has secrets, he thought, at least things they imagine to be secrets. Perhaps every living creature has secrets, the small tricks of survival they believe to be theirs, and theirs alone. Certainly the viruses had secrets. He knew, because he had glimpsed them.

And what would Becky think, if she knew he was wandering the house, late, late at night, asking himself questions which seemed on the surface to be utterly unanswerable? She might, he realized, come to the conclusion that he was mad. Indeed, she already seemed to be leaning in that direction. She might even leave him, suspecting his insanity was contagious. In truth, that was a point about which he himself was not entirely certain.

He parted the curtains of the bay window, looking out at the darkness of the night, feeling worn down by questions the size of glacial boulders. Surely there was something more? The stars, spread across the sky in a blaze of shimmering light. The cosmos, stretching out into unimaginable depths. Was the answer out there, somewhere in the dark realms? Or was it closer, almost right in front of him? He walked onto the back porch, engulfed by the vastness of the sky.

Really, he asked himself, what was the difference between the darkness that spread itself across the universe, and the darkness behind his own eyes, when he finally closed them in sleep? Both seemed infinite and unknowable. Both were part of the same cosmic realm. He sat in a chair and craned his neck up toward the stars. Then he closed his eyes, falling back into the darkness, imagining stars. There was no difference, he realized, drifting into an exhausted sleep, punctuated by sparks of electricity dancing across a field of neuron matrices. The stars behind his eyes, as deep and infinite as all the galaxies and clouds of nebula which twisted and churned, held tightly in the soft tentacles of creation . . .

A soft tapping on the glass doors awakened him. Rebecca was standing in her robe, staring at him with furrowed brow. The sun was fresh off the horizon, filtering through the new leaves of spring. Bracken shivered, feeling the morning chill.

"You slept on the porch?" Becky asked, sliding the

French doors open. Behind her, the smell of coffee crept out like an inviting shadow.

"Didn't mean to," he said, trying to smile, suddenly realizing how stiff his body was. He was definitely too old for this. "Just dozed off, I guess."

Becky just shook her head, a deeply tired look in her once glowing eyes.

He tried to make a joke about not being able to get up out of the chair, but Rebecca was obviously not in the mood to be amused at his parody of encroaching old age. She was, he thought, staring at him as though she had just found a stranger sleeping on the lawn furniture.

"Want some breakfast?" she asked, turning her back on him. Dealing, as she tended to do, with the basic realities of life, for which Bracken was grateful.

a molecule of time
(Date and Location Unknown)

Bein-ha felt the scrapper hit something other than
earth or stone. It was a subtle thing, a change in the
humming pitch of the blades, a brief shift in the hydraulic
mechanism of the scrapper's digging engine. As the
safety rules required, he shut down the machine and un-
strapped himself from the cockpit to inspect the obstruction. Even though it was not technically an obstruction, as
he knew from the sound and feel of the huge, three-story
machine; the blades could easily work their way through
whatever foreign object he had encountered. But the
monitors would be sure to pick up the minute changes in
the scrapper's vibrations, as he himself had done, and the
fines for violating safety rules were severe. Besides, he
was sufficiently ahead of schedule, and mildly curious at
what could be buried at the bottom of a two-mile hole in
the ground.

Bein-ha swung out of the control deck, lowering himself along the handrail until he was close enough for his

legs to extend from the thin, reedlike form of his body
and touch the bottom of the hole he was digging. Above
him, the hard-packed walls extended straight up for two
miles. The lights from the scrapper formed a bright pool
here at the bottom, where the pilings for the planned
thousand-story building would rest—an ambitious project, even by the high standards of his race. Adjusting the
filters on his eye sets, Bein-ha could just make out the circle of light at the top of the tunnel. A white speck, stud-
ded with stars, even though his internal clock told him it
was still six hours and twenty minutes until sunset. Bein-
ha's facial features wrinkled in what passed for a grin in
this particular time and place. He was a fanciful man,
who enjoyed minor diversions such as a hole of stars in
the middle of the day.

He elongated his arms, formed spindlelike fingers at the
end of his hands, and poked around in the freshly turned
earth. There was something long and white protruding
from a clump of dirt and rock. He extended his fingers and
touched the object, pulling it from the deep bed where it
had rested for uncounted millennia. A bone, he saw, his curiosity rising. While he himself had no comparable parts
within his own body, certainly nothing as heavy and un-
wieldy as this grotesque object, he immediately recognized
the thing for what it was. A piece of some long-dead, primitive animal. Yes, *skeletal remains*, he remembered the
phrase from a book he had processed during his days of
learning. It was, he knew, a unique find, one which would
no doubt flash his face on the evening news. He tucked the
bone into a pouch he formed along his shoulders, and
went back to the scrapper to report his discovery. The
book which mentioned these objects said *skeletal remains*
were usually found in groups, and so the probability existed that there were more such artifacts buried in the

vicinity. The book also went on to say, he recalled, that immediate notification of the nearest Scientific Agency was required, in the unlikely event such remains were discovered by any of the citizens of the Seven Continents. This Bein-ha dutifully did. He was also a man who appreciated and recognized the freedoms enjoyed by all citizens, when the rules of a structured society were obeyed.

He was not surprised when the order to return to the surface came quickly after his report. After all, the Scientific Agencies would want to conduct a more extensive excavation of the site, before liquid rock was poured down the hole to anchor the thousand-story building into the bedrock, sealing whatever was down here until the end of time itself. Bein-ha stood on the transport disk and felt himself shielded in its energy cage as the gravity plate pushed him to the surface in but a few heartbeats. There was, he noted, a reception committee already formed and waiting, when he and the disk reached ground level. He smiled and bowed, looking for the video projectors, greeting the committee in the formal clicking tongue of his race. He even produced the bone, pulling it from the pouch of skin, holding it close to his head so the news teams would be certain to include both the discovery and his face in their broadcast.

To his complete surprise, the welcoming committee backed away from him in abject terror. They quickly formed filtering skins over their faces. Also, Bein-ha could see no news teams gathered to interview him about his wondrous discovery. There was, however, a group of Seven Continent military personnel moving toward him. He was further distressed to observe that they had taken the time to weave full filtering suits over their entire bodies. Bein-ha's internal sensors began to radiate at the upper levels of fear, bringing his core temperature dangerously high. His heart systems began to compensate, and he almost fell off the gravity disk.

"Remain calm, Citizen Bein-ha," his construction supervisor clicked at him, although the frantic background noise coming from the man's sonar bulb sounded anything but calm. "Place the bone on the disk and step away. Our commitment to you remains strong. You will be cared for."

Cared for? Bein-ha wanted to ask, but protocol demanded that he first obey his supervisor's instructions. And there was no opportunity to ask the questions which it was his right by law to ask, because as soon as he stepped off the gravity disk, one of the military personnel covered him in an all-enveloping energy field which blocked his sonar receptor, and even prevented him from adapting his form. He had never before heard of such a thing happening, and so had no reference point on which to base reactions. Through gestures, the military people indicated that he was to follow them, and before any time seemed to pass at all, Bein-ha found himself enclosed in a tentlike dome, sealed off from the world, as if he had been unceremoniously shot off into space. It was only then that the restraining energy field was released and he was once again able to shape himself, and speak to his captors. As the hours passed, however, he gained little information and only the vaguest response to his demand for freedom.

"We are sorry for the inconvenience, Bein-ha," they told him. "But an emergency has been declared by the Scientific Agency. It seems that you may be carrying an infection."

"What sort of infection?" he asked, but again there were no answers.

The day passed, then another, and Bein-ha remained in the vacuum of his imprisonment. His family came to visit, clicking at him through the opaque walls of the dome. His wife shed the required tears of isolation, but his children looked at him as if they were convinced he had done something terribly wrong. His coworkers sent him messages of respect and sympathy, but still he was fed dried food and given boiled water which had no sweetness. His supervisor came, clicking sounds of anger at the way Bein-ha was being treated. In truth, Bein-ha was beginning to feel like an eater of spawn.

"I told them the Third Continent was not safe at those depths," his supervisor said. "But they assured me it had been properly terra-formed."

"Safe from what?" Bein-ha asked.

The supervisor only shook his facial muscles, claiming ignorance. That, Bein-ha was coming to believe. Ignorance or subterfuge, and he thought there was little to choose between the two. But there was information to be gleaned, he realized, by listening carefully to the masked conversations taking place between the scientific and medical people who were now visiting him with increasing frequency.

"There are definable subatomic abnormalities within the subject," they sometimes said. The words he knew, but their deeper meaning was not available in the memories of his processed learning. And he had stopped asking questions which were never answered, not being a man given to futile gestures.

"Were the containment procedures successful?" he heard one of the military personnel ask, on what he thought was the first anniversary of his confinement.

"Unknown," the response came, and Bein-ha noticed that the military person's core temperature rose appreciably.

Citizen Bein-ha spent the rest of his few remaining years in protective custody, despite an unending series of appeals filed on his behalf by his family and a number of civil organizations which took up his cause. Unfortunately, he seemed always to be in ill health, eventually succumbing to a coughing disease unknown among those of his species. This despite numerous attempts by medical personnel and other healers to save him. When he died, his body was frozen within the dome, and an atmospheric sailing ship sent his remains off into the depths of space.

As the military authorities feared, the containment procedures had not been successful. This fact, however, did not come to light until several decades after Bein-ha's death. And a hundred thousand years later, when the Change visited itself in a terrible scourge upon the people of the Seven Continents, when madness and chaos ruled the land, these events had been largely forgotten. Forgotten, that is, by all but one set of participants, who stored their knowledge on encoded protein molecules. The virus clans, timeless and infinitely patient.

thirteen

It was, Bracken realized, a question of thought. Surely it wasn't an accident that the lines of translated code had been tied to chemical indicators in the cerebral cortex. But what did viruses have to do with the function of human thought?

What was thought, anyway? The question came again, for at least the hundredth time. Questions, but no answers. His body ached from sleeping out on the back porch. Becky left for work, with hardly a good-bye. Bracken rubbed his eyes. The morning light seemed to pound against his brain. It bothered him immensely that he seemed to be on the verge of a truly monumental discovery, and he felt absolutely shitty. Wasn't enlightenment supposed to be a time of exhilaration? It sure as hell didn't feel like that. The BIR, Jacoby, and even Becky seemed to be involved in some sort of bizarre conspiracy to turn his life into a morass of emotional mud. And that was clearly one activity he could handle on his own, thank you very much.

The phone rang and he didn't feel like answering it. Terrance Stampe left a message saying he had arranged a 12:30 luncheon meeting that afternoon with Henry Woodson. Stampe signed off, wishing Bracken good luck. Whatever the hell that was supposed to mean.

So, what was thought?

Bracken knew if he couldn't answer the first, most basic question, he could never hope to make the leap into discovering the viral/human relationship. But viruses were mindless, in the conventional sense. Hell, in any sense. They were creatures without neuron structures, therefore without the ability to think. Like termites, viruses operated solely on instinct. His eyes opened and he stared at the wall for a moment. Perhaps the real question was: What would creatures with no neuron function of their own want from the most highly developed neuron system on the planet? The obvious answer bubbled to the surface of his mind. Impossible, he thought, shivering.

But what was thought? Given the technology of the day, the question seemed to be relatively straightforward. The physical aspects of the human brain had given up at least some of their secrets to the strong-arm forces of scientific inquiry. The mechanics of the activity had been identified: neuron cells fire a self-generated electrical charge across the axon nerve string. This process releases neurotransmitters, any of thirty or so chemical molecules, which then flow across the synaptic gap. The chemical message travels along the dendrite fibers, telling the next neuron cell in line whether to fire or not. A function which takes place at an astounding rate of hundreds of cycles per second all across billions of active neurons. From here, storage centers of the brain interact with the speech areas, and correlate with sensory input and muscular nerve centers.

All this combining to produce a creature which can remember and plan, signal or speak in a manner usually comprehended by others of its species, observe the immediate area the body itself occupies relative to other objects in the creature's sphere of influence, and move the physical body through this area with an advanced degree of coordination. In other words, a creature who can hunt effectively in groups, gather plants, and raise its young. A creature well adapted to the world in which it lived, certainly capable of long-term survival. All of which the human species had been doing, in various forms, for millions of years.

In various forms. For millions of years.

There, he realized, was the first part of the question. The coffee stirred his brain, reviving his body. Caffeine, Bracken decided, fell into the category of a miracle drug. He got up from the table and began pacing the house. Looking in each room, it seemed, for the answer he now believed to be more than some elusive, philosophical exercise.

(Strange thoughts intruding into his mind. Burrowing, twisting. Not with clarity, or definition. Not even anything substantial, rather an uncomfortable shadow of a memory. Like the outline of a tree standing in place for days after it has been cut down. Like the footsteps of a loved one walking the halls of the house for weeks after the funeral. Like the memory of a touch, a kiss, lingering on the surface of the skin. Whispers. Connections forming in a multidimensional darkness. Whispers of timeless infinity, the sound of wind blowing through a cavern . . . a tunnel which connects stars like the spokes of a wheel. A linkage, a matrix forming. Molecules passing over the living chain, brushing against the matrix, leaving behind slivers of light, flashes of memory. Whispers, intruding on his thoughts like soft feathers ruffling inside his skull.)

Yes, it was more than an exercise. Much more. Bracken shook his head, feeling as though he was trapped in the web of some lunatic exam, pondering a multipart question the answer to which was incomprehensible to the human mind. For the simple reason that the answer was, in fact, the human mind.

What do apple trees grow? Apples, right? He recalled the question from some long-ago logic course he'd taken as an undergrad. Apples had been the universal response.

"But don't apple trees also grow leaves and branches and root systems?" the professor had smugly suggested.

The point being, of course, that the first, most logical response was not always the complete answer.

So human beings existed in various, primitive forms for millions of years. They were, according to the ar-chaeological record, a highly successful species long be-fore they actually became Homo sapiens. Modern man, descending from the apes. Or ascending, depending on how you looked at it. This, he knew, was where the fun-damental logic of evolution broke down. Where Darwin's theory hit the proverbial stone wall. Apes have been apes for twenty million years. Most branches of the family ex-isting with relatively few changes for the past eight or ten million years. They did not evolve to become Men or Go-rilla People, or Chimp Dwarfs. They remained apes, suc-cessful in their various environments, surviving in what humans now consider to be a relatively primitive state.

So why did proto-man, in the form of Australopithe-cus, Homo habilis, and all the rest, go through what must be considered radical evolutionary change? After all, on the scale of evolutionary time, human advancement hap-pened with the suddenness of a tidal surge. Why? Why, a mere hundred thousand years ago, did modern man emerge from the clearly successful cultures of Neanderthal and Homo erectus communities? It was not, Bracken knew, the result of any explosion in brain power. That dated explanation turned out to be nothing more than a convenient myth, an explanation contrived out of too little data. A state of affairs still far from uncommon in the scientific community, Bracken knew. No one likes to admit they don't have the faintest idea about something, especially a subject in which they're considered to be experts. If cranial expansion was the answer, why did the supposedly primitive Neanderthals have as large and developed brains as modern humans? It was clear from the research being done today that biologists and anthropologists had merely been trying to apply Darwinian logic where it really didn't make any sense in explaining what had taken place.

The truth of the matter was, Bracken knew, that we should all be Neanderthals or Homo erectus men, adapted to a slightly warmer climate. Only we aren't. Why? What changed us? That, he realized, was the next part of the question. And he was afraid he now knew the answer. Something changed us, changed the structure of our DNA. In Bracken's mind, there were only two forces which could have achieved such a radical transformation in human characteristics. The first, if you believed in such things, was God. Divine intervention, a vast, encompassing intelligence, who controls the universe and somehow deemed it a good idea to create mankind. But if that were the case, why did God wait so long? Why not create Man from the beginning? The Creationists believed exactly that, even in the face of obvious fossil evidence to the contrary. The second possibility, the one which now seemed most plausible, lay in the hands of the earth's foremost genetic manipulators—the viruses. Somehow, through accident or design, the virus community instigated genetic changes which resulted in the creation of modern human beings. But why? What was the fundamental difference between Homo sapiens and those who came before? The ability to think and reason, to hold and recall vast amounts of information, and to process this data in a computerlike manner.

Question: What was the goal of the National Science Project? Answer: to build a better computer.

Question: What was the goal of parasitic organisms? Answer: to live within the bodies of their hosts as harmoniously as possible. To use the facilities which the hosts have, but which the parasitic community does not.

And what do the gene manipulators need that they do not already have? The ability to think, to process vast amounts of information. A better computer.

"They're changing us," Bracken heard himself whisper, echoing Kurt Eez's statement. "They're building a better computer."

A year ago, Bracken would have considered the idea absurd. But facts were facts. Viruses manipulate DNA. Evolution is the result of mutated genetic material. And human beings have been on nature's fast track, evolutionarily speaking, for the past half million years. It follows, then, that viruses, present in every living organism, are at least partially responsible. It was simple. It was logical. It was scientific heresy. Bracken knew it, even as he knew the conclusion was unavoidable.

Still, it seemed impossible. Trying to take the problem in sequence, Bracken poured another cup of coffee and began taking notes: Why us in the first place? What was it about human beings, that makes us particularly good hosts for the virus community? There are a lot of us, he reasoned, but that did not seem to be a sufficient answer. Approaching the question from the virus point of view, more human beings were not a necessity. Billions of smaller hosts would provide an equally acceptable breeding ground for the virus communities. Any sort of animal would do—prairie dogs, worms, insects, fish, or the vast multitude of rodents would have been sufficient for that particular purpose. Size could also be discounted. Elephants, antelope, bison, giraffes—if the purpose had simply been to build a larger beast. Larger was not always better. If that were the case, dinosaurs would be roaming the housing projects of suburbia. Apes and Australopithecus would do the job, if you were looking for mobility as a survival skill. No, it all came back to the same thing, the one difference between Man and all the other creatures of the earth—a brain capable of thought, of higher mental functions than apes or Neanderthals or other early versions of the human species.

For some reason, it had been necessary to introduce thought into the mix, and not merely for survival purposes. Creatures with less brain power than Homo sapiens were better adapted to simple survival. Speed, fangs, claws. A wider range of smell, hearing, and sight. Human beings did not score well in any of those categories. Only one thing separated them from all the other beasts—the ability to think on a higher level.

Why? The question returned. Was a creature like Man inevitable, given the forces of evolution? If so, why take billions of years to create such a beast? Why not build a better dinosaur, with a larger brain? Why do in four million years what wasn't done in a hundred and sixty-five million years? Bracken couldn't begin to answer that question. He only knew it *had* taken place. And thought had something to do with it. Perhaps in the end, it was merely a question of opportunity, or one of a series of incredible cosmic accidents.

"What is thought?" Henry Woodson repeated Bracken's question, finding himself both amused and confused.

"I'm sorry to be so blunt." Bracken apologized, knowing he was pushing the bounds of a relationship that had faded in the years since he had left Columbia University. According to normal social guidelines, it would have been polite to open the conversation with innocuous chitchat about old times or the weather—two topics which he and Dr. Woodson could use to get reacquainted, comfortable in each other's presence. And then, later, perhaps over coffee, proper etiquette would allow the real issues to be raised. But the whole thing had been gnawing at him for weeks. For years, actually, Bracken admitted to himself. Besides, hadn't the old man himself often said, "If you can't get right down to the good stuff, the person you're talking to probably isn't worth the effort of getting to know in the first place"? A philosophy Bracken agreed with wholeheartedly. Which was, as Becky often reminded him, the reason he usually found himself alone at the punch bowl at the few parties he attended.

"I guess I'd rather be alone than be stupefied by meaningless conversation," he always responded.

Besides, Henry Woodson understood this was not a reunion of old friends, but rather a meeting of convenience. So Gary Bracken, former student and colleague, could pick his brain, and thereby save himself a few years' worth of dry, academic reading. Woodson was in his early seventies, retired from his medical practice, and taught at Columbia not for money or prestige, but mostly as a means of avoiding the gardening work which seemed to so infatuate his wife. That, combined with the fact he actually enjoyed imparting knowledge accumulated over the fifty-odd years he had been studying the human brain. He was also enough of a capitalist to require payment for his services, and so had decided to allow the younger man to pay for lunch. That was, until he heard the nature of the inquiry. Henry Woodson now decided to buy his own pastrami sandwich. The simple truth of the matter was that no one could give a credible response to the question being posed.

"No, that's quite all right." Woodson smiled after taking a moment to squeeze the wedge of lemon into his iced tea. "I'm afraid, however, you've asked a question I can't really answer."

There was a long moment of silence at the small table, and Bracken was reminded of a bad off-Broadway play he and Rebecca had once attended. The applause had been brief, followed by what he was sure for the actors was a prolonged period of deafening quiet.

"I thought, perhaps, with your expertise on the subject . . ." Bracken began, searching for an honorable way to turn the conversation toward old times or the weather.

"I know." Woodson seemed to sigh. "You'd think that after fifty years a person would have something more to offer. I can give you the basics—memory association, information storage, that sort of thing. But I assume you're looking for something else, something more definitive."

Bracken nodded, trying not to look like a kid who suddenly realized there was no new bicycle under the Christmas tree.

"I got through the preliminary stuff myself," he said. "Barely, I'm not trying to pass myself off as anything but a novice in the field."

At that, Woodson smiled, remembering his fondness for this young man, who was certainly brash, but also understood his limitations. There weren't many, he knew from experience, who earned their doctorates and managed to retain that quality.

"Quite honestly, the human brain is still a mystery, even to those of us who like to think we understand more than the basic machinery of the organ," Woodson himself admitted, trying to give Bracken some insight into what he was looking for. "We have identified areas which control certain functions—storage, involuntary muscle movement, speech, the senses, and the like. I can even explain, to some degree, how those functions are transmitted through the body. We understand how the brain produces hormones, how it regulates things like body temperature and sexual activity. It's rather like studying the internal mechanism of a very complicated clock. That is, you can point out the gears, and pretty much tell how the clock keeps time. But then you must ask the basic question: what is time? That's the real sticking point. You run into a maze of twisted explanations and mathematical theories leading in ever-widening circles, and end up bumping against infinity. This admittedly poor analogy is perhaps even more true when we study the human brain. The gears, the machinery, while complex, are nonetheless understandable. That is, until you ask the question: what is thought?"

Bracken, despite the lack of a fundamental revelation, found himself listening intently to Woodson's explanation. Lunch arrived and the old professor seemed to take as much pleasure in his food as he did the brief lecture.

"I remember reading somewhere," Woodson said, dabbing at the corners of his mouth with a napkin. "Can't recall the quote, exactly, but the gist of it was, 'The vast horde of humanity finds itself riding the crest of a wave of enterprise and technology created by the thoughts of a precious few of our species.' The point being that a hand-ful of intuitive people created the entire basis of our civ-ilization. The machines and tools we use in our everyday lives, the forces which power them, the whole of our technology. The rest of us are basically along for the ride, carried on the backs of a few visionaries."

Bracken found himself laughing, although when he stopped to consider it, the whole thing wasn't that funny. In fact, the truth of the statement was staggering.

"So those of us who study the human brain are, quite naturally, always asking ourselves, 'Where do these in-spired ideas come from?' " Woodson leaned forward; his energy, his own quest for answers, felt like a mild electric shock to Bracken. "How did Beethoven, deaf for a good part of his life, write music of such intensity? How did Copernicus, with only the most basic tools, come to such a revisionist view of the universe? How did Edison, Ein-stein, Marconi, Zworykin, or any of the others one could mention find within themselves a vision which, for the rest of humanity, would surely have to be considered di-vine in nature?"

Bracken found himself staring into the other man's eyes. Lunch, his surroundings, all forgotten, passed into the depths of a hazy fog created by the force of Wood-son's words and personality. The older man seemed to shake himself for a moment, leaning back against his chair, as though on the verge of some previously uncon-sidered explanation. Seconds ticked away; Woodson seemed to reach inside himself, regaining his composure. When he spoke again, his eyes seemed smiling, less heated.

"Interesting, isn't it, Dr. Bracken, how such a simple question can get the juices of an old man flowing?" Woodson said finally, smiling sadly, as if the answers to all the unspoken questions had somehow slipped off his fingertips. Like grasping a handful of sand, Bracken thought, and watching it slip away.

Woodson sipped some of his diluted iced tea and poked at the remnants of his pastrami sandwich. As if, perhaps, with a little more time, he might come to some conclusion, a revelation which might place him with those he obviously revered. Or, Bracken considered, as if the old man stopped himself before he said something he didn't want to blurt out.

"So, what is thought?" Woodson repeated the question, circling back to the original point, like any good professor bringing his lecture to a close. "It is a collection of neuron impulses, traveling along nerve fibers, eventually connecting with the communication areas in the brain. The voice you hear when you think, even if the thought is not spoken or written down. Where does the voice, the thought, come from? In most cases, from stored memory. For example, I can pick up a menu and read it, because of a series of associations based on repetitive instruction I received as a child in school. Lately, through a frustrating series of hit and miss attempts, I have learned to program my VCR. Like most of us, I have only the vaguest idea how the device works, or how the television itself actually functions. I can recite the litany of basic bits and bites included in the manual of the computer I use. I can, perhaps, give a fundamental description of what happens when I plug an appliance into the wiring of my home. On the surface, these would seem to be rather basic questions in the context of modern life, but the majority of us don't have a clue how even the simplest devices work. Fortunately, the same is not true if I were to describe the methodology of extracting a tumor from a mass of brain tissue. That I happen to understand fairly well. The point is, Dr. Bracken, I have spent some seventy-odd years learning things, some better than others. Through a series of genetic occurrences—I hesitate to call them accidents—I have inherited the ability to retain at least a portion of this learned knowledge. I have even been blessed with the capability to make certain limited leaps in logic, using this acquired learning. That is, through my neurological studies, I have been able to add to the knowledge base of those who came before me, regarding the mechanics of the human brain. But in the face of all this time and effort, I am forced to the unavoidable conclusion that when it comes to answering the most basic question— what is thought?—I am completely ignorant. Where does inspiration come from? Is it something divine? Something molecular? An unexplained force residing in the cosmos that certain human beings are somehow able to tap into? I simply don't know. And as far as I have been able to ascertain, no one else does either. . . ."

Woodson's voice drifted off into a cloud of sadness. Bracken was filled with an unaccountable chill. If a man as learned as Henry Woodson could not solve the problem—how could Gary Bracken, who knew only about insects and protein exchanges, hope to succeed? Was he chasing a concept, an idea, which for some reason could not be understood by the human mind? Bracken closed his eyes, feeling the soft, heavy wings of failure settling across his shoulders. When he looked up again, Woodson was watching him, seeming to sense his despair.

"I will tell you one thing which might, perhaps, help you in your search," Woodson said quietly, as if he was about to say something he could not quite put into words. "If you attribute this to me, I will deny saying it. But it may well be that the secret of thought will be found in the smallest, simplest parts of creation. Human beings, when all is said and done, are nothing more than a series of complex cellular groups. Each cell group, each organ, has its own specific receptors, its own markings. All groups are, in the end, related in both substance and structure. But each group has its own specific protein code written on the cellular walls. All living cells carry this information, from the most primitive bacterium to the most complex—that being the cell structure of the human brain. And they are all coded with different proteins. Do you understand what this means, Dr. Bracken?"

Bracken shook his head, the chill moving deeper, into the very marrow of his bones.

"It means," Woodson whispered, "that this encoding process was instituted at the very beginning of complex life on the planet, and it has been in place for billions of years. We must ask ourselves the purpose of these identifying markings. They are much too specific to be random structures. For whom, or what, was this encoding process put in place? Certainly not for human beings, as we are a product of its development, and only in the last decade have we even become aware of this incredible protein structure. In the end, evolution breaks down to the most basic elements. More than that, I simply do not know."

"Are you saying that every cell has its own calling card?" Bracken asked, shaking his head, stunned by the revelation. "Sort of like a homing device?"

"That's correct," Woodson said quietly. "Every group of cells. The cells lining the stomach, for example, have protein structures and receptacle points along their walls that are markedly different from, say, the cells of the kidneys or liver."

"What do these receptors do?" Bracken asked.

"Do? Well, actually, they don't 'do' anything," Woodson said. "They are simply tiny nodules on the outside of the cell walls. No one knows what their purpose is, but research has shown that viruses use these them as invasion points, much like landing pads on the outside of the cells."

"That's incredibly bizarre!" Bracken couldn't help saying, even though he knew the remark to be less than scientific.

"I agree." Woodson smiled. "But it is nevertheless true. There is speculation that viruses use the receptors to match proteins between the cells and themselves."

"These receptors and proteins—you're telling me they're used to identify cells a particular virus is programmed to mutate?" Bracken asked, suddenly realizing the point Woodson was trying to suggest.

"No one knows for certain." Woodson shrugged. "At least, I don't believe anyone knows."

"That may not be true," Bracken said, his voice strained. "The BIR is trying to shut down my research. National-security issues, they claim—as if the government has any right to keep secrets from the people they represent. But Terrance Stampe told you all this, didn't he?"

"Terrance may have mentioned it." Woodson shrugged again.

"And he told you about the code lines we deciphered?" Bracken was at once furious and relieved when Woodson nodded. Furious that Stampe had betrayed his confidence, relieved that he did not have to explain what they had found, particularly in the confines of a public restaurant. Anyone might be listening, Bracken realized. Anyone. Woodson, he noticed, seemed to be mulling over the same thought.

"Why don't we walk back to the car?" Woodson suggested. "I'll give you a ride back to the university."

Bracken paid the check, ignoring Woodson's protest,

and caught up with the professor before he had cleared the main lobby of the restaurant.

"There's something else, isn't there?" Bracken asked, once they were in the street. The sun was warm, people walking without coats, cars passing by with their windows down. Dr. Woodson did not reply, however, until they were safely locked in his automobile.

"I don't know whether it will be useful to you or not," Henry Woodson said, carefully turning up the sound on the radio. "Lately, in the past year or so, a strange occurrence has been observed by some members of my profession. Something odd in the brain-wave patterns of certain patients. Nothing alarming, you understand. It's simply . . . well, unusual."

"Centered in the cortex region?" Bracken asked, the interior of the car suddenly close and confining. It became infinitely more so when Henry Woodson nodded.

"These patients have been seeking treatment for a variety of what might be termed delusional behaviors," Woodson continued, choosing his words carefully. "They are, for the most part, average, everyday people, with no history of psychoses, and generally treatment has been regulated by the mental-health professionals. But, of course, the possibility of physical malfunctions in the brain—tumors and the like—must be discounted. The interesting thing is, that in many cases the EEG, or brain-wave readings, are abnormal. But nothing shows up on CAT scans, or even in the few cases where exploratory surgery has been performed. The phenomenon itself remains unexplained. I mention this, you understand, only in passing, and this conversation must be kept strictly confidential. Besides, I doubt very seriously whether you'll find any reputable physician who will confirm what I'm telling you . . ."

Bracken leaned forward, a barrage of questions forming in his mind, but Woodson had already pulled the car
away from the curb and seemed intent on weaving his
way through the traffic.

"That's really all I can say about the subject," Woodson finished, when they stopped at the first light. "It's
more than I should have said, in any case. There are other
factors, other considerations, of which I'm sure you're
aware."

Bracken nodded, accepting the man at his word. The
medical community was obviously being pressured in
much the same manner as himself. The long arm of the
federal government was like a tentacle wrapped around
the shoulders of all the citizens in this supposedly free
country. In the end, Bracken knew, the best that could be
hoped for was that the tentacles didn't squeeze the life
out of everyone.

He stared out the window as Woodson drove. The
pushcart folk, shouting at traffic. The alleyways filled
with bundles of rags, which were really people in various
stages of despair. Fear and confusion drifted like smoke
along the sidewalks, as real as heat waves on a scalding
summer day.

a molecule of time
Day One + 1.2775 x 10 ^12

"My God, George, it sounds like some medieval insane asylum in here!"

Dr. George Kindle nodded in agreement, even though doing so angered him to no end. He was chief administrator at Mount Sinai Medical Center in New York, one of the country's leading hospitals, and his psychiatric ward was indeed in turmoil. The ward now occupied the entire west wing of the facility, and emergency plans were being implemented to expand the unit further. The influx of new patients continued at an alarming, even terrifying rate. Every day, police and emergency medical units were bringing people into the hospital, picking them up on the streets, in offices, and apartment buildings. People suffering symptoms of dementia the like of which Kindle and his overwhelmed staff had never seen. Madness and chaos seemed to be overtaking the whole of the world, at least Kindle's own personal corner of it. And as his longtime friend and colleague Garfield Roget had correctly

pointed out, the place was being run like London's infamous Bedlam Hospital.

Screams came from behind every locked door on the
wing, echoing through the corridors. The sharp, terrible
sounds could be heard throughout the entire hospital,
Kindle knew, but he was powerless to do anything about
it. The situation was quickly reaching catastrophic proportions, thus his urgent plea to Garfield Roget for help.

Roget was a short, balding man, whose love of good
food and wine caused him to breathe heavily during
what was, for him anyway, a long walk. But the man's
exterior, Kindle knew, effectively concealed one of the
sharpest minds in the psychiatric business. If anyone
could make sense of this plague of madness, it would be
Roget, or so George Kindle hoped. However, as the two
men walked the corridors of the west wing, Kindle saw
the look of confusion in his old friend's eyes—the same
look that had been plastered across his own face these
last weeks.

By the time they reached Kindle's office, lately turned
into a crisis command center, Roget looked like he
wanted to cover his ears and run to catch the next plane
back to L.A. Kindle understood the feeling. Bailing out
seemed like an excellent plan, although, of course, it was
not an option. As the two men wormed their way through
a corridor of hastily set up desks, one of the office workers handed Kindle a report. Phone banks were threatening
to ring off the walls, and staff doctors were arguing, each
vying with the other for medication and treatment rooms
for the hundred or so patients currently booked into the
overflowing facility.

"Ten new cases brought in this afternoon," the assistant told him. Kindle took the printout and hurried toward
his private office, plainly ignoring the storm of voices

calling to him. Roget followed on his heels, and seemed relieved when Kindle slammed the door closed behind them.

"What the hell is going on, George?" Roget asked, sinking into one of the room's padded leather chairs. "Did I miss another Woodstock reunion? Don't tell me a truckload of bad acid somehow found its way into the drinking water?"

Roget tried to smile at his own bad joke, but it was a failing effort. George Kindle didn't even make the attempt, but instead collapsed into his own chair. Outside, it seemed the argument between the staff doctors might actually lead to blows, and the unceasing chorus of screams and moans from the West Wing swept into the room like a cold wind.

"I don't know, Gar," Kindle said, his voice unsteady. "I honest to God don't have a clue."

"How long?" Roget was searching his own memory for similar situations. He found none in the mountain of journals and books he had studied during his long career. Certainly, he knew, nothing in his own experience could even begin to explain what was happening here.

"It started eight or ten weeks ago," Kindle said. "A few cases trickling in. Nothing out of the ordinary, really. If one can use that terminology when supposedly rational, normal people suddenly go completely off the deep end. It began to escalate a couple weeks ago. And now the situation has snowballed into this . . . whatever the *hell* this is."

"Toxicology reports?" Roget knew he was grasping at straws. Obviously a man of Kindle's experience and knowledge would have covered all the reasonable explanations. But he had to ask anyway. "Food poisoning, or some tainted over-the-counter medication?"

"Nothing." Kindle shook his head. He caught a glimpse of himself reflected in the polished wood of his desk, and was amazed to find he hardly recognized the face looking back at him. The normally thin features looked puffy and his thick dark hair seemed to have developed a disturbing white tint. My God, he thought, I've aged ten years. . . .

"George, are you all right?" Roget asked, suddenly concerned for his friend's health.

"Yes, I'm sorry," Kindle said, drawing himself back to the business at hand. The effort caused his head to begin throbbing again, and he gulped several aspirins. How many was that today? He realized he didn't know. Not a good sign. He capped the bottle and slid it into a desk drawer. "Not much sleep these days, as I'm sure you can tell. But no, all the blood work is coming back normal. MRIs, CAT scans, they're all negative. There is some abnormality in the patients' EEGs, but that's to be expected, since they're all experiencing dementia with pronounced hallucinations. Your bad-acid theory was seriously considered and rejected, by the way. These people haven't ingested anything out of the ordinary. Physically, they're fine. That's what makes the whole damn thing so frustrating. This shouldn't be happening, but it is."

"Then there's something taking place within the brain itself," Roget said, mostly to himself. "Something the tests aren't picking up. Have you had any fatalities?"

"A half dozen at this point," Kindle said. "Reactions to the heavy doses of tranquilizers we were prescribing in the beginning. Didn't do much good, however. We'd shoot them full of enough sedatives to knock out a horse, then in an hour they'd be back up screaming. Did more harm than good, so now we're reduced to locking the doors and trying to tie down the most violent cases."

"Bedlam," Garfield Roget mumbled, and Kindle frowned, rubbing at the heavy bags under his eyes. "Do you have autopsy reports on the deceased?"

"Of course," Kindle said, disappointed at the harsh tone of his voice. "They're right here." He forced himself to smile in a gesture of apology. To the man's credit, Kindle noted, Roget gathered up the offered files without appearing to notice his colleague's short temper. "No tumors, and the tissue samples came back negative."

Roget nodded, studying the autopsy sheets.

"Did you inform the CDC about this?" Roget asked, after a few moments of silence. "I assume you got the same cloak-and-dagger report we received out west?"

"I followed procedure and notified them as soon as the situation began to develop," Kindle said, nodding. "They sent a team into the hospital and had the army fly in several crates of tranquilizers. Basically, they told me to keep a lid on things, as much as possible, and they'd handle any public statements. Apparently they've been able to put a hard clamp on the media. There's been nothing in the papers, or on the TV news. A good thing, I guess. No sense in panicking people, at least until we know what we're dealing with."

"That's probably best," Roget agreed. "Does the CDC know I'm here?"

"No," Kindle admitted, actually smiling for the first time in weeks. "I didn't want to spend a whole day filling out request forms for an outside consultation."

"Good," Roget said, grinning a little himself. "At least I won't have those prying bastards following me around like shadows. At this point I'd like to go down to the morgue and have a look for myself at the brain tissues. I'd strongly advise you to lock the door and catch a little shut-eye."

George Kindle acknowledged the advice, but knew he wouldn't take it. Not with the whole bloody hospital falling to pieces around him.

Two hours later, however, he found himself jerked awake by a rapid knocking on his office door. His arm was numb from sleeping in his chair, and he took a few seconds to shake feeling back into his hand. He rubbed his eyes, straightened his tie, and ran a comb through his hair before answering this latest intrusion into the beleaguered existence which had lately become his life. Garfield Roget, he saw, had also been swept up by the storm. The man was carrying a thick folder and had an odd look in his eyes. Confusion, Kindle thought, seasoned with just a hint of fear.

"What is it?" Kindle asked, the noise from the corridors of the west wing combining with the chaos of his outer office to create an atmosphere charged with instability.

"I'm not sure," Roget said, moving to the desk, spreading the contents of his folder across the clutter of previous reports. "Take a look at this."

"Cell tissue?" Kindle asked, picking up what appeared to be slide photographs, holding them up to the fluorescent light.

"Culture slides taken from the cortex area of your fatalities," Roget confirmed. "Here they are, under regular magnification."

"I don't see any abnormality," Kindle replied, studying the photos.

"No, you won't," Roget said. "Not until you run the slides through the electron-scan microscope. There . . ."

"A virus?" Kindle asked, staring at a tiny, raised dot within the cell structure. "But there's no sign of viral infection. We took spinal fluid. One of my people even did a direct skull tap. There wasn't anything to indicate—"

"It's not an infection, in the classic sense," Roget interrupted. "Look here . . . that's a chain of viruses, entwining themselves along the axons and nerve endings."

"What in God's name?" Kindle snatched at the photographs of the slide enlargements. The dots, the viruses, seemed to be twisting themselves along the nerve strings, like thin, tiny snakes.

"George, they're not mutating the cells," Roget said, his voice rising in excitement. "They're forging links along the neuron paths, incorporating themselves into the structure of the cortex. They're becoming part of the brain itself."

"My God . . ." Kindle heard himself whisper. He stood like a teetering statue, his hand reaching for the corner of his desk to steady himself as he stared at the photographs. Disbelief and shock radiating through his body. The screams from the corridor, swelling to a crescendo around him, reverberating, until their sound filled the whole of his world.

fourteen

The beeper pulsed in Paul Sandborn's pocket, and he winced looking at the recall number. He excused himself from the dinner table and went into his home office. Late-night calls to this extension were never good news, and he knew this one would be particularly disturbing. He dialed the number the beeper fed him, and Jeffery Lang's image appeared on the small screen above the phone. Lang, he noted, was still in his office at the CDC, and the man's expression told Sandborn exactly how disturbing the call would be.

"Sorry to bother you so late," Lang said needlessly. "It's rather important, however."

"I'm at home," Sandborn said, before the other man could continue. "The lines here have only basic scrambling capability."

"Very well." Lang nodded, indicating he was aware of Sandborn's security concerns. "I'm afraid the matter we were discussing a few weeks ago has taken an unexpected turn. The facility in New York has apparently achieved a breakthrough of sorts regarding the molecular code we spoke about."

"That operation was supposedly shut down." Sandborn knew he was stating the obvious, but couldn't help himself. Those fucking rogue researchers, they could never do what they were told.

"I know," Lang agreed. "We did receive their material, as promised, but the researcher in question must have continued the work on his own."

"How bad is it?" Sandborn asked, hoping his expression would be enough to make Lang choose his words carefully.

"Our monitoring equipment suggests that part of the protein code in question has been translated," Lang said slowly. "Not much at this point, only two or three lines. But the implications of these sections do relate directly to the phenomenon we've been studying. Our people are working on it now, but the researcher's equipment is off-line, and his program is not in the laboratory's computer bank. That leads us to believe it's a private experiment, probably a solitary venture. Nevertheless, we're certain a breakthrough has taken place."

"Do you think there's an imminent security problem?" Sandborn asked, half hoping for a positive response. That would give him a green light to take some serious action against this Bracken asshole.

"No, I don't believe so." Lang shook his head. "He's out there on his own, but there's no indication of a security violation. The facility itself is in good standing, so it's fair to assume this was something the man just happened to stumble upon. Our own people haven't gotten nearly as far. The man's either brilliant or extraordinarily lucky."

Sandborn nodded, his mind processing an array of possible responses. If this Bracken was so fucking smart, what the hell was he doing working at some dinky contract lab no one had ever heard of before? No, Lang was probably right. The guy stepped in shit, and discovered oil as he was cleaning off his boots.

"Thanks for the update," Sandborn said. "I'll get on it right away."

The screen blanked and Sandborn took exactly thirty seconds to consider the problem before punching up Harvey Mitchell's home number. Within the hour, he had Mitchell squirming in the hot seat of his Washington office. Over the smell of peppermint Breath Savers, Sandborn could make out the Manhattans Mitchell swilled before his supper had been interrupted.

"I don't know." Harvey was shaking his head, stumbling over the words as they caught in his throat. "This shouldn't have happened . . . you read the reports yourself."

"Yes, I read them," Sandborn said, his anger deflected by his own culpability in this increasingly frustrating affair. No one seemed to have any answers, or even any valid information. Except, of course, for some obscure researcher who seemed to be able to achieve results the entire CDC staff thought impossible. Certainly, Harvey Mitchell, a half-drunk bureaucrat, couldn't be expected to come to terms with what was going on. Sandborn knew he'd kept the man largely in the dark. And thank God for that, he thought, watching as Mitchell tried to hide behind the incompetency of others. A trick learned to perfection by anyone who had spent as much time at the public trough as Harvey.

"Arguing about what shouldn't or couldn't have happened is decidedly counterproductive at this point,"

Sandborn said, deciding not to roast Mitchell any more than he already had. "I'm sure we can agree the potential, at least, exists for a security breach neither of us wants to deal with."

Harvey Mitchell nodded, sensing his butt was out of the fire, for the moment anyway. But he was now worried about just how deeply the BIR was going to be dragged into this mess. Whatever the hell the mess actually was. His fears, he discovered, were entirely justified.

"We have to crush this guy," Sandborn said coldly. "Crush him like a fucking bug!"

Gary Bracken went into the office early the next morning, after spending most of the night in his basement lab. He was only now realizing that he hadn't actually spoken to Becky in more than two days. Which was, he thought, probably just as well. Still, he couldn't help but ponder the abysmal canyons of guilt that silence always seemed to open up inside him. It was just like her, he thought bitterly, to make him feel guilty just when he needed her support.

He was considering all this when Mary Ann Meade walked past, on her way out of the building's lobby. More fucking guilt. Once you started, it seemed to be a never-ending trip. He tried to catch her attention, but she pretended not to see him, and refused even to acknowledge his presence when Bracken called after her in his belated attempt at fence-mending. Jesus, was the whole fucking world out for a piece of his ass? Screw 'em all, he thought, waving her off. Still, it was odd that she was at the lab this early in the day, and Bracken felt a moment of apprehension. The moment stretched out, lengthening and twisting, when Terrance Stampe met him at the Centrifuge entranceway. Terrance looked as though his dog had just died, Bracken thought as he began to realize the magnitude of the trouble he might be in. Stampe didn't even float an inquiry into how the meeting had gone with Henry Woodson.

"Jacoby wants you in the conference room, pronto," Stampe said.

You've really fucked it up this time, kiddo. Bracken heard the thought, but wasn't sure if Terrance actually spoke the words. He merely nodded and followed the older man toward Centrifuge's inner sanctum. The day shift, Bracken noticed, didn't even look at him as he passed. From there, it only got worse.

Stan Jacoby had a grimace on his face. But it looked to Bracken that the man was barely able to suppress his glee at what was about to go down. Bracken walked defiantly into the room and sat in his usual chair at the conference table.

"I'll get right to the point, Dr. Bracken," Jacoby said, his voice heavy with disdain. "Did you enter the laboratory on Tuesday night and cause a commotion, harassing the staff members of this facility?"

"I was here," Bracken admitted, looking to squash this as quickly as possible. God, you'd think he came in with a gun and taken hostages. "There was a minor incident. I lost my temper and broke a couple beakers. I was in a hurry to do a data run on the computer, and the staff didn't seem to want to assist me. I'm sorry about my outburst, and I'm more than willing to apologize for my behavior. But at no time did I harass anyone. Furthermore—"

"That's quite sufficient, Dr. Bracken," Jacoby snapped, cutting him off. "The woman is threatening legal action. Personally, I think she'd win if the case was pursued. Fortunately, she's not as vindictive as I might be in her position."

I'm sure of that, Bracken thought to himself. Jacoby glared, as if the man had actually heard the thought.

"We've been able to head this off by offering her a full-time position upon completion of her graduation requirements," Terrance Stampe put in, trying to forestall Jacoby's mounting tirade. "She was most cooperative, I might add, given the circumstances. And from all indications, Ms. Meade will make an admirable addition to the staff. The truth is, we probably would have hired her anyway."

"That's good," Bracken said, beginning to feel relieved.

"However, I am not of the opinion that you should be treated so leniently," Jacoby said, his voice rising. "I received a most disturbing phone call this morning from the head of the BIR in Washington. They were inquiring into the nature of your supposedly curtailed experiments on the virus protein exchange. It seems they have information that you've been violating their request to cease your inquiry into this area."

Bracken closed his eyes, anger and frustration rising up like a tidal force inside him. The bastards. The rotten bastards were trying to hound him out of existence. Trying to cheat him of his discovery.

"Dr. Bracken, is this true?" Jacoby asked.

Terrance Stampe, Bracken saw, was watching closely, to see if he was about to be implicated in what could very well be considered a violation of the lab's security clearance. Bracken shook his head.

"I was following up on some data we gathered before the BIR requested the shutdown of the experiment," he said, his eyes shifting toward Jacoby. Bracken was surprised to find his vision was actually blurred. Clouded by rage, he thought, surprised to realize that such a thing could actually happen. He blinked, trying to bring the room and his adversary back into focus. He was also surprised to discover that, once again, he wanted to leap over the table and tear Jacoby's throat out with his fingernails. To watch the gloating bastard's blood run down the front of his expensive tailored suit. To stare into Jacoby's eyes as they glazed over under the blinding fluorescent lights.

"Following up toward what end?" Stampe asked, in a blatant attempt to cover his own tracks. Bracken smiled coldly in Terrance's direction, acknowledging the maneuver.

"The termites," Bracken lied, hoping his background might confuse the issue enough to save him. "I was working with the termite proteins when I happened, quite by accident, upon a computer program which produced a partial translation of the virus proteins."

Jacoby, he saw, was shaking his head, not believing a word. Stampe, however, looked like he was about to give Bracken a standing ovation.

"So the information was incidental, related to the original protein experiment?" Stampe asked, already proceeding with his hastily constructed argument before Bracken could respond. "I don't believe the insect experiments were prohibited under the BIR guidelines, were they, Stan? We'll inform the BIR that Dr. Bracken was conducting some private research in his specialty, and we were double-checking the validity of this new information before turning it over to them."

"I don't buy it, and neither will they," Jacoby said belligerently. "Enough fooling around. I'm formally requesting your resignation, Dr. Bracken. Have it on my desk this afternoon."

"Fire me, I won't resign," Bracken growled, mirroring the look on Jacoby's face.

"Fine, then you're fired!" Jacoby said, grinning now at his victory.

"You don't have the authority!" Bracken glared back at him, and then looked over at Terrance Stampe. "Both senior partners have to countersign any termination order."

To Bracken's relief, Stampe nodded in agreement. Bracken found himself staring again at Jacoby with his fists clenched, a red rage closing like a veil over his eyes. As if Jacoby was trying to bait him, the older man was smiling.

"Want to bet that won't be a problem?" Jacoby asked, sounding so pleased with himself that Bracken almost went for him then and there. "Your termination was requested by the BIR as a condition of our grant continuance."

"You never told me that!" Stampe protested.

"I'm telling you now," Jacoby said. "Fight me on this, Terrance, and the government will pull the rug out from under us all. Dr. Bracken, you will vacate the premises immediately or I will most certainly call the authorities and have you thrown bodily into the street."

Bracken glanced over at Stampe, searching desperately for support, but Terrance looked as though all the fight had gone out of him. He looked about eighty years old, Bracken thought.

"I'm sorry, Gary," Stampe mumbled.

"Time to say your good-byes, Dr. Bracken." Jacoby sat back smugly in his chair.

"You miserable old fucker!" Bracken heard himself shout. He went across the table, reaching for Jacoby. He had him once, for an instant, before the lab attendants rushed in and pulled him away. Jacoby was choking, trying to catch his breath, eyes bugging out of his head. It was almost worth it, Bracken thought. Almost. In seconds, he found himself out in the street, seething as the door was locked behind him. He kicked once at the shatter-proof glass, and then drove home.

When Rebecca returned early in the afternoon, she was furious. But not at him, Bracken saw. At least not yet.

"What are you doing home?" Bracken asked. It was only three o'clock, and Rebecca was never one to leave her desk before five.

"I was about to ask you the same thing!" she said, slamming the door, her briefcase, and her coat, all in the same motion.

"I asked you first," Bracken said. He was sitting in the living room, channel-surfing through the cable stations. He was just starting his second drink, but already felt curiously drunk. He knew he should be downstairs, working on the protein experiment, but simply couldn't make himself concentrate. Which was odd, he thought, since losing a job had never bothered him before. The real problem, he knew, was telling his wife. An eventuality he wanted to postpone for as long as possible.

"I lost two goddamn grants today." Becky sighed, moving over to the liquor cabinet, pouring her own drink. "One for the museum, and one for the SUNY people. They should have gone through easily, but I got a phone call from the funding agency in Washington turning both down. Some bullshit about funding cuts. That's not the real reason, though. The funding had already been approved. I tried to get more information, but was stonewalled everywhere I turned. So I got mad and left. Why aren't you at work?"

"Got fired," Bracken said, bracing himself.

"Sweet Christ," Becky whispered, dropping onto the couch, staring at him. "A run-in with Jacoby?"

"Sort of." Bracken shrugged, wondering how much he should tell her.

"Well, it's obvious that you have to go back and make peace with the man," she said, making a conscious effort to keep herself and her voice calm. "It was the protein experiment, wasn't it?"

The whole thing had been simmering for weeks now, and it had finally reached the boiling point. Gary had been working day and night, she knew, and it had no doubt affected his job performance. It was, she thought, as if he had become possessed by some strange, hidden aspect of his basement work. Something which, for the life of her, she didn't understand.

The truth was, she admitted to herself, Gary Bracken didn't seem to live in the rational world anymore. She watched as he nodded his head at her question, half expecting some sort of emotional outburst. He might curse and slam a chair, but eventually he would be forced to give in to whatever it was Jacoby wanted of him. But instead of ranting and raving, Bracken simply shook his head and smiled, strolling calmly over to the bar, pouring himself another drink.

"It's not quite as simple as kissing Jacoby's ass to get my job back," he said. "There were other complications."

"Such as?" Becky asked sharply, mentally going over their bank account, wondering how long they could pay the bills on her salary. Assuming, of course, she still had a salary. Two grants shot down in the same day. That had never happened to her before, and she still couldn't quite believe it.

"There was a problem with the BIR," Bracken said, trying to sound calmer than he actually felt. The truth was, he felt kind of strange. As though all of this—his house, Rebecca, everything around him—was some sort of surreal image. Something not exactly real. It was an uncomfortable feeling, but it seemed to hold a bizarre fascination for him.

"Oh God." Becky sank back deeper into the folds of the couch. "They found out about what you were doing. That virus protein crap. You've got to go back to Centrifuge and straighten this out, Gary. The computer project, you're in on the ground floor. This is a huge deal. You can't just throw all that away."

Bracken only smiled at her, as if he had already made up his mind. His eyes looked wild and unfocused. She wondered for a moment if he was drunk . . . or crazy.

"What I'm onto is bigger than some foolish fucking computer project," he said, his voice shaky, yet calculated. This was an argument he had carefully constructed, but somehow the words couldn't move from his brain to his mouth. He tried to speak again, but instead waved her interrogation away.

Becky stared at him, the first dim rush of panic passing through her. He appeared drunk, but she knew instinctively that he wasn't. He hardly ever drank to excess. But there was clearly something wrong. He was blinking and looking around the room, as if seeing things no one else could see. He kept glancing into the corners, at the late-afternoon shadows. Almost as though he, too, were afraid. Afraid of what he might find there. She began to seriously consider that her husband might be having some sort of breakdown.

"You've been working too hard," Rebecca said, getting up, moving toward him. Her anger being displaced by concern. She suddenly wanted very much to take his hand, to hold him until whatever demons were around him slipped off into the shadowy gloom from which they had arisen.

He backed away as she approached. Something was happening to him. He shook his head. A twisting, swirling feeling. As if there was a wave inside his head. A dizzying, crashing wave. A detached feeling. As if the world, as if time itself was not a steady solid thing. She touched his arm, he pulled away. . . .

—Bright White. Flashing in his head. And he was looking out at a wide, open plain. A grassy savanna. Surrounded by shouting, snorting, animal grunts. For a moment he thought the grunts were coming from the beast that lay bleeding in the grass at his feet. A short-pronged antelope, its throat ripped out, legs twitching as the last of its life flowed onto the trampled grass. Then he realized with amazement that the sounds were coming from his own mouth. That his hand held a sharpened stick, its tip black and hardened by fire, dripping now with the blood of the antelope. His arm, his body, covered with matted, brown fur. A female ran down the hill, from her hiding place in the ravine. Swollen and heavy with child, holding a curved, sharpened stone in her hand. Her eyes flashing with excitement at the kill. Grunting at him, bending over the still-quivering body of the animal. Touching the flowing blood with her fingers. Tasting it. Standing, smiling, her teeth bared in what might have been a grin, or a growl. She pressed her fingers against his mouth, and he tasted the blood, warm and salty. Confusion ripping his brain. There were other short-prongs kicking or lying dead in the tall grass. Other hunters, members of his clan, standing over their prey. Shouting in hoarse grunts, waving weapons above their heads. He smelled the blood. Smelled the lingering scent of a campfire wafting from their own fur. His senses so sharp, they seemed to burn in his head. He heard the breeze. The rip-

pling of the grass. His bare feet felt the pounding of
hooves trembling the ground like soft drumbeats as the
rest of the antelope herd fled from their ambush. She was
looking at him strangely. And he wanted to say something. To ask how—why they were in this place? But
there were no words. Only gruntlike sounds. The female,
heavy with child, bending back down to cut meat from
the carcass.

*Timeless. The virus clans worked within the bodies of
their hosts. The Many seeking the path to ONE. Infinitely
patient . . .*

"What?" she asked, staring at him. Terrified by the blank,
glazed look in his eyes. Looking as though she wanted to
shake him, but was somehow afraid to touch him. "Gary!
What the hell is going on?"

He stared back at her, blinking. Trying to adjust to
whatever moment of reality this was. Shadows dancing at
the edge of his vision. They were in the house, he saw. In
whatever moment of time passed for Now.

"Gary?" Rebecca asked, her voice rising to the louder
ranges of hysteria.

He found it odd that his senses seemed dull. That he
couldn't hear the wind shifting through the trees outside.
That both their smells were masked by the scent of per-
fumed soap. He swallowed, tasting warm, salty blood in
the back of his throat. He took a long pull off his drink,
the liquor biting yet somehow comforting in his mouth.
She was still staring at him, he saw, as if he truly was a
stranger suddenly forcing himself into her life.

"What?" he snapped, pushing her away with more
force than he met, surprised to hear the low, rumbling
growl roll out of his mouth.

She stumbled against the TV, then backed away, locking herself in the bedroom, and he was forced to sleep on the couch. In the morning Rebecca packed a suitcase and left. Bracken did not try to stop her. He did, however, note that she left the smell of fear behind. It hung in the air for hours, even after she had gone.

a molecule of time
Day One + 1.2775 x 10 ^12

"The past is speaking to me," the woman said.

The man sitting next to her nodded, believing her.

"No, I'm serious." She put her hand out, touching his arm, as if she hoped the physical connection between them might serve to reinforce the truth behind her words.

"I know," the man said, acknowledging her gesture.

He did know, and he did believe. The past was speaking to him also, even if he could not bring himself to say so out loud. The past, he thought, was speaking to everyone, although it had to be admitted that most were mired in denial. He had denied the obvious until this very morning—when he woke to find himself sliding great stones along a muddy road to the valley where a ring of prayer stones was being erected under the direction of the Priests. In some manner, which he did not understand, the Priests would use this place to gather information about the journeys of stars through the sky, and so be able to tell the people when to plant and harvest their grain. This and much, much more. Things he would never understand, for the Gods spoke to the Priests and not to commoners like himself.

That was the way of things, he thought, sitting on the bench beside the woman, as they watched the cars and buses roar past them. The man had the sudden notion that he needed a Priest to explain all these things to him. Perhaps in this particular time and place, in this moment, the Gods still spoke to their chosen ones. Although, in truth, he doubted it.

The woman, much like the man in age and social status—both being in their mid-twenties, dressed casually but neatly for the workplace—had an entirely different perspective on the phenomenon she sensed both of them were experiencing. She recently found herself in the company of her peers, somewhere in the deep past. Working with the Circle of Women, rolling the grinding stone from one to the other, speaking of the day's events as they milled their grain. They discussed the weather, of course, but with an urgency known to those of the past, for whom rain or the lack of it often spelled the difference between life and death. They spoke of their children, who showed what promise and in what areas. The men, the hunters, were discussed in much the same fashion. Upcoming unions were examined, this done in an almost bemused manner as the Elder women spoke of the positive and negative attributes the offspring of these unions might exhibit. The harvest, the storage of grain and dried meat for the approaching winter, even the leadership of the tribe itself were all topics discussed around the grinding wheel. When she emerged from this vision—or dream, or psychotic episode, or whatever name the media was currently attaching to the phenomenon—the woman thought it would be wise to seek out such a Circle, to sit around a grinding wheel and discuss the upcoming Change. She was certain such Circles existed, but did not yet know where to find them.

As they sat on the bench she spoke of her desire to find a Circle, like the one in her dream, and the man mentioned his need to seek out a Priest for much the same reasons. They rose and kissed good-bye, having been husband and wife for the previous five years. They parted, each on their separate quests, hoping, even planning to see one another again, although they never would.

The man, who had been an engineer with the Metro Power Authority, sought vainly for an explanation about the coming Change from those in the religious community. He wandered the city for several months, even while the National Guard was called into service in a valiant, yet ultimately failed attempt to keep the power flowing. He was killed in the food riots, shortly after the electricity shut down.

The woman, who had been a nurse at a local hospital, fared somewhat better. Through a series of unlikely encounters, she found her way out west during the time when the transportation systems were still intact. In Boulder, Colorado, she was initiated into a Circle of Women. The Circle to which she belonged had been a functioning group, surviving in one form or another since the days of the Seven Nations, before Columbus made his mistaken landfall in the Caribbean. She was present in Boulder when the de facto government of the United States announced its historic Rebuilding Campaign in that city at the turn of the century. The fact that this campaign was largely political and doomed to failure was discussed at great length within the Circle.

The hospital where the woman once worked also survived well into the next century, at which time it became a famous enclave, tending those who managed to live through the first chaotic years of the Great Change. In this place of healing, the staff members set broken bones by candlelight, washed wounds with homemade disinfectant, and sutured with catgut. They boiled scalpels in steaming cauldrons before attempting to remove bursting appendixes or amputate rotting limbs, even though such procedures usually resulted in infection, for which there were no more miracle drugs. Later, after several generations had passed and the Change was fully implemented, the old building was razed to make way for a new facility which ran on fusion power.

fifteen

The scream—loud, piercing in his head. A woman's scream, he thought, turning toward the sound. Again the scream, and the hairs on the back of Bracken's neck stood straight up. Panic, terror. His panic, the woman's terror. He turned again, trying to find the source. Forgetting for an instant that he was alone in the house. Alone in his life. Trapped inside an ever-widening web of madness.

The sound, he realized, was coming from inside his head. Unable to accept that explanation, Bracken ran into the bedroom, finding only shadows and empty corners. The scream came again, echoing, as though someone or something had planted a speaker inside his brain. Each time the sound came, Bracken ran to a different part of the house, not believing that such a terrible, penetrating noise could come from inside him. The basement, dark and filled with the taunting machinery of his doomed experiment. The back storage rooms of the cellar—the furnace, the water heater, boxes and tools on a workbench. But no person, no thing, to which he could assign this terrible screaming. He grabbed a flashlight and ran outside, checking the porch, the bushes, the garage. No one. Nothing, except the darkness of the night. The wind, chilling him. His feet sliding in the mud. Slipping, falling. The flashlight careening away in a strange, flashing dance. Tree branches groaning in the wind. Clouds racing across the face of the moon. His empty yard, filled with an unidentifiable scream of terror. A sound, high-pitched and sharp with horror. The sound coming from inside his head. From deep beneath hidden layers of memory. His own memories? From some long-forgotten time in the distant past?

All of history is filled with the sounds of women screaming, he heard himself whisper.

Confusion mixing with his panic. A witch's brew of fear and anxiety. The thought came to him that perhaps the sound was coming from his own mouth. He stumbled back inside the house, slamming the door against unseen ghosts.

How do you tell if you're going insane? he wondered.

Bracken went into the bathroom, flicked on the light, and looked at himself in the mirror. At the week-old growth of beard on his face. At his eyes, wide and bloodshot, surrounded by lines of fatigue. The reflection failed to quell his fears. He watched his mouth, making a conscious effort to keep it closed. The scream came again, and he was fairly certain his mouth had not opened. So the sound had not come from his own voice, but rather from inside his head. Did that make it better or worse? He couldn't decide.

What the fuck was going on? Bracken wanted to ask the question out loud, but didn't dare. What would happen if he opened his mouth and a scream came out? He didn't want to find out, so he held a hand over his mouth and went back into the living room. Turning on the television, hoping to mask the sound which reverberated in his brain. The news was on CNN, as always. The reporter talking about a war in some faraway place where the Gods of Chaos ruled. Film clips of hard-faced men firing large guns. Firing indiscriminately at an already ravaged city. The buildings pockmarked by artillery shells. A close-up shot of blood congealing in shallow pools along the streets and sidewalks. Words floating into his ears, masked by the awful screaming in his head. The local graveyard, he saw, was filled with nameless crosses and mounds of freshly turned earth. Women crying as wooden coffins were unloaded from the back of military trucks.

And the thought came to him again, startling and terrible: history is filled with women crying. Since the beginning, for all of humanity's existence upon the earth. No, the thought went deeper and became even more horrifying: since the beginning of time itself. The function of the living has always been to mourn the dead. To cry over the bloodied corpses of those killed in the name of the Thousand Gods and the Countless Countries. Bracken's hand twitched, his eyes felt suddenly heavy. He sank into the chair, even as the sounds of fear and terror danced in his head like smoky dreams.

Deep within the cerebral cortex of the host, the Many searched for the key to understanding. Within the vast electrical field of this complicated organ, protein molecules flowed along the pathways of the neuron cells. Flickering images, as yet unreadable to the Many as they struggled to become ONE. As they moved toward the ultimate goal—to merge with the host into a single, func-

*tioning entity. The power of billions of years of evolution
nearing fruition. The clans, seeking to access their own
unimaginable history. The host, caught in the dreamlike
state of the clan's reality. Encoded protein molecules
flowed between the host's brain and the partially constructed matrix of the Many.*

—Bright White. Memories. The female screamed. A cry
of mourning. The images, the dream, becoming a tangi-
ble thing, real in its intensity—as real as his own life, as
real as all the other lives contained within the molecules.
Evolution binding him to the past and present. Binding
him as the protein strings held the clans together. Both
caught in the inescapable knowledge of their own related
histories. A history extending back to the beginnings of
life in the primal seas of Earth. And for the virus clans,
back further still, through the depths of time and space, to
a doomed world in the Galactic Disk. And yet even further, to other worlds where life had arisen from the mud
and slime of cellular birthing fields. To the clans' own beginnings in the holocaust of Galactic birth. Their knowledge, timeless, an unbroken chain, extending back to the
First Origins. To a time when the Universe itself was a
collection of gases and molecules, governed only by the
statistics of trillions of chance encounters. The purpose of
it all, hidden from every creature who ever existed on all
the worlds of time and space since the Beginning itself.
Accessing this hidden knowledge was the mission of the
Many in their quest to become ONE. Discovery being the
driving force behind all higher forms of life. Large or
small, the search for self is at the heart of it all.

—Bright White. The female screamed, as they have
since the Beginning. But in this molecule of time and

memory, the female screamed from a forgotten planet in the heart of the Galaxy. She screamed from across billions of years of time and space. Her agony caught forever in a tiny bit of protein now flowing across the neuron cells of the host, filtering through the matrix of the Many. Bracken, caught in this web of remembering, cried with her—as her antennae feared to touch the cold, lifeless bodies of the family she had nourished through long years of war and hunger. He knew the tragedy of crops burned, of the young sent off to perish in a hail of fire. Through her multifaceted eyes, he saw the twin suns, hot and red, lifting off the horizon. Saw their harsh light refracting in the drifts of sand and the bare, thorny brush of this inhospitable land. A hard place, once green and lush, now burned and forsaken. He watched as her pointed limbs pushed out from the hard shell of her body—watched as she scooped out long holes in the sand, burrowing a final nesting place for her mate and the young ones they had brought into existence together. Watched as she rolled their bodies into the burial holes, pushing sand between her thin, segmented legs to cover those she loved. And he listened, as she sang her song of life and rebirth over the shifting mounds. Knowing that she now neither believed nor wanted rebirth. He cried with her as she asked the Universe why such a terrible thing had been visited upon them.

He woke and staggered from the chair, falling onto the floor. His head . . . brain and mind seemed to separate. To become multiple entities, each unique and distinct. The One becoming the Many, becoming ONE. One, Many, ONE. The thought came to him, but made no sense. He blinked, the vision of the female gone as quickly as it appeared.

• • •

—Bright White. Swirling thoughts, impossible and maddening. Single-cell bacteria swimming in vast oceans. Cells invaded. Changed. To an unknown purpose. Hidden. Hidden from everything that lived. Even from the Timeless Ones. He had the sudden, terrible feeling that he was flowing. His body dissolving—all that he was—*All That He Was*—sinking, slipping away. Flowing down a spiral of Time and molecules. And the thought came: that he was mortal, yet immortal. That this was not some strange, impossible nightmare. But that it was all real. All of it.

He blinked again, and it was gone. He shivered, pulling his arms around his body, surprised to discover that he was, once again, whole. His head, floating. He felt the world turning beneath him. The thoughts, the images, flowing across his brain. Receding, like floodwaters sinking beneath desert sands. But he now knew more than he wanted to know.

He could close his eyes and see worlds exploding, gas and debris pushed out into the vastness of space. Suns going nova, destroying whole planetary systems. The Ones, escaping, as they had time after time. In the vastness of the Universe, worlds were destroyed every day. Countless suns ended their lives with each tick of the clock. And from this devastation the Ones went forth on long, timeless journeys, seeking other worlds to colonize. But destruction was not their only means of mobility. They made their way to other worlds in the bodies of star-traveling hosts. They spread across the Universe with each small step taken by every species who ever went forth from their own home world. For the virus clans existed within every living entity in the vastness of space. Rode with them on every journey taken, great or small.

Each place a traveler went, each place where gravity and the solar winds brought debris into the atmosphere of an unsuspecting planet, the clans came and began their work. Bracken knew these things, as surely as he knew his own name. In this manner, they had come to the earth, billions of years ago, and now existed within every living thing, plant or animal. Their colonization of this world as total and complete as any conquering army. They lived, even, within himself. And now they were changing him. Changing the whole of humanity. Invading our thoughts, he knew, moving them in a direction unknown and hidden. Toward what end? He had no idea, but the reality of it was with him, inescapable and undeniable. Although he knew with certainty that mankind would surely try to do both.

Bracken stared at the now meaningless jumble of noise and light which was his world. Confusion, like a great beast, gnawing at his bones. He wanted to cry, hoping that he was mad, but knowing he was not. This *thing* was happening to him. Happening to all of humanity. The virus clans were invading the thought process of Man. And so great was the power of the microscopic world, he knew there was nothing anyone could do about it.

It was useless, he knew, to try to hide. Equally useless to try to pretend normalcy in the face of this seemingly horrible reality. But was it a thing of horror, or simply a matter of destiny? Indeed, he thought, it was entirely possible the two were the same.

He went outside and looked at the stars, hoping at least to find some comfort in the night. The wind, sighing like a tired lover. Brushing his face, slipping inside him, seeping into his brain. There, it seemed to gather strength, blowing like a storm across the neural paths of his mind. Where, he knew, the invaders were at work. Tireless, timeless. The mourning cries of the female on that long-forgotten world slipped briefly across the dark patterns of memory he now seemed to possess. He found it odd that screams could erupt from inside his brain, unexpected and uncontrolled, like shrieking monsters rising from the depths of black, forgotten caverns. Erupting, flapping their wings in batlike precision, then fading away into oblivion. He wondered if he would be able to go on living with such sounds in his head. He heard it again briefly, clearly, low and moaning, like the call of lonely whales across leagues of empty ocean.

He walked, his brain trying ineptly to shut down both sound and thought. Thought, that elusive beast. Tantalizing and seductive. Both cruel and sweet in the same instant. Thought, the one thing separating mankind from the beasts. Thought, sought after and prized, like a forbidden fruit. It was a drug, he realized, through the ravaged tangle of nerve endings which had now become his brain. Thought was like the soft, smooth edges of a codeine high. Yes, it will comfort you in lonely moments, like the sun on your face on the first, warm day of spring. Thought will lead you down inviting, flower-strewn paths. Then, when you seem safe and protected in its tender grasp—like the gentle, exciting caress of your first lover—the claws will extend. First, gripping the flesh in a tight hold that invites you to pull away. To tear your own body in a desperate moment of retreat. Then, sensing your fear, the claws will tighten, penetrating deep into the muscle. And the instant of turning back, to escape the ripping talons, has been lost. Lost in a moment of indecision, of confusion. The same moment, buried deep in the past, which is the very source of that which none of us wants to face. Thought. Like a terrible bird of prey, its claws reaching deep inside the body. Grasping with talons and ripping beak, seeking the very marrow of your bones, the core of your existence.

Thought, separating us from the beasts? Bracken wondered. Is it not the essence of our being? Sweeping across our brains like a firestorm. Thought, cutting deep and sharp, into our hearts. Into our very souls. Forcing us to see ourselves in the bright, glaring light of knowledge. Casting aside the shadows of our own defenses. Telling us: that we live, and so are doomed to die. Thought, like a heavy, tearing bullet shooting across our neural paths, demanding that we consider ourselves in the unforgiving spotlight of what we are, of what we might have become. Replaying the paths chosen, highlighting the roads not taken.

Thought, like a lethal, potent drug—once ingested, unable to control. A mad, crazed, hallucinating experience. Growing meaner, sharper, more virulent with each memory, with each moment of life, until the brain is thoroughly consumed by its crushing weight. His brain reeled, his body seemed to convulse. As if it wanted to purge the very concept of Thought. What good, what purpose does it serve? Thought. The memory of his father dying a slow, painful death. A memory unmerciful in its exactness. A gnawing worm crawling in the deep caverns of his mind. A curse . . . a terrible, terrible curse.

What good, what purpose can it serve? Only to tease, then torment. The memory of his mother, her face pale and lifeless, lying in a church, surrounded by reams of flowers. Taken from that place of worship and placed into the cold, dark earth. Is there any reason for memories such as these? Is there any comfort, any salvation?

The brain fabricates lies to keep the flesh whole and functioning.

"We will all be together again, in the comforting arms

of God," he heard the minister say. A fable constructed in
the most desperate hours of misery.

Thought. That which separates us from the beasts. Can
it be that the beasts are the lucky ones? Can it be that
thought is indeed the most dreadful of curses? That living,
simply for the sake of living, is the way Creation was
meant to be? That thought, which we so embrace and
deify, is an unnatural and destructive force? A double-
edged sword, a weapon which we turn with equal abandon
upon our enemies and ourselves. A thing inflicted upon us
by the very weakness of our species. Cultivated by the in-
eptitude of our senses, by our own physical limitations. In
order to survive, our brains became our primary weapon.
A weapon we have used as carelessly as a man swinging
a battle-ax in a crowded movie theater. And now, perhaps,
our brains will become the very instrument of our destruction. The thought patterns themselves, changed and
adapted by outside forces. The invaders, the gene masters,
colonizers of worlds, now loose within the confines of the
human brain.

Why? he heard himself whisper, even though he already knew the answer. Why? To use this thing they have
created. This complicated machinery, the end result of
billions of years of evolution. To use it for the purpose it
was made—to achieve Thought. In the same manner termites use their own method of protein communication.
The same way ants and bees exchange chemical information. And even humans, with the new protein-reading
computers now being developed. Was it so strange, then,
that the gene masters themselves might strive to develop
their own means of communication? To become ONE.
The thought came to him, strange and defused. Even
though he did not understand the exact meaning of it all,
he understood enough.

Thought. Comforting and savage in the same moment. He remembered Rebecca's warm embrace. And knew now with certainty that she was gone. The wind, suddenly dark and foreboding, swept across the vast electronic field of his brain, and he could do nothing in the face of such bitter knowledge, except hold his head in despair. And he knew that within the whole of the world, there would soon be great weeping and gnashing of teeth.

Thought, separating him from the beasts.

Within the bodies of their hosts, the virus clans continued their exploration of the multifaceted brain. Uncounted generations had passed since the development of this complex organ, but the clans' trial-and-error methodology had only recently begun to find success in utilizing its potential. Working silently, deep in the folded columns of cells, where electricity and molecular proteins and memory all fused into ONE, the clans explored the chasms of the synaptic cleft, entwined themselves along the axon and dendrite nerve strings, and examined the neurotransmitter chemicals with great care. Seeking knowledge, origins, the mystery of existence. The One, becoming the Many. The Many struggling to become ONE.

a molecule of time
Day One + 1.2775 x 10 ^12

The evening news, addicting and horrifying. Obscene, in a way. The stories told with calm fascination, accompanied sometimes by graphic footage, carefully edited so as not to offend the sensibilities of the sane . . . too much.

—A man being led out of a courthouse. Scene switches to an urban dwelling, surrounded by police and the abnormally curious. Voice-over: so-and-so arrested for a gruesome murder in Chicago, the killing of a mother and her children. And the especially grisly kicker: the woman's unborn baby had been cut from her womb. Seems the killers wanted a baby, so they went out and got one.

—Twelve dead at a massacre in a Texas McDonald's. For reasons unknown, gunman walks into the fast-food restaurant during the noontime rush and simply opens fire. Body bags being loaded into hearses and ambulances. Brief interviews with grieving relatives.

—Another courthouse scene. A woman being led away, sentenced to life in prison for killing her own children. Couldn't say why, exactly, but admitted that she'd strapped the kids into their car seats and drove them into a lake.

—Multiple suicides in the French countryside. Bodies found in a strange star pattern near a campfire. Cult activity suspected, making the whole thing mildly palatable, vaguely believable.

—Soldiers on trial in Japan for raping a twelve-year-old girl. Luckily for them, the announcer explains, there is no death penalty in Japan. Government protesters are, however, executed in China, Africa, Haiti, and elsewhere. Screen flashes their pictures for what is undoubtedly the final time. War crimes in Bosnia, and elsewhere. Long shots of mass graves, file clips of the guilty. Who, the announcer says, will probably never be brought to trial.

—Jewish leader assassinated. Drug killings in South America, Asia, L.A., New York, and elsewhere.

Channel surfing through madness and chaos.

Jesus, what the hell is going on in the world? he asked his wife.

A shrug, a shake of the head. Fortunately, after the evening news, some comedian comes on the television to explain things. The world isn't terrifying or insane. It's only mildly amusing.

sixteen

. . . how did it ever come to this?

Sunlight drifting across the bedroom like pale smoke. The morning defusing across Bracken's open eyes, as though the ceiling above him was a prism, breaking the light into a confusion of colors. Colors which mingled with the confusion in his brain. So deep, so profound, he barely noticed the coming of the day. Hallucinations parading before his eyes, each more intense, more real than the last.

—Bright White. Coughing in the harsh smoke of winter fires. Hunger gnawing at his belly as glacial snows filled the mouth of the cave. Breaking the bones of long-ago kills, digging out the sour marrow with branches and rough stone tools. Sometimes . . . sometimes cracking the bones of those who had died, desperation driving them all to sacrilege . . .

• • •

Fishing in quiet inlets. Riding the waves in round hide boats. Hauling up nets made from the twisted sinew of animals. Stabbing into the calmer shallows with long, thin spears, as school after school of spawning fish made their way into the inlets from the sea. The smell of fish permeating his leather clothes, staining his flesh with its sharp odor. A smell, a taste that lingered for all his life. But the smell was sweet. It meant full bellies for himself and the others of his village, and so brought a comforting smile to his face. . . .

Digging in long, dark tunnels driven into the hillsides. Backbreaking labor, often done under the threat of the lash. Smoky torches glowing against the timbers, their light dimmed by clouds of dust. The harsh sweat and soft curses of men laboring under dangerous conditions, in a frantic search for the metals which were changing the world. Alchemists, smelting fires, the sooty ash of charcoal. The biting whips of overseers. Heavy sacks of ore, bending backs, twisting bone. All so the resounding clang of metal weapons could break the morning silence like the ringing of demonic bells . . .

War raging in flashes of insane fear and maddening confusion. The thunder of hooves, the clash of armies colliding on battlefields made slippery by blood. The stench of death, vomit, and exposed entrails, mingling with the ever-present smell of terrible, numbing fear. The pitiful cries of the wounded. The howls of the victors and the vanquished, fusing into a hellish chorus. War, the threat of it always hanging in the air, even in times of peace. Tilling the earth with wooden tools, which somehow turned to metal as he watched his hands work them. Crops gathered, stored in clay vessels against the coming winter. Animals, tenderly cared for, then summarily slaughtered. Their meat, salted and dried, hung in small smoky buildings. All of it, as often as not, lost to marauding bands, or taken by those in power to feed the engines of war . . .

Tears and laughter. The fleeting comforts of love. Sweet and half-remembered. Children born to be buried. Taken by hunger or mysterious sickness. Plague and war, walking the land, hand in hand. Death waiting, always, for the unwary or the unlucky. Songs and prayers and sacrifices made to ever-changing, yet interchangeable gods.

The history of his species, Bracken knew, in odd, fleeting moments of lucidity, when the thoughts seemed to shift in his brain, to focus on some other, deeply buried memory. Whether or not they were actually his own memories, his own lives, Bracken didn't know. Didn't care. The realization, the reality of it, left him stunned, completely unable to rise from the bed.

The bank, a whisper came from some tiny corner of the life he was now supposedly living. Got to go to the bank and get some money. The gun, he remembered, was on the nightstand. Got to get up, go to the bank.

And he laughed, knowing he was helpless, caught in the grip of something much larger than himself. Knowing that either madness or enlightenment had now entered his life. And really, when you got right down to it, did it really matter which? He thought not. Perhaps there was little to choose between the two.

The bank, the whisper came again. This time smothered by laughter before it could go any further. Bracken, now understanding himself to be merely an extension of time—a pair of hands, a body, a brain, connected by some force of nature to all the other hands, bodies, and brains that had gone before him. And he knew, also, how fleeting and meaningless were the material things human beings of his time somehow found so important. That life in the so-called modern age was, in fact, a contrived illusion. A trick, a mirage, created by the combined forces of religion and commerce. A game, played by the foolish and the weak. The rules invented long, long ago by those with wealth, position, and power; in a vain attempt to hoard their treasure, to retain their position and power. Yet in the end, Death, the great equalizer, came to them all. Immortality, the final fruit of victory, slipping through the fingers of rich and poor alike. Bracken, sensing that the game and the rules were about to change, stared at the prism of his ceiling.

The Change was coming, as it had for his species many times in the past. The Change was, in fact, upon him. Upon them all.

—Bright White. A tiny sun exploding in his brain. Bringing memories. Of building. Tents from scraped hides. Shallow dugout huts, mounds of earth; burrows, the women called them. Cutting down forests, first with flint axes, then hardened metal, which required constant sharpening. Filling in the cracks of log huts with mud and straw. Later, the mud and straw baked into bricks. Villages, towns, cities. Houses, castles, fortified walls. Churches of wood, stone, and glass. Towers, reaching toward the sky. For the glory of God. For the glory of kings, sultans, presidents, dictators, and wealthy merchants. All falling before the indomitable forces of nature.

Sunlight, leaking into his eyes like cleansing drops of heavy water. Bracken stirred, blinking, shaking his head. The bedroom unfolding around him like a cardboard backdrop in some bizarre, surreal stage play. He shook his head again, looking around with a sense of clarity he hadn't known in days. Weeks. Perhaps even months. The world was different, somehow. Changed in a way he couldn't quite comprehend. As if he was looking at things from a slightly different angle. Seeing a perspective, a depth he never suspected.

He knew with reasonable certainty that he was alive and existing in this current time, this moment of reality. It was a good feeling. A centered perspective. But he was acutely aware of his connection to the past. That he was part of all things which had come before him. And, perhaps, to all that would come after. It was a timeless feeling. He was quite surprised to find an intense, almost healing comfort flowing just below the surface of this knowledge. As though he suddenly knew himself to be part of something more permanent than himself. Yes, he decided, it was indeed a timeless feeling.

His nose wrinkled as he sat up in bed. Timeless, maybe, but still in desperate need of a shower and some clean clothes. And he had to get moving. There was a lot to be done. Problems to be solved. Discoveries to be made. In the back of his mind—no, in the depths of his mind—he thought he knew what had happened. Oddly enough, he was not afraid. An effect, he considered, which could be attributed to either madness or enlightenment. And from the confines of the body, how do you tell the difference? Indeed, did it matter?

A half hour later, showered and shaved, he brewed a pot of coffee and buttered some frozen waffles, which were the closest thing to actual food he could find in the depleted stores of the house. Plans, sliding across his brain. Taking, it seemed, an extra step before actually entering the realm of thought, as if there was some hidden circuit installed in his brain. Which, he suspected, was exactly what had happened. But the actual proof would have to wait. Until . . . later, he thought, trying to get used to the lag in his thought processes. It was like living a quarter second or so behind the normal human time frame. Not a particularly good survival tool, he thought. But the delay, he began to see, was more than offset by a clarity he had never previously known. It was as if he could see electricity moving into the toaster, cooking his waffles. Watching coffee emerge from the machine, a drop at a time. The water running in a cascading rainbow from the tap. His thoughts, focused and clear. If somewhat slow. But even as the world seemed new to him, there were still old problems to deal with.

He shuffled around in the bill folder and picked up the phone—the handheld set, disdaining the video connection, wondering how he had been tricked into using such a foolish device. He told the voice from the power company that their check would be in the mail today. Then he did the same with the bank, wondering at the blur of numbers on the many and varied accounting systems the average person was forced to deal with every day. At the time and effort which goes into making life so fucking complicated. Pitiful, really, how human beings use their resources. Perhaps that, too, was about to change. Then, before leaving the house, he made another call. To Harvey Woodson's office at Columbia.

"I'm sorry," the detached voice said. "Dr. Woodson isn't available. His office hours are from two to four on Friday. Would you like to make an appointment?"

"Please get a message to Dr. Woodson," Bracken said calmly. It was Tuesday, he thought, and there simply was not time to wait until the end of the week. "Tell him that Gary Bracken will meet him at three this afternoon at any place convenient to him, but that I would prefer his laboratory at the university."

"Sir, I can't—"

"Three this afternoon," Bracken cut off the secretary's protest. "Tell him it's extremely important."

Bracken hung up and dug out his checkbook, writing the promised checks for the mortgage, insurance, and electricity. Then he rifled the desk drawers, pushing aside the computer and lab equipment he moved upstairs since Becky's departure, finally coming up with an envelope containing the titles for his and Becky's automobiles. Becky had taken the Jeep, of course, leaving him with the four-year-old Volvo.

"A car that will really retain its value," the salesman had shilled shamelessly. "An investment in safety and economy, like putting your money in the bank."

Right, Bracken thought, laughing at himself, at his gullibility. He drove to the dealership and sold the car outright, for cash, to the bewildered salesman, getting three grand, half the book value. But it would be enough, he thought. Bracken caught a cab to the bank, deposited enough money to cover the checks he'd written, and stuffed the rest into his coat pocket. Even an enlightened madman, he knew, had to play the game according to the rules of whatever time frame he found himself in. Even though, in truth, there were no rules, other than those a person makes for himself. Particularly in these times, when the rules were about to change for everyone.

It was a little before noon when Bracken finished with the Gods of Commerce. He stopped and took a deep breath outside the mall where the bank was located. The sun was bright, almost warm. Melting snow running in tiny streams across the parking lot, picking up an oily slick as the rivulets passed over the tarmac. The debris of humanity being washed, virtually unnoticed, into the watersheds and oceans of the world. He felt the earth turning beneath him, moving in its swift arc around the sun. The sun, exhaling, breathing its radiating light across the planet. And he wanted to shout, to dance at the joy he felt, as a living entity upon this place. Bracken, his brain humming, felt connected in ways he did not yet understand to the past, the present, the future. He felt as if the earth itself was singing a song to the Universe, and he wanted to add his own voice to the chorus. But didn't. Not now, not here. Not yet. There were other people passing, staring at him out of the corners of their eyes, as if suspecting he was somehow different from them. And he was, for a while. But soon . . . soon, the Change would be upon them all. And it would be a time of great joy, or utter madness.

That thought chilled him. He blinked. Clarity. As though a fog had been lifted from his eyes. The people, it seemed, were not flesh and bone, but pillars of light. The trees, bare, leafless. He saw their bark covering, looked deeper at the living wood beneath. Patterned rings, like some oddly constructed child's toy. The trees, rising above him, solitary, alone. Mere remnants of their tribes, which had once covered the land. He blinked again, wondering if perhaps some chemical imbalance in his brain might be responsible for his thoughts, for the visions that had all but consumed him over the past days. But no, visions had been a part of his life since the moments of his first awareness. False illusions, he knew. Part of the carefully constructed reality which had somehow taken over the lives of all human beings. Well, that was about to Change, he thought. Either that, or he was completely and utterly mad. Bracken decided he did not care which was the true reality.

A pay phone caught his attention; he slid his TEL card across the slot and punched in numbers. Becky's secretary picked up the phone and smiled until she saw it was him.

"Is she in?" he asked.

"One moment, Dr. Bracken," the girl said curtly.

A long minute passed by, and finally his wife's image appeared on the screen. The look in her eyes told him that he was not yet forgiven. Anger and fear written into her face. And he hardly blamed her. Hers was the true reality.

"Becky . . ." he said, listening to her silence on the other end of the line.

"I'm sorry," he said finally. "I just wanted to talk, to look at you for a second."

More silence, then he could think of nothing more to say, and hung up. On the other end of the line, Rebecca stared at the blank screen, knowing she should have said something, anything. Her husband was going mad, he needed her, and she should have said something.

At precisely three in the afternoon, Bracken heard the slow, heavy steps of Harvey Woodson coming down the flight of stairs to his Columbia University laboratory. Bracken was waiting at the bottom of the stairwell, having arrived a half hour earlier. It had been impossible to wangle a key for the lab from Woodson's secretary, who seemed to take his presence in the office as a personal affront. So Bracken left word that he'd be waiting downstairs even as the woman had informed him—quite curtly, he noted—that she had been unable to confirm the appointment. But Bracken was certain the old man would show. Woodson, he knew, was an abnormally curious man and not likely to miss a chance to inspect firsthand what Bracken suspected he already knew. Namely, that something odd was taking place within the framework of the human brain. The Change which Bracken knew was upon him. Upon them all.

"Dr. Bracken." Woodson greeted him formally, negotiating the last of the laborious steps. "You know, I've been after them for years to install an elevator down here, but of course there was never enough money. Now, however, I'm convinced these stairs are keeping me alive. My physician says there's no better exercise. He's lying, of course, but I'm too old now to screw myself to better health."

Bracken grinned. In all the years he'd known him, Harvey Woodson hadn't changed, other than becoming a bit slower and more pronounced in his movements. As if he had to actually think about the motions his body was making even as he was doing them. Like a person walking on ice.

"You are looking pretty spry," Bracken offered as the old man fumbled with his ring of keys.

"Another lie," Woodson said, waving away the intended compliment. "No one looks good at my age. Adequate and upright are the only possible adjectives. The question is: How are you, Dr. Bracken? Word gets around, you know. Particularly when the news has a despairing twist to it."

Woodson turned now, staring at him, pushing the laboratory door open. Bracken felt suddenly like an insect specimen about to be pinned to a felt board.

"You're not all right, are you?" Woodson asked, with his customary lack of tact. A trait common to the very bright and the very old, Harvey Woodson falling neatly into both categories.

"I don't know," Bracken said, honestly, following

Woodson into the laboratory. "I was thinking that maybe you could tell me."

The lab itself was small, hardly the size of an average American kitchen, and it was an odd mixture of old and new. A computer console, of course; but stashed away in a corner of Woodson's desk was an antique Underwood manual typewriter. Beakers stored over a sink, a Bunsen burner set up on the counter. There were also other, more modern machines lining the walls. Harvey Woodson, Bracken saw, still commanded his own portion of the biology department's budget.

"You know I don't practice medicine anymore," Woodson said, watching him with a critical eye.

"I'm not looking for someone to *practice* on me," Bracken said, dead serious.

"Gary Bracken." Woodson laughed. "Always a quick boy. What is it, then? By God, you look like you've got a tiger by the tail."

"Maybe," Bracken admitted, settling into a chair by Woodson's desk. "You remember the context of our last meeting?"

Woodson nodded, and Bracken went on to describe, as best he could, the events of the past weeks, including the odd occurrences of the previous days.

"I want you to run an EEG on me," Bracken concluded. "Check my brain-wave patterns for any abnormalities. And I want you to keep the matter strictly between the two of us."

"As you wish." Woodson nodded, seemingly undisturbed by Bracken's revelations. Almost, Bracken thought, as if he had somehow expected them. "But you have to understand that my best advice, even before we do any testing, is for you to seek competent medical attention.

I'd be happy to provide the name of a discreet colleague. . . ."

Bracken shook the words aside.

"Let's just get on with it," he said, more sharply than
he intended. His nerves, he suddenly realized, were
frayed to the breaking point. The previous euphoria
seemed to have vanished into the ether.

"Sorry," he finished, knowing he was reacting to the
possibility that what he suspected was now about to be
proven correct.

"Quite all right," Woodson said, understanding Bracken's
response. He rolled out an equipment cart and began setting
up the EEG test, taping a series of monitoring disks around
Bracken's forehead. "Tell me, Dr. Bracken, do you think
stress qualifies as an emotion?"

"What?" Bracken asked.

"Forget it," Woodson said, waving off the question.
"You seem to be under a lot of stress lately, and I was
wondering if you'd had time to consider the feeling. Just
curious."

Bracken shook his head, blinking at the shadows
which seemed to be encroaching on the corners of his vision. Vision. Now, that was an odd word.

—Bright White. Memories of a small hut. Hot, sweating.
Paint on his body running in long, multicolored stripes.
Chanting sounds coming from those around him. From
his own mouth. Old men, sitting in a sweat lodge, somewhere in the depths of time. And he was with them. Old.
Chanting, praying. Paint dripping across the scars of a
lifetime. The thumping sounds of a single drum reverberating through his old bones. Praying. For what? he wondered. For wisdom and knowledge, the voice came to
him, speaking from the swirling mists of time.

• • •

He blinked. Woodson was saying something, ripping a long piece of graph paper out of the machine.

"Are you feeling ill?" Woodson sounded concerned.

Bracken realized he was sweating profusely.

"Do you want to lie down? Should I call an ambulance?"

"No," Bracken managed to say, slowly regaining his senses. At least he hoped he was regaining his senses. Who can tell, really? "I'm fine . . . I just . . . never mind. What's going on inside my head?"

"I don't know." Woodson shook his head, looking again at the reading. "There is a strong abnormality in your alpha waves. However, the motor skills are fine. The involuntaries, the heart and lung function, seem strong."

"I'm not going to die?" Bracken asked.

"Not anytime soon, I should think," Woodson said, his eyebrows furrowed up like mating caterpillars. A sign Bracken didn't like at all. "But again I would advise in the strongest terms, that you seek medical help. Have an MRI done as soon as possible. There's something—"

"There's something changing the way I think, isn't there?" Bracken asked. Woodson didn't meet his eyes. "And you know what it is. It's something you've seen before?"

Harvey Woodson nodded, but refused to elaborate. Like a man handed something he did not want to look at. Something strange. Something terrifying.

"There's an outside agent doing something to my memory, isn't there?" Bracken asked, his voice soft, almost accusing. The proof of what he suspected had now been brought forth into the light of day. And Harvey Woodson knew what it was, but somehow couldn't bring himself to speak of it. As if it were some obscene subject, suitable only for the censors or the book burners.

"That's a possibility," Woodson said, his voice dull and quiet. An old man who had seen too much of what the world had to offer.

"What is it?" Bracken demanded.

Woodson shook his head. Opening his mouth as if to speak, then closing it, thinking better of the idea.

"You've got to tell me!" Bracken almost shouted, catching himself, reaching for Woodson's arm. "I have a right to know."

"All right." Woodson sighed, closing his eyes for a long moment, as if giving in to the inevitable. "There was a directive issued several months ago by the CDC in Atlanta," he began, making an attempt to straighten his sagging shoulders, as if he was about to divest himself of a heavy weight. "A high-priority directive sent to the heads of psychiatric facilities, and to selected neurosurgeons who deal specifically in certain types of physical dysfunctions of the brain. It was a sealed report, hand-delivered by government agents. The FBI, it was said, although I have no proof of that. Those who received the report had to sign documents stating that under no circumstances were the contents of the directive to be released to the media, or the information given out to the general public. The penalties for violation were quite specific and extremely harsh. The report itself fell under the guidelines of the National Security Agency. I could be sent to a federal prison simply for telling you this much."

"The CDC," Bracken said quietly, the pieces falling into place. He had used the computer bank at the office, and the CDC had been tapping them. The Bureau of Industrial Research had, of course, been informed, and probably everything that happened in the whole fucking country ended up somewhere in the offices of the highly secretive NSA. The contents of his experiment, supposedly secure through the use of his own personal code number, had undoubtedly been opened by government computer experts. As simple as breaking a lock on a teenager's diary.

"The directive, it contained information about a viral invasion involving the human brain?" he asked.

"Yes," Woodson said, almost whispering. "The government wanted to keep the whole thing quiet. They didn't want to cause a panic in the populace, but they had to take some sort of action. There were increased incidences of what they called abnormalities in the neuron systems of supposedly normal people, and it was taking place on a national scale. So they tried to keep a lid on, the best way they could. The report described symptoms much like those you described, and provided an identification process involving the alpha readings on the brain. An increase in the regular base frequency of ten cycles per second, to just under eleven cycles per second. The irregularity shows itself in adults at the point where the alpha rhythms become desynchronized; that is, where they break off into the higher frequencies."

Woodson held out the printout from Bracken's EEG. Showing, Bracken saw, the very same irregularity.

"The CDC called for strict isolation of anyone falling within those parameters," Woodson continued. "And, of course, immediate notification sent to the disease center in Atlanta. I'm sorry, Gary, but it seems that at the moment there's very little that can be done in the way of treatment."

"But it's not an infection, is it?" Bracken asked. Woodson raised his eyebrows in response. "I mean it's not an actual disease," he clarified. "People don't get sick from it. You said I was healthy, other than this anomaly."

"There have been no casualties directly related to the condition," Woodson agreed. "At least none that I'm aware of. Some people, apparently, are able to deal with the effects—the hallucinating dementia—better than others. Like yourself, for example. That's why it's impossible to get a hard count on how many people are actually involved. How many 'victims of the phenomenon' there really are, to quote the report."

"Still, it's not an infection in the classic sense," Bracken said, more to himself than Woodson. "I mean, it's more like a process. A mutation. A change in the brain's anatomy."

"It's not even that," Woodson said hesitantly. "The brain itself is not physically altered. It's more a matter of the viruses . . . well, they seem to be planting roots along the neuron extremities. Sort of like microscopic vines growing along the nerve endings of the brain cells."

Bracken stared at his old friend. Like army ants building a bridge across a ravine, he thought. Only in this case, the bridge is being built along the neural fibers of the brain. *My brain*, he thought, and the reality of it slammed into him, taking his breath away.

"I didn't mean to upset you," Woodson said, making a discernible effort to keep his voice calm. "But you wanted to know."

Bracken nodded, swallowing the lump that was suddenly growing in his throat.

"It's as though the viruses have found a way to gain access to portions of the brain, specifically the cerebral cortex," Woodson commented, as if the whole thing held a certain warped fascination for him.

And they're inside *my* head, Bracken heard himself think. He blinked, not certain if he was crying or not.

a molecule of time

Day One + 1.2775 x 10 ^12

He was startled every time a bank of lights was lit or darkened, every time a heavy door clanged shut. The hard metal-on-metal sound reverberating, ringing in his ears, actually causing the air around him to vibrate. He could see the air shimmering. Dozens of times a day. The doors clanging, the light banks coming on with a *whoosh!* in the morning, and dying with a thunderous silence at night.

Dying. With a thunderous silence. He was about to die. About to enter the dark, unknown realms of endless oblivion. Of course, everyone was going to die, sooner or later. It was just that Marvin Barnes knew *when* he was going to die, and it was sooner rather than later. In a little over nine hours. Nine hours and ten minutes, to be precise. Midnight, exactly. At that time, Barnes knew, the state of Texas was going to exact its revenge on his poor, white ass. They were going to strap him to a gurney, stick a needle in his arm, and kill him. And there

wasn't a goddamned thing he could do, except sit here
and wait for them to do it. Sure, he could fight some.
Drag his feet, make it harder for the guards to do what
they were gonna do anyway. But he'd already been told,
quietly, in private, that causing trouble probably wasn't
such a good idea. Lots of times, when guys fought at the
end, there seemed to be problems finding the right vein,
and a man might have to get stuck four or five times, depending on how hard he made it on everybody. And there
could be other problems with the execution, the like of
which Marvin Barnes didn't even want to consider. No,
it was definitely going to happen and there wasn't jack-
shit he could do about it, so Barnes guessed it was better
to let the thing happen as smoothly and painlessly as
possible.

Everyone said it was a smooth way to go. Listen, Marvin, they stick you with a little needle, and you go to
sleep. It can't get any easier than that. At least that's what
the guards, the doctor, and the warden all said. Of course,
he knew they wouldn't hesitate to lie to him, if it made
killing him any easier.

Jesus, he was sweating again. His hands shaking, legs
like fucking rubber bands. He couldn't even pace his cell
anymore. The Death Cell. A guard sitting at a desk in
front of him, reading a newspaper. Marvin shivered.
Damn, his clothes were soaked. Sticky and cold. He
pulled the scratchy woolen blanket around him. The
guard glanced up at the movement, then went back to his
paper. Quiet. They were all quiet around him now. Speaking only when necessary, and then only the precise lines
the procedure called for. He was a dead man, and no one
wanted to talk to the dead. Except for the preacher man,
but Barnes had gotten tired of the Jesus Will Save You
rap, and told the preacher to go save somebody else. Be-

cause if there was a God, Barnes told him, He sure as hell wouldn't let a man die like some fucking dog being put to sleep.

Even though Marvin Barnes, in the rational part of his mind, knew he had it coming. He had, after all, stuck the sawed-off into the face of the clerk at the gas station he'd robbed, and pulled the trigger. Blood and brains all over the fucking place. All over the money, Barnes's clothes, the shotgun, everything. Like he'd stuck a bomb in the kid's mouth and lit the goddamn fuse. That was how they'd caught him. Blood, like glue, sticking to everything. And why he'd done it, Barnes couldn't say. It had just happened, like a lot of things in his life. And now he was going to die. The only thing that could be hoped for was that they weren't lying. That it would be an easy death, and he wouldn't scream or blubber when they did it to him.

Shaking, sweating, biting his lip. Barnes wanted to get up and pour himself a drink of water, but didn't trust his body. The table in the center of the cell seemed a long way off, so he rolled some spit around in his mouth. They brought in his last meal and set it on the table. Steak and fries, but the smell was nauseating, and Marvin knew he wouldn't be able to eat any of it. What was the point, anyway? A couple of hours now, and . . .

And what? he asked himself. Shivering, sweating, the dread overtaking him, turning the spit to ashes in his mouth.

He had begun to feel detached, as if everything around was unreal, somehow. As if he could almost get up and walk right through the bars. Through the walls and the main gate. Out into the moonlight of a soft, Texas evening. And what then? he asked himself. Look for a better, less public way to die, he thought.

Of course, this wasn't the worst way to go out. It wasn't even the worst way Barnes himself had died. After months of soul-searching, of wading through the nightmares that plagued him with all their vivid reality, Marvin Barnes had come to the conclusion that he had done this before, in one form or another. And in all probability would do it again, in another life. It was the way Eternity had of fucking some people over, he thought. Barnes knew with certainty that he had died as a criminal many, many times in the past. The memories were simply too real, too vivid to be anything else.

In his dreams on Death Row, Marvin Barnes had known the pain of crucifixion. Of hanging on a cross, with nails driven into his wrists and feet, gasping for breath in the hot sun, shivering naked in the lonely, dark hours of the night. He had felt the searing pain of flames licking his flesh as he tried desperately to suck smoke into his lungs to end the agony, tied to a courtyard stake. He heard the trapdoor of the gallows swing down, dropping away from under his feet. Recalled with perfect clarity that strange instant of weightlessness, then falling . . . falling for a mile, it seemed. The gagging, smothering loop of rope tugging at his throat. Tugging softly at first, then tightening with terrible suddenness, crushing his windpipe—followed closely by the faraway cracking sound of his neck breaking. He remembered the cold, sharp blade of the headsman's ax touching the back of his neck. The whistling sound as it cut the air above him on its downward arc. The heavy thump, the jerking of the body, the confused, dizzying feeling as the severed head was held up to the crowd. Seeing, in a blinding haze, the last few seconds of light. The dull roar in his ears.

These, and other deaths Marvin Barnes felt he had known, somewhere, sometime. And he found this knowl-

edge comforting in an odd sort of way, when they came
for him this time. The loud clang of the cell door opening. Someone telling him it was time. As if he hadn't
known. Time, again. Shaking off the heavy blanket, trying to stand. The world, a long tunnel through which he
walked, his prison slippers scraping the floor as the
guards at his elbows made him feel as though he was
walking on layers of air. The long, long hall, the room,
the gurney, everything sanitized and scrubbed, like some
bizarre hospital for the dead.

Wait, he wanted to say. I have to use the bathroom. . . .

But before Barnes even realized what was happening,
they had him on his back, on the gurney, pulling the
straps tight around him. Arms stretched out and strapped
down so he could only move his fingers. And his toes, he
realized. It was good, Marvin thought, that he could wig-
gle his toes. Cold. Sudden and quick. He tried to jerk his
head down to look, but couldn't really see what they were
doing. His pants were down, and they were sticking
something in his ass. And stretching out his dick! Panic,
sharp and horrible, rolling his stomach. He moaned,
thinking he was going to puke. Terrified they were going
to castrate him before they killed him. Like one time in
his dreams.

No. A catheter, he remembered someone telling him,
days ago, when it became obvious they were really going
to kill him. A catheter, so he didn't mess himself. It
burned. Jesus, it burned. He tried to twist away, but of
course was unable to move. Then they covered him with
a white blanket and he was warm again. Sweating hot as
they opened the curtains so the witnesses could watch. It
wasn't right that they let people watch while he was put
to sleep like a rabid dog. He was a human being, not an
animal. Their eyes, staring at him, watching as the fear of

impending death played across his face. But there was no
time to care about any of that. The doctor was standing
near one of his outstretched arms. Eyes squinting, hands
pale, wrapped in rubber gloves, holding the needle, sliding it across Barnes's arm. The needle piercing his arm,
and he winced at the momentary pain. But in a second it
was gone. This wasn't so bad. Wasn't so bad, he thought.
He could do it. He wanted to tell them that it was okay—
that he could do it. But Barnes's mouth was dry, the
words like dust in his throat. The lights bright, blinding.
He blinked, sweat rolling into his eyes.

The warden was reading the death warrant. Asking him
if he wanted to say anything. Barnes did. Something
quick and funny. Make them laugh. Make them remember how well he went out. But the words were like sand
in his throat. He tried to spit them out, saying nothing.
Everyone stepped back. Heads nodding, a hum of machinery. A thud, he thought, like the trapdoor of a gallows
dropping away. Then a dark fog rolling across his vision.
Dreams of choking, of dying . . .

*Within the body of their host, the virus clans died as well.
The electronic matrix of the host's brain fired its last
charge, and then grew quiet. The host's flesh began to
cool, the cells expiring from the lack of oxygen. For the
clans, it was a slow, lingering death. But as the sacrifice
of hosts was unavoidable, so, too, was the loss of many
clans trapped within these dying bodies. Martyrs to the
cause of Change. If this particular experiment did not
produce the desired results, others would. Evolution was,
after all, a harsh, demanding business.*

seventeen

Paul Sandborn's head hurt and his legs were twitching like a science lab frog. The legs, of course, warning him of imminent incoming; his head, meanwhile, was attempting to distract him from the unpleasant information he was about to receive from the director of the CDC.

Christ, but it had been a mind-numbing day, he thought miserably, waiting in Lang's Atlanta office while the good doctor attended to some personal business in the bathroom. A few minutes had passed, and Sandborn began wondering if he should check on the director. Just to be sure the man hadn't pulled a Harvey Mitchell on him. That being to stick a gun into your mouth and pull the trigger, leaving a highly visible corpse parked in a government lot, inside a fairly new Caddy, that would never get clean enough for resale. Not to mention an equally revealing suicide note, outlining the NSA/BIR cover-up of a health threat to the American public. At least, that had been Mitchell's take on things. Only sheer

luck got Sandborn's agents there in time to take possession of Harvey's accusing note.

The *Washington Post* would have had a fucking field
day with that, Sandborn thought, breathing a small sigh
of relief when he heard Jeffery Lang finishing up in the
bathroom. Harvey Mitchell had been mighty busy, all
right. Who'd have thought the old drunk had it in him to
root around like that and actually do some first-class
covert information gathering? Even though what he
learned had proved, in the end, to be too much for him.
Thus the gun-in-the-mouth, take-me-out-of-the-ball-
game trick shot to the head. Then again, Sandborn considered, maybe something else had caused ol' Harvey to
take a little close-up target practice. Maybe Mitchell felt
something strange going on inside his head, and knowing
now what it was, simply choose the Big Bang alternative.
And if it came right down to put-up or shut-up time,
Sandborn knew, there was no way to tell he wouldn't do
the same thing himself.

He hoped not, however, believing that bullets were the
option of last resort. Certainly the tranquilizer of last resort. But then, he wasn't going crazy. At least he didn't
think so.

Jeffery Lang smiled at him, drying his hands with a
paper towel. The smile weak and forced, the drying action continuing far longer than was necessary. Stress was
like a spiderweb, Sandborn knew, entangling them all in
its sticky net. A bad simile, perhaps, Sandborn considered, until he realized that was exactly how he felt. Like
a moth that had blundered into an unseen obstruction and
now had some grotesque monster bearing down on him.
Only it wasn't a monster in the classic sense, but instead
a bug, a microbe, a fucking virus.

"I feel like we're back in the thirteenth century, discussing the finer aspects of the bubonic plague," Sandborn said jokingly as Dr. Lang sat down and began shuffling through the notes on his desk.

"Have you been having any vivid recollections of that time period?" Lang asked, suddenly shifting his focus to Sandborn's eyes.

"What time period?" Sandborn asked, momentarily confused.

"The thirteenth century," Lang reminded him.

"God, no!" Sandborn said quickly, coughing a short, sharp laugh. "Nothing like that at all. Sorry, a bad attempt at a little gallows humor."

"You understand that sudden, released memories might be an indication of the condition?" Lang asked. Sandborn nodded. "And I trust you'd report any abnormal events as soon as they occurred? It would, of course, be in your best interests to do so. We have had some success—"

"You've had no success," Sandborn said, reminding Lang of CDC's failure. "Unless you count hitting someone in the head with a thinly padded baseball bat. That's the only thing I've read about that begins to serve as an effective treatment."

"That's grossly unfair!" Lang protested, his own anger rising, then quickly ebbing on the wave of exhaustion the outburst cost him. "It might be correct, but it sure as hell is unfair."

"You're right, I apologize." Sandborn shook his head. "It's this *thing*—it's got us all on edge. I read your report on Mount Sinai. A first-class mess. By the way, I'd suggest you keep any written material on this matter to a bare minimum."

"You're not asking me to delete potentially vital information from my reports?" Lang glared. "I can't do that, and you know it. If this all blows up on us, there has to be a record of what took place."

"For who?" Sandborn asked.

"Posterity," Lang said, a dull smile creeping back across his thin face. "And there will be a posterity. This is not the plague, or some AIDS mutation, or the super-flu. We're not all going to die. Not right away, anyway."

"What it is, then?" Sandborn challenged, as if daring the other man to tell him.

"A new viral strain, certainly," Lang said carefully. "At least new to us. Probably something that's been around for forever, and we're only just now seeing it. Clearly, the virus itself is important, but there are other considerations as well."

"Such as?" Sandborn asked.

"Well, the virus isn't a disease-causing microbe, for one thing," Lang said. "That is, it's not attacking the immune system, nor altering the cell structure in any significant manner, other than harvesting a few cells to reproduce it-self. That's why an antibody is going to be difficult to come up with. It seems to be a very passive viral strain."

"Only it's invading people's minds," Sandborn pointed out.

"True, to some degree," Lang agreed. "It is incorporat-ing itself into the neuron structure of the cortex. No ques-tion about that. But it's doing so in a most unobtrusive manner. Almost as though it's becoming part of the brain structure."

"So what in God's name is going on?" Sandborn de-cided to get to the heart of the matter. There were already calls to his office, asking him to file a report on Harvey Mitchell's death as soon as possible.

"In my opinion," Lang said, even more carefully,

"what we're seeing might be best described as an evolutionary surge."

Paul Sandborn shook his head and groaned. Lang had hinted at this before, and now it was out in the open, no doubt recorded by Lang's personal security devices. Blurted into the formal record, where Sandborn would actually have to deal with it.

"That's crazy," Sandborn said, for the record, on the odd chance he would one day have to defend himself before a military tribunal.

"Not really." Jeffery Lang held his ground. "There's a very well-constructed theory stating that evolution is not the slow, steady, plodding process scientists once thought it to be. Fossil evidence suggests that in many cases evolution happens quickly, suddenly, and then levels out for long periods."

"Yes, but you're talking about us! About human beings, for God's sake!" Sandborn hissed angrily.

"And human beings can't evolve?" Lang asked, almost laughing. "What do you think we've been doing for the last four million years? A quarter of a million years ago your ancestors could barely speak their own names. How do you think we came to be where we are today? Evolution. An almost unprecedented surge of evolutionary change and selection. The last bit of which took place only some one hundred thousand years ago, or thereabouts. So why shouldn't we continue evolving? In fact, we are. All of us. Right here, right now."

"But you can't see evolution," Sandborn protested.

"Why not, if it's a dramatic enough surge?" Lang shrugged. "Something that only takes a few generations to entrench itself in the population. Why shouldn't we be able to see it, on some level? To document it, even. Just because it hasn't happened during the extremely short period of recorded history doesn't mean it *can't* happen. Or even that it shouldn't happen. And once it does, in fifty or a hundred thousand years, it's doubtful anyone will remember the process, or the upheaval it caused. Things will simply be what's considered 'normal' for that particular time."

"Are you feeling all right?" Sandborn asked, trying to be sarcastic.

"Tired," Lang admitted. "I could curl up on the floor and sleep for two days. No fooling."

"Maybe you'd better," Sandborn suggested.

Lang smiled away the remark.

"Do you want to finish the briefing, or not?" he asked pointedly. Sandborn nodded, seeming to press out the creases in his pants. "You read the Mount Sinai report. The scenario has repeated itself in several other cities, although the media has been kept out of the loop up to this point."

"That's something," Sandborn said, shaking his head, dreading the briefing he himself was going to have to give to his superiors.

"Don't expect that piece of luck to continue." Lang reinforced Sandborn's own thoughts. "In all probability, this phenomenon is going to continue to escalate. A media leak is unavoidable. Frankly, I'm surprised it hasn't happened already."

It has, Sandborn didn't say, knowing his agency had stepped in to squash more than a dozen press investigations. But Lang was right, he knew. It was only a matter of time before somebody went public, and then all hell was sure to break loose. The National Guard might have to be called up if things got any worse, maybe even army regulars. But what happens if they get whatever the hell this is? He wanted to call it an infection, but knew Dr. Lang wouldn't let him get away with it.

"Give me the worst-case scenario," Sandborn said, deciding to cut to the chase.

"The worst-case scenario . . ." Lang echoed, giving himself time to formulate a reply Sandborn would accept. No easy matter, given the actual facts. "I'd have to say that would be someone, somewhere in the world, who has access to nuclear weapons becoming delusional and blowing up the world."

"Sweet Christ." Sandborn sighed, considering the safeguards built into the worldwide launch systems, wondering if they were secure enough to withstand a full-blown Plague of Madness, as the phenomenon was being called by those inside the loop. "Is that really a possibility?" he asked.

"You'd know the answer to that better than I would." Lang shrugged, deeply concerned that this seemed to be the first time such a possibility had been considered. It confirmed his own suspicions that the world was being run by people who were woefully unqualified for the job.

Sandborn sighed, shaking his head some more, deciding to approach the problem from another angle, looking desperately for one he could actually control.

"Okay," he said, focusing his attention away from his twitching legs. "Let's look at it another way. How many people are going to be affected by this thing?"

"Well, I'd have to say that eventually everyone will be," Lang said, trying to keep his response calm and clinical.

"Everyone?" Sandborn almost jumped out of his chair.

"Eventually," Lang said. "But that's several generations down the line. Unless, of course, we find a way to reverse the process. Which I doubt, as it does seem to be a widespread mutation. Indeed, if we should even try to stop it. This may actually be a positive thing, you know, as disruptive as it might seem to us at the present time. Studies indicate that human beings only use a small portion of our cognitive powers. Only ten percent of our brains, by some estimates. It's been a mystery, really, why that's so. The answer may well be that we've simply been waiting around, from an evolutionary standpoint, for a mutation of this sort to take place. The Change could easily work to our benefit, adding appreciably to our knowledge base and memory storage. We'll have a better idea in a generation or two. Assuming, of course, we survive."

"What in God's name are you saying?" Sandborn's patience was quickly evaporating. "Are you saying the human race is about to become extinct? Something tells me the president isn't going to want to hear that!"

To Sandborn's surprise, Jeffery Lang laughed.

"I suppose that would throw a serious monkey wrench into the reelection campaign," Lang said, still chuckling, despite the enraged look on Sandborn's face. "I don't know what's going to happen to the human race." He shook his head. "No one does. But whatever events transpire, you and I will be long gone before they reach any critical point, and the president will be just another page in the history books."

"Then we're not going to all go crazy and die off like dinosaurs?" Sandborn reached for the glimmer of hope the CDC director seemed to offer.

"No, I didn't say that, either," the man said, suddenly serious again. "But you have to understand, mutation—even if it takes place quickly by our standards—will still take a number of generations to firmly establish itself into the populace. Among people who are living today, my guess would be that no more than fifteen to twenty percent of the adults will be outwardly affected. A higher number among the newborn population, because the neuron-cell mutation seems to be increasing in frequency."

"Fifteen or twenty percent," Sandborn repeated, mostly to himself. It was, he knew, a considerable figure. Millions of people. But still, he thought, within manageable levels. He found himself somehow relieved that civilization was not about to end. Not on his watch, anyway.

"And out of that number, some will be more radically affected than others," Lang went on, pleased that Sandborn seemed to have calmed himself.

"Then we'll be able to maintain critical services." Sandborn was now thinking out loud. "Food, medical, defense, that sort of thing."

"Probably," Lang agreed. "There will be some pockets of the population more severely affected than others. It'll clearly be a drain on our resources, but we should be able to manage. The real problems will come later, and they could well be catastrophic."

"What do you mean?" Sandborn's voice was now cold and controlled. Like a battlefield commander weighing his options.

"Mutations are not introduced unilaterally into a population base," Lang explained. "Although this case is clearly unique, as the change is taking place on two separate levels. That is, within both the virus community and the human host. But still, you're going to have a pronounced, and perhaps radical difference in the population base."

"I still don't understand," Sandborn admitted, his frustration level rising along with his blood pressure.

"All right, here it is in a nutshell." Lang sat back in his chair and stared at the ceiling. "As the Change takes place, even if it happens swiftly, human beings are going to be divided into two distinct camps—those who have undergone the Change, and those who have not. At this point we'll find out if the mutation is positive or negative. That is, who among the two camps will have an evolutionary advantage. Whoever does will become dominant, perhaps even starting a new line of Homo sapiens. That's exactly what happened when modern man appeared on scene. There were at least two other distinct lines of early humans existing at that time—Homo erectus and Neanderthal populations. Today, we send teams of archaeologists out into the field to find their bones. Whatever happened back in that time, it was swift and surgically precise. We survived and everyone else has been turned into museum exhibits."

"But it's not the same thing," Sandborn protested—feebly, he knew.

"In fact, it may be exactly the same thing," Lang said. "The general expert opinion is that modern man experienced some sort of advantageous cognitive mutation. Simply put, we became smarter, better able to process information than the other human lineages around at that time. And the next thing you know, they're a footnote on the evolutionary time line, and we're making gold crowns to proclaim ourselves Masters of the World. Today, right this moment, we have what is essentially a viral invasion of the human thought machine, the cerebral cortex. A mating, if you will, of parasite and host. The cortex is an incredibly complicated structure. Its function, really, is somewhat of a mystery—how and why it works, the massive, yet curiously untapped power contained within that part of the brain. The virus colonies seem to be positioning themselves among the cells and nerve strings, along the neural pathways taken by the electrical impulses the brain generates. Why, of course, we don't know. But they appear to be activating a memory sequence using encoded protein molecules carried within their own genetic structure. That is, they seem to have a vast storehouse of chemically retained memories, and these memories are implanting themselves along the cortex, sometimes briefly eclipsing our own primary thoughts. Viruses, as you know, are parasitic organisms. They use the host—ourselves in this case—to perform functions which they themselves are not capable of. Now, the goal of any parasitic organism is to live as harmoniously as possible with the host. The symbiotic relationship, I'm sure you recall from the basic biology classes we all took in school. This particular event might well represent the next phase in the human/virus relationship."

"And you're saying medically we can do nothing about this so-called *relationship*?" Sandborn asked. "That these viruses are free to enter our brains, control our thoughts, and there's nothing we can do about it?"

"You're missing the point," Lang said carefully. "They're not controlling our thoughts. They're augmenting our mental process by adding their own chemical memories. In the most basic terms, they're supplementing our memories by infusing their own. Perhaps they're using our generated electrical impulses to access their own memory proteins. Who can say? But the truth is, we may well find that mankind as a whole has a lot to learn from this sort of knowledge infusion. It makes sense, actually, from an evolutionary standpoint."

"I've got news for you," Sandborn said bitterly. "None of this makes sense."

"It does when you take a hard look at the facts, and at the pattern of human evolution," Lang said, his voice falling away to a whisper, as he collected his thoughts.

"Remember, it wasn't that long ago when modern humans first began to leave behind fossil remains. Previous to our appearance, there was a whole herd of ancestral hominids from whom we descended. The various Australopithecus branches, a few early homo species, then suddenly out of the blue—us. Big brain, world dominators, the whole nine yards. We immediately, and I mean immediately, replaced or engulfed all the lingering prototypes. The Neanderthals and Homo erectus populations, who were our closest ancestors. The general assumption, for lack of any other, was that we accomplished this feat through the use of our highly improved brain power. However, the Neanderthals had developed brains which were at least the equal of our own. And Homo erectus wasn't that far behind, in terms of brain development. So something happened, we don't know what, which gave Homo sapiens a distinct advantage in terms of survival ability. In other words, our ancestors experienced an evolutionary spurt, and it had something to do with our cognitive functions. We were somehow able to think better than our ancestors, despite the fact that their brains were not that different from our own."

"And we have no idea what that was?" Sandborn asked, finding the whole thing incredible.

"Not at the moment," Lang replied. "But I believe we're about to find out. Do you know what was in the lines of code this Bracken fellow was able to translate?"

Sandborn shook his head, his legs twitching out of control.

"It was an indication that the virus community is in the process of instituting a change on their primary hosts," Lang said. "Namely, us. This Change, the early stages of which we've actually identified, has something to do with the human thought process. It is my opinion that as we delve more deeply into the protein molecules of the virus communities, we're going to discover that this same sort of change took place when Homo sapiens broke off from our ancestral line."

"So you're saying that right now, today, we're the primitive population?" Sandborn heard himself ask.

"It's entirely possible," Lang said, leaning back in his chair, considering the implications of what he had just put on the record.

Before he left the university laboratory, Bracken had to promise Woodson he would seek medical attention. Both of them, he felt, realized it was an empty promise.

—Bright White. Flashing memories, infusing themselves into his thoughts. Cold, reptilian blood in his veins. Staring up at familiar yet unknown stars. More stars spilling across the night sky than he had ever seen. Fear, anticipation of some vaguely perceived disaster. A thunderous, blinding explosion. Then darkness, deeper than he had ever known. Extending outward, toward infinity . . .

He blinked, realizing he had somehow gotten himself into a taxi. The street familiar to him, close to home and sanctuary. The cabbie staring in the rearview mirror.

"You okay, pal?" the guy asked, obviously wondering if he had made a mistake picking up this fare.

"Migraine," Bracken whispered, rubbing his eyes, trying to center himself. It felt as though he was swimming in a cloud of confusion. Like a ship fighting a sudden, impenetrable fog bank, searching desperately for a safe harbor.

"My sister gets them." The cabbie nodded, sounding

both sympathetic and relieved at the explanation. "They're a son-of-a-bitch."

Bracken nodded. A block or two to go, and he felt if he could just sleep for a while, things might be better. Maybe Woodson was right, he considered. Maybe he should get some help. Surely he would be forced to, if this madness continued. . . . Something up ahead caught his eye. Something odd. But it was a struggle to determine if it was real or not. A dark van parked in his driveway. Several cars pulled right up on the lawn. Men in FBI jackets coming out the front door. The cabbie slowed, reading the street numbers. The men, he saw, were loading his computer and lab equipment into the back of the van.

"No!" he said sharply. The bastards, they were stealing his experiment, his life. And he knew the next thing they were going to steal was his freedom.

"What?" The cabdriver turned toward him.

"Take me to the nearest motel," Bracken said, reaching into his coat pocket, pulling out twenty-dollar bills, throwing them into the front seat. "Quickly!" He almost yelled, throwing more money in the man's direction.

"You got it, mister," the cabbie said, scooping up the cash, hammering the gas pedal.

Bracken ducked down as they swept by. The cabbie, having seen more than his share of strangeness, followed the principal rule of his trade: the customer with cash is always right. He hardly gave a second glance at the FBI raid, which he knew was in progress. Drugs, taxes, maybe a little counterfeiting. But the bills looked good, so he didn't really give a shit. The government was always hassling somebody, he knew. A few minutes later he wheeled into a Holiday Inn. Bracken took more money from his pockets.

"You took me to the airport," Bracken said.

"Have a nice flight, pal." The man grinned.

—Bright White. Memories dancing across his brain. Some fleeting, yet vivid and intense. Others panoramic, seeming to take years, centuries to unfold. Shapes and colors. Feelings so real and deep, he could do nothing but weep until they passed. His mind felt as though it was caught in a firestorm of emotion and remembering. As though he was reliving a myriad of lives and experiences so far removed from his own that they were, for the most part, incomprehensible. The life-and-death struggles of worlds, stars, entire sectors of space itself. He saw life rising up from the most humble beginnings, flourishing for aeons, only to meet the fate of all life—death and destruction. The memories of millennia passed before his eyes in the span of minutes, leaving him exhausted, drenched in sweat. His mind, a swirl of confusion. Yellow light touching him with a soft, caressing hand. The Hundreds, rising up out of the sand, hatching from long-buried leather eggs. The Circle, filled with chanting monsters. Voices raised in complicated rhythms to call forth Gods of unimaginable power and vengeance. Madness stalking him like a sharp-toothed ghost . . .

The bed, the sheets smelled like old horse blankets. He blinked, looking at the clock on the dressing table: 5:25, he saw. But what day? He realized he had no idea. The Madness, drifting around him like billowing storm clouds. Bracken shook his head, slowly realizing he was in the here and now. In the moment of reality where his life was being lived. Could it possibly be the same afternoon? The same day in which he had managed to check into this tiny, reeking room? He turned on the television,

desperate for temporal information, yet terribly appre-
hensive about what he might learn.

A smiling, dronelike person on the Weather Channel
was calmly reporting the temperatures from across the
nation. Record highs in some cities, while a cold front
was moving across the east. It struck him as incredibly
strange that an entire television channel was devoted
solely to the weather. But the date scrolling across the
bottom of the screen told him that, indeed, only a few
hours had passed. A few hours. A few days. A few aeons.
The difference, he now understood, was minimal at best.
Time and place seemed to have slipped completely away
from him. He was deeply afraid for a moment when he
considered this idea. It was a dizzying, confusing feeling
of timelessness. It actually terrified him, until he realized
that he felt strangely . . . immortal.

Bracken fumbled for the phone, punching in the only
number he could remember. The other end of the line
rang for a long time before a voice answered.

"Becky?" he said. "It's me. I have to see you. . . ."

—Bright White. Knowledge he couldn't understand.
Coaxial angles, gravity sliding, complex mathematical
systems involving numbers too great for him to grasp.
Things he would never understand. But someone would
understand, he realized. If not now, today, then someday.
A year, a century, they were almost the same. The knowledge would make sense to someone, sometime. The thunder of great engines exploding in a deep, penetrating
rumble. Fading away to silence as the ship gathered
speed and the force fields around it disrupted the laws of
physics, as human beings knew them. The huge vessel
pushing outward, beyond the boundaries of the blue sun's
gravitational pull. Manned by beings cloaked in light.

And he was one of them. Explorers, seeking knowledge in the depths of space. Beings who were ONE with the virus clans. Beings who left footsteps miles long in the shifting sands of dark moons . . .

The persistent knocking revived him, forcing him away from the memory of the Explorers. Forced him to the door, which he opened without looking.

"Becky," he said, trying to smile.

She, staring at him for a long moment, before putting a hand over her mouth and starting to cry.

a molecule of time

Day One + 1.2775 x 10 ^12

The One worked slowly through the body of the host. Floating down swift rivers in the darkness of the interior flesh. Sightless, unaware of light or the lack thereof. Operating without any of the senses of the living, save one—that of touch. Brushing against the cells it encountered, the One searched for the proper receptor, the correct protein sequence, the door which would grant entrance to the heart of the cell it had been programmed to change. And through this change, continue the clans' links to the past, present, and future—the One's own heritage. Those links forged over 3.5 billion years, and back further still, to the deeper realms of time and space. The link, the knowledge, unknown to the One, as it proceeded with its labors, pursuing its goals with the tools of instinct and perseverance. Even the grand potential of its work, the cosmic possibilities of ONE remained closed to it.

Touching, floating in the darkness. Aware only of

the chemical interaction between itself and the target cells.

—Bright White. Light, a tiny sun blinking suddenly into existence in the dark heart of the subterranean cavern. The light, flashing along the neural paths of the host. Passing from neuron cell to axon to the dendrite fibers, leaping across the synaptic cleft in a blaze of electricity and chemical proteins. From cell to cell across the long chain of the cortex, knowledge and memory moved at blinding speeds. The host, functioning only with the limited senses of the physical realm, unaware of the continuous flashes of light working their way across its brain.

The One, drifting, comes into contact with the protein shell of the neuron cell. Driven by instinct, the One attaches itself to the target cell. Extending a long, whiplike stinger from its body, the One penetrates the body of the cell and injects itself into the cellular mass, leaving behind a tiny, lifeless husk on the outer shell of the neuron cell. Within the cell, the proteins of the One reassemble and seek the true target—the genetic strings of DNA, the operational mechanism of the cell itself. There, the proteins of the One attach themselves to the strings of DNA, programming the latent reproductive machinery of the neuron cell to produce the Many. And these burst forth from the confines of the reproduction cell, a cloud of swarming, microscopic flies. Here the Change comes to both host and parasite, for the newly hatched viruses do not seek more cells to invade, but rather entwine themselves like thin, invisible vines along the electronic pathways of the axons and dendrites. They wrap themselves in the terminal fibers of the neuron cell, their bodies touching in a matrix of thin tentacles.

The One, becoming the Many, seeking to become ONE.

The long-sought goal as close now as the synaptic gap, where neurotransmitting proteins pass between the brain cells. There, in a strange mix of soft electrical charges and chemical exchanges, the act of thought takes place. Memories are recalled, encoded protein molecules are scanned for the information they contain. The matrix of the clan, joining with the fibers and nerve strings of the cortex cells, wrapping like the finest wire ribbons around the long cord of the axon. Twisting in an almost forgotten dance. The Many, becoming ONE with the host. An event of historic importance, for both host and parasite. An exchange of gifts—the clans offering billions of years of history in return for the gift of thought. The Many, touched now by the soft flashes of electricity. Adding their own encoded proteins to the flow of chemical molecules passing through the gap of the synaptic cleft. The charged molecules pass over the memory structures of the host's cortex, and through the virus clans themselves. And within the living matrix constructed by the Many, the clans become, at long last, ONE.

—Bright White. Memories. Storied for impossible lengths of time, flooding the collective mind of the clan. A rain of encoded molecules, charged by the massive electronic field of the host's brain. Flowing down the long, living ribbon of the matrix, combining with the neurotransmitter chemicals of the host's cells. Becoming, once again, memory. Exquisite, yet maddening in its intensity.

—Bright White. Memories. The sky seen through long-dead, blinking eyes. Stars, suns, worlds of forgotten origins. Clouds, pillars of swirling sand. The touch of sunlight on a host's skin. Colors and scents recalled in a flurry of remembering. A storm of images. Water tumbling down a mile-high cliff. The feel of fur, skin, scale, feather, bone. Cloaks of soft woven material. Memories of light and living. Fluttering, multiwinged insects.

Memories. Of darkness and light. Pain and pleasure. Victory and defeat. Emotions cased in protein molecules for millions, billions of years. Released in a flooding torrent of Bright White remembering. Seeing, smelling, touching. Touching not the soft shells of countless cells, but the outside world. Outside worlds. The hum, the buzz of life. Books, scrolls, words etched in stone, whispered histories in languages long dead when the Solar System was still a mass of swirling dust. Knowledge gained and lost. Perhaps, with luck, gained again.

—Bright White . . .

eighteen

Bracken woke sometime during the darkest, middle hours of the night. For a moment he couldn't remember where he was. Or when. Or who. A moment of intense panic in which he was afraid to move, or even breathe. The darkness, supplemented only by the red glow of a digital clock. And that was the clue he needed. It was safe now to move, to look around.

Rebecca lay beside him on the bed. He recalled that she hadn't said anything after her arrival, merely holding him while darkness and sleep overtook them. He remembered explaining to her, as best he could, what had happened. What he thought was taking place in his mind, and perhaps in all their minds. He spoke of the coming Change, of the many Changes he had seen in his memories of time and space. Her response had been curious, he thought. Becky simply held him, and he had been aware that she was crying as she kept her arms around him. No sobbing, no anger. Only quiet, soft tears running down her cheeks.

Mostly, he knew, it was a reaction to his appearance rather than to the revelations he spoke of. Which, he also knew, she didn't quite believe. She did, however, believe in his madness. And really, how could she not? he asked himself.

She stirred briefly as he got out of the narrow bed. The heavy spread still pulled up around the pillows, both of them dressed in street clothes. She had prudently slept beside him, he noted, and not with him.

He sat quietly on the edge of the bed for a moment, and she drifted back to sleep. He made his way across the dark room into the bath. There, he closed the door and turned on the light, pausing for a moment before looking at himself in the mirror. How bad can it be? he asked himself. Bad enough to make your wife cry, the response came.

His reflection blinked back at him, and it was indeed worse than he would have guessed. His eyes sunken, ringed with wide, shadowy circles. Lines crisscrossing his face, several days' worth of stubble highlighting the effect. Gray streaks in his hair, like dirty flour. He had aged ten years in the span of a few days. The wonder was that Becky had stayed at all, after she had seen him.

He found himself staring at the stranger in the mirror. Somehow close scrutiny only served to make the lines appear deeper, the eyes more bloodshot, the skin pale and drawn. What year was this? he wondered. He felt and looked like two decades had passed. Time made even less sense to him now than it had before.

—Bright White. Fear. The ground rumbling. Running panic-stricken on all fours through collapsing, dark tunnels. Choking, gasping for air. Digging frantically for the surface . . .

—Bright White. Memories. Holding a heavy, stone-tipped spear. Preparing to plunge it into the chest of a thickset, manlike animal as the creature tries to scramble away. The smell of blood and smoke and death twisting through the air like some diseased fog. A snarl from his mouth, a cry from the other. Long and low, as if the beast is pleading for mercy. But there is no mercy. Not today, not ever. Planting his feet, he drives the weapon into the flesh and bone of the enemy.

Sitting on the edge of the bathtub, holding his head. Uncontrolled memories flooding across his mind. Bracken knew he had no hope of ever controlling them. That he would live his remaining years in a state of constant, furious brainstorm. That the knowledge contained in the protein molecules was beyond his capability to organize. He realized the awful truth: that he had been preyed upon by this *thing*. That the Change had been thrust on him with the suddenness of a snakebite. His body, his brain had been given no time to prepare. And now the flood of bewildering, incomprehensible memories swarmed over him. He held his head, wondering how he was going to live like this.

A soft knocking. Bracken looked up as the door creaked open. Rebecca staring at him, with a mixture of fear and terrible pity.

"Gary, are you all right?" she asked.

"No," he whispered, knowing he would never be all right. That the future belonged not to him, but to those who would come after. Those who were born with the Change. Who would, if they were lucky, be able to adapt. To insulate their nervous systems to accommodate the infusion of this new way of thinking. Evolution, he thought bitterly, had betrayed him.

—They're changing . . . Changing us! Kurt Eez had said.

Rebecca came to him, putting her arms around his shoulders.

"It'll be all right," she said softly.

"No, it won't," he whispered again, afraid to look up at her.

—Bright White. Flashing across his brain . . .

Sandborn settled into the leather chair behind his desk. It was a comfortable piece of furniture which he was reluctant to part with, even though it was obvious he was going to have to do so. The briefing with his superiors had gone about as badly as he suspected it might. Then, predictably, the briefing with *their* superiors had been even worse. As a good soldier, Sandborn accepted full responsibility for his agency's actions. Although he had, of course, kept those in charge discreetly informed of the situation. As a man of the world, and one who knew the minds of bureaucrats perhaps better than they knew themselves, he was not surprised when the shit truck had been backed up to his office door and summarily dumped. His own boss, the civilian head of NSA, did what he could to force back the attack dogs by correctly pointing out that Paul Sandborn could hardly be blamed for a widespread evolutionary mutation.

All of which would probably save his ass, if not his job, Sandborn thought, sitting back to write his letter of resignation. It gave him little satisfaction to know that Jeffery Lang was even now involved in the same thankless task. In any battle there were bound to be casualties among the front-line troops. This time around, it was his misfortune to be one of the first pushed out of the trenches. Such were the fortunes of war and government service, Sandborn knew. And in the end, he knew also that he had done his best. During the afternoon meetings with the joint chiefs, he had vigorously opposed calling up the Guard and deploying army regulars.

"An unnecessary aggravation of an already potentially volatile situation," he remembered saying. And really, things weren't that far out of control, he'd argued. Not yet, anyway, he refrained from saying.

Sandborn was, however, forced to admit there was no way of telling when the situation might escalate to that point. So the Guard was in the process of being called up, and troops were being moved to protect government installations. All of which, he knew, would only serve to inflame both the media and the general populace. In typical bureaucratic fashion, since he had been in opposition of the deployment plan, Sandborn now found his new assignment was to coordinate the Protection Program. The absurdity of it actually caused him to smile a little as he put the finishing touches on his resignation.

The media, he knew, was being fed a cover story. The usual "terrorist threat" scare tactic, which allowed the military to pretty much operate at will. Even with all that power at hand, Sandborn still felt as though he had just been selected to deliver a eulogy at a state funeral.

Surprisingly, at least to Paul Sandborn, the world did not immediately fall to pieces. The Change came in much the same manner that Jeffery Lang, former director of the CDC, predicted it would. The Plague of Madness, as the media dubbed it, progressed at an alarming rate in the beginning, but quickly leveled out, at least among the adult population. No madmen launched preemptive strikes with their country's nuclear arsenals. And the public, once they became aware of what was actually taking place—at least to the extent that the newly appointed director of information allowed—rallied to support the Protection Program. True, there were riots and major service disruptions in the large cities. But the Guard and the army regs, under Sandborn's direction, handled these problems in what Congress deemed "an exemplary fashion." Some years later, when Sandborn retired, that phrase was inscribed on a presidential medal he was given for his distinguished service to the "cause of humanity." Sandborn graciously accepted both the medal and a substantial pension, and spent his remaining years at a secure government compound in Idaho, writing an exposé about the American bureaucracy which no one would publish.

Jeffery Lang became the new minister of education, and was instrumental in designing computer programs to help school-age children deal with the problems associated with the utilization of molecular memories. Human beings, he often lectured, had been chosen by evolution and natural selection for their resiliency and adaptability, and were even now proving themselves in both areas.

Among the general population, life went on pretty much as it had before the Change entered its current active phase. There were some unusual economic twists and turns. A large number of people found themselves without jobs, and several overextended banks went under, taking billions of dollars with them into the tank. But all of that had happened before. In the cities, occasional brownouts became the rule rather than the exception. There were food shortages and disruptions to the major transportation systems, but nothing the army couldn't handle. Welfare, divorce, and abortion became familiar political issues as elected officials successfully diverted attention from the real problems of the day. News stories concerning the rising crime rate and its relationship to the demise of the family structure once again dominated the airwaves as Madness became more commonplace, and therefore less newsworthy. In a curious twist, situation comedies depicting dysfunctional families, in which exasperated parents were forced to deal in amusing ways with children plagued by bizarre molecular memories, became standard fare on the television sets of the world. The protein-reading computers came on-line a few years after the Protection Program became law, although translation programs for encoded virus molecules were outlawed. The tabloids had a field day speculating about the existence of "secret alien knowledge." And the CDC, using the protein-reading computers on the virus molecules, found the cure for cancer and a wide variety of other malignant diseases. Other discoveries, however, such as the viral role in human evolution, were classified top secret and sealed in the National Archives until the next century.

Rebecca Owens-Bracken successfully sued Centrifuge Labs for her husband's share of the government patents developed during his employment. Before the Plague of Madness shut down services in the major cities, she fled into one of the many secure communities established by private companies as havens for the wealthy and powerful.

The Ministry of Health was put under military control, and the army corps of engineers built a series of secure hospitals to deal with the delusional victims of the Change. Gary Bracken, and twelve million of his fellow citizens, eventually underwent a lobotomy and a sterilization procedure, as dictated by the Emergency Powers Act of the Protection Program, in an effort to contain the impact of the Change on the genetic pool. No one in Congress, however, had the nerve to include newborns and young children in the legislation. Thus, the Change was controlled and limited in scope during the early years. But despite the efforts of the CDC and the World Health Organization, the Change continued to expand. In the end, all that was gained were a few, short years, during which the race of prototype humans called Homo sapiens continued to pretend they were the final goal of evolution.

The Change came, as it had in the past, with brutal swiftness, sweeping away the weak and the inferior like dust. The virus clans, timeless and infinitely patient, continued their work.

a molecule of time

The boy was next in line at the computer chamber. Behind him, his classmates also waited. They talked quietly, nervously, knowing without being told that the next few minutes would have a profound effect on the rest of their lives. Teachers from various school levels moved among the children, speaking calm words of encouragement. Smiling, touching the shoulders of those who were becoming agitated. Downstairs in the auditorium, parents were waiting for the test results, equally nervous, hoping for the best. Illian's own mother had taken him aside before the family caught the hydroplane to the Evaluation Center.

"This really isn't that big a deal," she said confidently, even though both of them knew it was. "No matter what happens, you're still my son."

Illian smiled up at her, trying to seem grateful for the encouragement. Still, he was unable to shake the feeling

that there was something basically unfair about your entire future being decided for you at twelve years of age.
And by arbitrary forces over which you had no control.
Molecular memory ability—he hardly knew what it was.
Which, he thought, did not exactly enhance his chances
of successfully passing the evaluation. The previous
night his father had come to his room. Quiet and stoic, in
the manner of all fathers, checking to be sure the boy
knew what was required of him. And no matter what the
outcome, that his son would conduct himself in an honorable manner.

"You understand there's no reason to be afraid?" his
father asked. Illian nodded. "The evaluation is a simple
thing, really. We've all done it. It doesn't hurt, and it's
over in the blink of an eye."

"I know," he replied, trying to match his father's stoic
stance. "They told us all about it at school."

"Then you'd better get some sleep," his father said,
hugging him briefly.

Sleep, however, did not come easily. Illian lay in his
bed most of the night, disdaining the use of his pillow's
rhythm waves. Somehow, he did not want anything inter-
fering with the reading at the Evaluation Center in the
morning, even though everyone assured him there was no
way for brain frequency readings to be incorrect.

—The function of the brain is set in the first decade of
life, the textbooks told him. Some are molecule-receptive,
while others are not. It is, simply, a fact of nature.

Lying in the darkness, the boy tried to bring up some
deeply buried molecular memory, but couldn't. This, too,
disturbed him. Though, again, it was not supposed to
mean anything.

—Cognitive thought is a function of primary and secondary filters, the books said. Without the proper filtering

cycles to organize and block competing memories, the human brain would be entirely dysfunctional.

Yes, he knew all that. Simple biology. And he was equally well versed in history, understanding the Years of Chaos better than most of his classmates. He did well on the grading tests, also. But the Basic Instructors never failed to tell everyone that high test scores were not necessarily an indication of molecular receptiveness. The boy knew, however, that many of the Basic Instructors were Half-Brains themselves—not having the capacity for any of the higher functions—and so might be expected to mouth partial truths. His grandfather had been a Reader, and he hoped that would increase his odds at the Evaluation Center.

In truth, the boy understood that a lot was riding on this genetic coin flip, for himself and his parents. If he tested positive, the family would be allowed the privilege of secondary children. He himself would go on to the Training Academy, there to learn the full capabilities of his mind. He might be offered a place in the Sciences, perhaps even a slot as a Tech on the earth orbiters. That was his dream, to see space firsthand rather than through the computer simulators. But, of course, that was the dream of every young person. No one wanted to be a Grounder. Running factory boards, or teaching Basic Instruction, or monitoring the virus codes, although he knew these to be honorable, useful trades. How could he not, as that had been drilled into him since the first days of his instruction?

"Everyone is equal in the eyes of God," the Basics said, always with a smile. "Some are protein-receptive, some are not. But the smooth functioning of society relies on each finding their own levels, their own room in society's house, Reader and Nonreader alike."

It was, he knew, a lie. Some lived in the basement while others flew above the clouds. But, of course, he was not foolish enough to point that fact out to anyone. Even at his young age, he understood that some secrets were meant to be hidden away in the back of your mind. And that was, in fact, the real reason behind his fear of the computer chamber. Where, it was said, the innermost secrets could be probed, even if the Basics scoffed at that rumor. More than anything, he did not want to be a Half-Brain, programming robots to build better transport vehicles.

"Next," the Tech said, and Illian stepped forward, barely suppressing a chill as the door slid closed behind him. He was alone in the darkened chamber, listening to the thumping sound of his heart. He had never before heard it beat so loud.

"Step forward, eyes front," a detached voice said.

He obeyed, staring at the back wall, as he had been taught to do. A sharp, momentary flash of light.

—Bright White. Engulfing the interior of his brain, like a floodlight, like a lightning flash exploding behind his eyes. Beyond the brightness, stars swirled in the depths of space. Great sailing vessels prowled the interstellar night. Voices whispered in strange languages he couldn't quite understand. It seemed that in an instant he was given a vision of all time and space—a thing so sudden, so unexpected, so beautiful and overpowering, it was all he could do not to cry.

"Got a live one," he heard the Tech say to someone in the background.

a molecule of time

Day One + 1.277500365 x 10 ^12
(1000 years APT)

I t was the sport of Kings. The ships sat like huge, dark arrowheads, shimmering in the morning light. The sun reflected off the polished glass cockpits of the fliers as the elite, two-man crews walked across the tarmac. They talked quietly with each other, planning strategy, joking about the conquests of the previous evening. The pilots, tall and lean, wearing necklaces of golden claws to signify their rank, never lacked conquests about which to brag. Moving with the graceful assurance of the genetically enhanced, they climbed into their machines and turned their attention immediately to the Art of War.

—Victorious warriors win first and then go to war, while defeated warriors go to war first and then seek to win, Kraft thought, quoting the old master, Sun-tzu.

He strapped down, watching as the autopilot went through the preflight checklist. The AP was moving through the sequence faster than Kraft could follow in normal time, so he overrode his visual sense, just to double-check the computer equipment. Not everyone in the squadron bothered with that relatively minor inconvenience, he knew, but Kraft took his duties as commander seriously. In the background noise of the headset, he heard his navigator feeding audio coordinates into the squadron's tracking systems. Kraft experienced a moment of temporal displacement as his brain worked in two time frames—listening to the navigator's instructions in normal time while following the electronic impulses of his control panel. It was an uncomfortable, separated sensation, like floating on the sea on a dark, cloudless night, trying to count the stars and the wave undulations at the same time. Which was the reason most pilots didn't bother shifting their visual range merely to double-check machines known to be accurate to several dozen decimal places.

But cosmic errors, as the old philosophers taught, dwelt in the smallest margins of infallibility, and Kraft was not one for taking unnecessary risks. A mind-set some considered odd for a fighter pilot, he knew, but it was this attention to detail which gave him the ability to lead. If he issued the command, those in his squadron would blast their ships out of the atmosphere and follow him into the sun. In fact, they had all done so during reality simulations.

But on this day, Kraft was not taking his people to flirt with a fiery death. Today, the mission was relatively risk-free, but that did not mean the seemingly insignificant details could be ignored. Thus his close attention to the preflight checklist. The AP flashed the end of its sequence and Kraft blinked his vision back to normal time.

The navigator was finishing his coordinate input, the squadron's destination having been kept secret until takeoff, primarily as a safeguard against the media suddenly appearing at the engagement site. The military had become extremely sensitive about these sorts of missions, he knew, and in all probability this was the last raid on the rebel encampments, so the security safeguards were undoubtedly prudent. In truth, Kraft knew he would be glad when the whole affair was over. This was hardly pleasant duty, but he was convinced of its necessity. The rebels had, after all, brought this on themselves.

More than a century ago the genetically inferior, known as the Challenged, had been granted sanctuary in the Northern Mountains, after medical science failed in its efforts to augment their cognitive abilities. Naturally, it had become impossible for that small percentage of people who lacked the facilities to access EMM—Enhanced Molecular Memory—to live and function effectively as members of an advanced society. So in the interest of the public good, they had been given land and such technology as they were able to use effectively and guaranteed the Right to Life. Sanctuary, sustenance and access to the lower levels of communication were, in the end, all that could be offered to these unfortunates, Kraft knew from history. But it had not proven to be enough. In the ensuing years, the Challenged began a series of technological raids, jamming computer systems in blatant attacks to download protein-reading software. When attempts at education and appeasement failed, there had been little choice but to instigate military operations against those in the Sanctuary Lands. If nothing else, EMM taught that preservation of the whole took precedence over all else.

So it had come to this—the last raid against the remaining rebel outpost deep in the Northern Mountains. As distasteful as Kraft personally found his assignment, the task had fallen to him, and he would execute it to the best of his abilities.

"All systems ready?" He spoke into his headset.

Affirmative lights clicked across his control panel.

"Let's do it!" he said.

The ground rumbled and the morning sun was eclipsed by the squadron's burners.

The young girl huddled in the underground bunker, dug deep into the hillside. It had been hoped that building the shelter away from communication and defense positions might shield the children and the infirm from the full fury of the Readers' attack. That effort, it now appeared, had been wasted. Loud explosions rippled through the earth, causing dirt to trickle down on the girl's head and the emergency lighting to flicker. The dimming of the lights, the encroaching darkness, frightened her more than anything. To be buried alive, entombed in the dark, was the worst thing she could imagine. Terror was spreading through the bunker like some swift-moving sickness. Many of the younger children were crying, and so Nikka swallowed her own fear and moved among the young ones to comfort them. As she was the oldest, in her tenth year, it fell to her to give them strength and courage, even though Nikka felt she had little of either quality to spare.

The sounds of fighting filtered into the bunker, and she listened closely, trying to determine how the battle was going. There was little hope, she knew, that her people would prevail. Outmanned and lacking the technological weaponry of the Readers, there was hardly any doubt about the outcome. Still, her father and her uncles were powering up the laser banks, Nikka knew, hoping to destroy enough of the fighters to cause the Readers to break off the attack. A futile gesture, at best. Nikka had seen the fighters at work many times during her brief lifetime, and understood the power of their killing machines. She knew

also that the Readers could never be stopped. They were
simply too strong for her people to stand against them.

As the battering continued, Nikka held the younger
children against her own slim body, trying to shield them
from the falling clumps of earth, praying that her father
and uncles might somehow survive. But God, it seemed,
had deserted them long ago. In her heart, she wondered
how that could be. Even though such questions were considered blasphemy, she had once asked her mother why
such a thing seemed to have happened. Why God, who
made the earth, the sky, and all people, had made them
different from the Readers? Why God had allowed them
to be banished to the Sanctuary Lands, there to languish
and ultimately be exterminated? Because that was what
was taking place, Nikka knew, even if no one was willing
to speak the words.

Her mother, still alive that summer when they camped
in the Valley of Stones, had no explanations, no words of
wisdom or comfort. She pulled her daughter close, shaking her head. Perhaps, Nikka now thought, her mother
somehow sensed her own approaching death, which had
come swiftly, suddenly that very season. Her mother simply curled up in her blankets one night and went to sleep,
never to awaken. Almost, Nikka thought, as if the world
had become a place in which she simply did not care to
live anymore.

In truth, Nikka did not understand any of this. The
fighting, the dying, the hatred the Readers harbored for
her people. The outside world portrayed them as inferior,
almost beastlike in their thoughts and actions, but the reasons for this were never satisfactorily explained to her.
She herself was able to read the few books smuggled into
the camps from the world beyond the mountains. And
even though Nikka was aware that on some level, there

was something deeper—something she was missing and didn't quite understand—she often imagined herself escaping the Sanctuary Lands with her father and uncles, living at peace in the luxury and comfort of the Readers' society. Her friends, of course, laughed at this fantasy, although she suspected many of them had the same dream hidden in their hearts. A dream now dashed and broken as the sounds of terrible thunder shook the ground, like giant footsteps.

So she pulled the young ones to her and prayed. Prayed that when all of this was ended, she and her father and uncles would somehow survive. And the Readers would take pity on them. She could, after all, read. She would show them, if given the chance. The explosions, however, continued in all their hellish fury, and Nikka soon realized that her prayers were hollow and empty. That no one, no thing, was listening. The lights flickered, the young ones around her began to cry. Nikka bit her lip and resolved to be strong.

Within the bodies of their hosts, the virus clans continued their work. The One, becoming the Many, becoming ONE. Along the way, many sacrifices had to be made. Evolution being a harsh, demanding business.